KU-666-698

Carol Birch was born in 1951 in Manchester and went to Keele University. She has lived in London, south-west Ireland and now Lancaster. Her first novel won the 1988 David Higham Award for Best First Novel of the Year. In 1991 she won the prestigious Geoffrey Faber Memorial Prize.

COME BACK, PADDY RILEY

Anita's mother was the mermaid in the Belle Vue Fair Freak Show. Vain and young, careless in her mothering, her children rolled with the rackety life. Into their lives came Paddy Riley, a young Irish lad whose cheerful motto was 'the only sin in life is to miss an opportunity'. Anita's mother, in a loveless marriage, was that opportunity and a delicious secret, until young Anita spun a jealous and tragic lie. Now Anita is married with two children of her own. Then Michael moves into an ancient boat down at the harbour. His presence excites her. Just like Paddy Riley . . .

CAROL BIRCH

COME BACK, PADDY RILEY

Complete and Unabridged

ULVERSCROFT

Leicester

First published in Great Britain in 1999 by
Virago Press
London

First Large Print Edition
published 2001
by arrangement with
Little, Brown and Company (UK)
London

British Library CIP Data

Birch, Carol, 1951–
Come back, Paddy Riley.—Large print ed.—
Ulverscroft large print series: general fiction
1. Adultery—Fiction
2. Love stories
3. Large type books
I. Title
823.9′14 [F]

ISBN 0–7089–4485–X

Published by
F. A. Thorpe (Publishing)
Anstey, Leicestershire

Set by Words & Graphics Ltd.
Anstey, Leicestershire
Printed and bound in Great Britain by
T. J. International Ltd., Padstow, Cornwall

This book is printed on acid-free paper

For Jan

At night a constant stream of Brylcreemed men and perfumed women passed along Anita's road on their way to the Longsight entrance of Belle Vue, where the Italian hot-dog seller had set up his stand. Fairy lights hung all over the funfair and in loops along the avenue between the sylvan enclosures of rare and exotic birds, running up towards the turnstiles.

Anita lived just across the road from the big perimeter wall with spiky glass on top. From the room she shared with her little brother Robin she could hear the sound the animals made waking up early in the morning, a kind of vast collective groaning yawn. Poor things! She would picture them: half lion, half tiger, Rita the tigon, gnawing meat wistfully in her cage; and the other big cats, pacing the bars, wild, malevolent green and gold eyes like boiled sweets; and the lovely gazelles, and those fierce-faced monkeys skittering about on their rock, and the hippo in its little bath opening its huge jaws to have a whole loaf of bread thrown on to its vast, soft, shifting tongue.

1

Belle Vue was a zoo, a funfair, a rambling place of gardens and lakes on a huge triangle of land in the middle of a poor, grey area near the middle of Manchester. There was a dog track, a stock car stadium, wrestling and concerts at the King's Hall.

Thirty years ago, Belle Vue was Anita's back yard.

The boy walked past her as she leaned on her trolley in Tesco, contemplating the cereals. A giant packet of corn flakes was cradled in front of him as if it were a baby in a sling. The sight of him bit into her like recognition and she found herself following him discreetly with her trolley. If there was a conscious thought in her head it was only that there was something in his face and she couldn't let him go, but she wasn't really thinking at all. He nearly took a turn down the wrong aisle but swerved back on track in a way that was both self-conscious and graceful: a fairy, an alien, the most beautiful child she'd ever seen with his skinny little body and solemn, hollow face.

She followed him till he joined up with a small man with greasy black hair who seemed to be his father. The man was like a monkey — not one of those mean little things with

2

spiteful, pinched faces, and not a stupid chimpanzee either — but a noble gorilla made human, or a man at the cusp of some lost link between species. He was ugly, she supposed, slightly frightening, and his face stayed in her mind until she encountered him again weeks later, this time among the freshly baked rolls and whole-meal loaves. The boy was squatting down by the lowest shelf looking up at him. They were getting a sliced brown loaf. Shocking, that thin-lipped, high-cheeked adult face on top of a small child's body. Steady-eyed, grave, unblinking as some babies. She stared. The father wore old jeans with a thin grey jacket and heavy cream-coloured muffler. His back was to her, so she moved round the stack to catch a glimpse of his interesting, ugly face. It was dark and troubled, with heavy features and thick sulky lips.

When they walked away down the aisle, the man with his basket, the boy stalking behind like a page, she had to force herself not to follow. It's coming to something, she thought, a woman of my age following young boys round supermarkets. I suppose it's just because he's a boy and I only have girls. Anyway, nothing to get excited about. She'd had this kind of *déjà vu* from the face of a stranger before, as if they'd met once briefly

3

on some far-flung shore or been intimate in a dream, forgotten till the memory was jogged. It made her giddy, but it meant nothing, of course: just something funny going on in the brain, a broken circuit or something. When she got to the checkout the man was buying something from the kiosk and the boy was bobbing up and down by the cigarette counter, just like any other daft child getting bored being dragged round the shops, except that his pale little face was so serious. It seemed like a named condition, this particular combination of bobbing and solemnity. Autism perhaps.

She was in a tremendous hurry. She always was. She had to pick up Sid from playgroup and Jas from school. As soon as she had them in the back they started fighting and she yelled for them to shut up, and sighed, and reckoned she was due a break to go and see her old friend Leah in London pretty soon. Surely? She drove through town, down the long Georgian ribbon of High Street with its shiny goods, determinedly interesting and mostly expensive. Yes, I will, she thought, driving through half-timbered Tudoresque at the lower end of town, past bungalows fronted by rose gardens, then the housing estate and the dreadful death-trap of the bypass she had to leap across before the peace of the high-banked lanes and the

4

square stepped tower of a church towering far out in the cornfields.

The sugar beet lanes were full of mud. Driving through them, it hit her why she had reacted so to the boy. He reminded her of someone she had known a very long time ago, a young man called Paddy Riley.

Oh, Paddy Riley! she cried inwardly. Oh, Paddy Riley!

Nearly thirty years ago. It must be.

———————

Anita's mother was the mermaid in Belle Vue freak show that summer because her family knew a man called Archie Bannister, who smoked a fat cigar and wore a trilby hat and a pale grey overcoat. In those days he ran a place in town called Archie's Chop House, where her mother had worked as a waitress after the war.

Anita didn't like Archie Bannister. Sometimes he was in their house, she'd seen him sitting by the fire in the rocking chair, but he never said a word to her or Robin. He was one of those adults who would no more consider speaking to a child than he would a chair leg. He had a smooth, shiny, pumped-up look and a sharp little nose, and he smelled of cold and money. His connection with Belle Vue was a mystery to

5

Anita, but that was why they could get in free, why she and Robin knew the place as well as they knew their tiny yard, and the street with the red Halt at Major Road Ahead sign, and the three alleys coming out over the road. It was also a mystery why he appeared in some of the earliest photographs of her mother and father together, standing in groups of long-forgotten people in front of the boating lake or the King's Hall, and how he came to know the tinker Deasys, that branch of her mother's spectacularly spreading family tree that travelled all over the north of England and the borders during the war years. 'I had a great war,' her mother used to say.

Not all of her stories were true. That about the Deasys was though, Anita thought, because she had memories, distant but vivid, of standing on the cobbles outside Exchange Station, with the people passing by trying to avoid them. She'd felt ashamed and hurt for her mother, for she was in desperation. 'Little bunch o' heather, sweetheart,' her mother was saying in the memory, 'come on now, change your luck. Your hair's a lovely colour, darlin'. That's a lovely baby girl you have there.'

———————

After that she kept seeing them everywhere. Funny, she thought, the way that happens.

She saw the little boy who looked like Paddy Riley along the sea front, or with his backpack coming home from school past the antiques and stylish clothes, the occult paraphernalia, organic meats and local crafts of High Street. He was always alone, older than his size and years. Lounging in the doorway of The Bookshop on the Quay where she worked at odd, ill-defined times, she would mark him walking along the crazy dark line of converted shacks and sheds that leaned against each other wearing their new faces all along the Quay: the Mustard Seed, the Co-op, the Curlew Restaurant next door, where the dark young man with the square jaw and white apron chalked upon a faded blackboard the menu for the evening to come.

She glimpsed the boy with his father in Boots; the man was at the Pharmacy, the child gazing wistfully at hot water bottle covers in the likeness of soft toys. Where is the mother? she thought. He has none, the little boy has no mother. Her heart turned over.

In the evenings when she went out, she'd catch an occasional chance sighting of the father. He was good for the odd day-dream. He looked different at different times. Once he was a rambling tarry sailor, once an

7

escaped convict. Once she even saw in him an awkward schoolboy with his fingers in his mouth. He was two tables away in the Dun Cow when she was out having a drink with Jane Jarrett, his face in profile amused by the company he was in, a mixed bag of colourful types and pretty people. Walking through town late one cold night with Charley, he passed her by in the harsh yellow light under the soldier clock at Jak's corner, a heavily made-up woman on his arm. His face was always a shock, as if she'd just turned a corner and come face to face with a tiger.

She was bigger than him, she noted. She was a tall woman, but she'd had small men before, it didn't bother her either way. Charley was a big lad.

It rained for a week.

Jasmine stayed home with swollen glands and runny eyes, and her eczema flared up. She lay on the sofa for three days with the dog, an old man of fourteen by the name of Basil. Anita drew the pair of them, the golden girl and the little red mongrel greying round the face, taking the results up to her studio corner and sticking them on the wall. One or two she would certainly frame up later. She made lemon tea in a jug like her mother used to make for her father, took Jasmine on her knee and sang songs to her — old pop songs, songs from musicals, old school songs, 'Annie Laurie' and 'Will Ye No' Come Back Again?' and, creeping in there after years in the void, 'Come Back, Paddy Riley, to Ballyjamesduff, come back, Paddy Riley, to me', which gave her a sharp little stab in the chest.

Standing at the back door smoking her cigarette, looking out on the first clear morning, she thought: I've always done my best to protect the children from myself, from what I used to be. All this I've given them, these woods to play in. I had nothing. The woods pushed up against the old grey wall behind, hulking, a shaggy beast taking over, scraping the windows at the back with its sly insistent fingers. The wall was falling down where the girls kept climbing over.

'Get ready!' she called, pinching out her cigarette, sighing and turning back into the kitchen. It was a terrible mess as usual. The walls had the look of plumage, so thickly pinned with notes and receipts and reminders they were. The sink was piled with dishes, the dog's bowl sat on the draining board, the central table was buried under files and journals and homework and rubbish.

Sid grumbled over her shoes in the hall. Jasmine was in Basil's den. She had asthma as

9

well as eczema, but it was nothing to do with the dog, they'd checked. Cats were out though. Anita worried about Jasmine. She wondered if she could have inherited some sort of respiratory weakness from Anita's own mother, the thought of whom, wired up to a machine, depressed her.

In the summer before the Grammar School, their Aunties Connie and Dymphna took them to see their mum being a mermaid, even though she'd expressly forbidden it. The funfair's sirens wailed, sideshow hucksters called and cajoled. Rattling, screaming, high in the sky a long chain of carriages hurtled itself over the alpine peaks of the great grey Bobs, fastest gravity ride in the world. I'd never go on that, Anita thought. Never. Connie wore a bright yellow sundress with thin straps that cut across her red-brown peeling shoulders, and she dragged their cousin Kevin by the hand, him leaning outwards and trailing his fingers on the ground so that he looked like a chimpanzee being walked. A Punch-faced effigy in a glass case laughed insanely.

The sun was very high. Under it the crowds seemed glowing, wilted, slowed down by heat, and the people shooting out from the

10

ghost train's doors covered their eyes and squinted in the sudden glare. They passed the Midget House, with its board bearing the legend: *Real Live Tiny People*! 'Roll up! Roll up!' cried the barker, sweeping his megaphone about like a bugle.

Near the King's Hall they stopped and bought candy floss. Robin was supposed to hold her hand but he kept pulling away, gently but persistently, smiling and strolling on ahead, his skinny back and jug ears insolent. She didn't care. Let him go. The candy floss stuck to her lips. In front of the floral clock they stopped while their aunties lit up their cigarettes and started to giggle.

'She'll go mad!' spluttered Dymphna, bending forward for a light. She wore tight tartan trews and a short black jacket and her black hair frizzed above her high forehead.

'Well!' Connie inhaled. 'What harm? We'll only stop a minute.'

'Jesus, Con, she'll do her nut!'

She tossed a match in amongst the red, white and blue clumps of flowers. The shiny Buddha sat above the XII, peacefully dreaming behind his smooth swirling eyelids.

They walked on between the fireworks lake and the ballroom where her father had met her mother at the outside dancing on the

11

boards. A hawk-faced man in a turban led the elephant there, plodding along with a swaying cargo of kids on top. They passed the Helter Skelter, the Indian Grotto, the Miniature Railway with the grumpy midget driving, just heading off with a clang of the bell and a hoot of the whistle towards the shine of the boating lake.

———————

Most of the time she could put her mother out of her mind. God damn these genes, she thought, you do your best but they're already there. And where does Jasmine get her nerviness from? Look at the state of her nails.

The clematis was coming out round the front door, crawling over the dull pink paint that peeled like sunburn on the walls. The sky was vibrant blue with big white fluffy clouds, everything smelt green and fresh, the breath of the air sweet. She chivvied the kids into the car and drove into town, dropped one at school and one at playgroup and went into work a little late. There like a shock was her pretty little ape-man, leaning his knuckles on the crowded table, negotiating with Alison over some books he was trying to offload. He wore his grey jacket and cream-coloured muffler, and his thick black brows jutted out

12

like thatches over his eyes.

Alison nodded hello abstractedly, moving her lips as she totted things up in her head. A red velvet top hung loose from her wide shoulders and big breasts, glowing in the musty brown of the shop. Alison too was all shades of brown, hair and eyes and the pigmentation of her face, though her ear-rings were huge and bright and looked like those big rock catherine wheels Anita remembered sucking in Blackpool when she was little. Alison's ear-rings were loud and kitsch at all times, as if all the wildness of her soul went into them.

Anita moved alongside her.

'Shall I leave them then?' he asked.

She felt as if she knew him, as if he belonged to her in some odd way, watched over by her as he was, all unknown. They should greet each other as friends.

'Yeah, you can do.' Alison sat down and started writing out a credit note. 'You can either redeem this later or use it for books. Whatever.'

Anita waited for him to look at her at last, but he didn't. He straightened. There was something of a threat in his lean, feral presence in their cosy, shabby shop.

'Have a look around,' Alison said.

'You chose the wrong time of the month,'

13

said Anita. 'We're always skint at the end of the month.'

He didn't respond.

She turned her head on one side to read the spines of the books he was offloading. Law mainly. Ex-student, mature student maybe. The Bookshop on the Quay didn't take everything. They'd made an attempt to specialise: art and poetry was Alison's thing, circus and fairs Anita's. But mainly it was a free-for-all. Thirty-five? she thought. Thirty-seven? Younger than me, at any rate, though that doesn't matter. He did not look at her. She pulled herself up and showed off her height, flung back her hair with her hands in a slightly exaggerated, slightly self-conscious manner and went into the back to put on coffee and a CD of Purcell chamber music. Lighting a cigarette to smoke quickly away from Alison's disapproval, she pouted seductively at herself in the mirror, sat on the stool, pointed a toe and stroked her leg to feel the stubble starting to grow back. Her soft pink sweater came down to her knees. Forty-two, she thought. Weird. Now Alison, she would never follow strange men around supermarkets. Alison goes circle dancing at the Old Schoolhouse. She blew smoke at the wall with its scribbled messages and coffee stains and postcards. He had something in common with Charley, she thought, though God knows what. They all had it, all her men, Rory Gotch and Mad John and Candy; she just saw them and thought: that one's for me.

The bell rang. He'd gone.

She came out. 'Do you want coffee, Al?'

'Go on,' said Alison, shifting her bulk about expertly in the small gap between the table and the wall, writing in her little book.

———————

The freaks were by Pepino's Circus and the Hall of Mirrors. A clown in a big checked suit sat smoking a cigarette and taking money on the steps of the booth, his face cracked under thick white paint, the whites of his eyes bloody above a shiny red nose. The freak booth was painted with garish pictures of the sea and rocks and a voluptuous mermaid sitting on one of them holding a comb and a glass. Never Before Seen! said the letters on the front of the booth, The One And Only Genuine Barbary Mermaid! See! The Incredible Tattooed Woman! See! From the Forest of Amazonia! The Unbelievable Snake Man!

They went up the steps. In the first booth was the Incredible Tattooed Woman, the toes of her spiky high heels just sticking out beneath a shiny purple cloak that covered her entirely. She smiled at them, did a little twirly

15

sort of dance from side to side then flung her arms out wide like a peacock unfurling its tail, so that the purple cloak shimmered around her like wings. She wore a dark blue bra and knickers. All the rest of her stocky body was dark too, a mass of birds and beasts and fishes and reptiles in blues and greens and reds and blacks, some bright and new-looking, some faded.

'Tut-tut-tut,' went Connie loudly, shaking her head, and Dymphna giggled.

To see their mother, you had to look through a little glass window. She was sitting quite far back on a fake rock with her tail in a tank of water. She didn't look anything like their mother, her broad, pink, apple-cheeked face scarcely recognisable without her normal short red hair. The aunties gasped because at first it looked as if she was naked to the waist, but when you looked close you could see a flesh-coloured bra covering her breasts under the cascading blonde tresses of a huge wig that billowed over her shoulders and down to her waist, where the silvery-green fish's tail began, slightly dented, bending a bit just before the tail fin. Her big, pushed-forward mouth was even bigger, slathered round about with ruby lipstick, and her eyes were like Theda Bara's.

'Oh my God, Con,' Auntie Dymphna

16

whispered with a laugh in her voice. 'Oh my God.'

They just stood looking at her sitting there doing nothing, flicking at her hair with a tortoiseshell comb now and again. She looked bored and self-conscious, but then she saw them and had to pretend not to notice. Anita saw her eyes turn cold and furious, then hurt.

Connie laughed slightly hysterically.

Their mother turned her face from them and stared stonily at the painted waves on the backdrop behind her.

They had to move on to make way for others.

The Unbelievable Amazonian Snake Man was a big bald shiny man like a wrestler, with a tiny moustache and a leopard skin. 'Oh Lord Lord Lord!' whispered Connie. A snake as thick as her waist hung heavy about his neck, and another slept in the corner.

'Oh Christ, there's another one!' Dymphna clutched Connie.

One coiled about a tree. It was like the picture of Adam and Eve in their mother's old children's Bible.

'Look at that,' said a woman with a powder smell and high heels coming along behind them. She was looking at their mother. 'Fake,' she said grumpily.

Anita looked at the people filing along the

17

little passageway, expressionless, looking and passing on, looking and passing on.

'Come, kid,' said Connie.

She'd seen the African Fantasy and the man with rubber skin and the bearded lady and the world's tallest man. She really couldn't say why she felt so peculiar when she came out, why she had to swallow a small lump in her throat, why she dreaded her mother coming home tonight. It wasn't just because she'd be angry. Anyway it wasn't Anita and Robin she'd be angry with, it was Connie and Dymphna, who leaned against each other outside the booth and laughed themselves stupid.

And then she saw the boy she thought of as the blue-eyed boy taking money for the Hall of Mirrors, yawning and picking his nails on the steps. Her face went hot and her chest shivery, she licked her lips, still tasting the sweet candy floss, and she forgot all about her mother and Connie and Dymphna and the two irritating little boys wrestling around like bear cubs at her feet.

She had seen the blue-eyed boy last week in the paper shop. Her mother had sent her for her ten Woodbine but there was no one behind the counter. Anita and the boy had had to stand there together in the empty shop waiting. He was buying Polos and the

18

Evening Chronicle. He was about eighteen and she was only eleven but she could get a crush like the end of the world. She could get a crush that skinned her heart and inflamed her mind, fluttered in her throat and wrists and made her miserable to be a child. She had had crushes that caused her to weep into her pillow, lie down in the rain on next door's garage roof for an hour refusing to hear her name called, sit gazing at the wall in a rapidly cooling bath, aching because of her silly little girl legs with sticking plasters on the knobbly knees.

———————

Anita's friend Lindsay said she knew him vaguely, his name was Michael, he used to be at the University. She said she thought he knew the Foremans, used to work with Dick maybe, something like that, and the boy's mother, well, she had a feeling the boy's mother might be in an institution of some sort.

'I suppose I can see what you see in him,' she said, leaning back to drain the wine from her glass.

The sightings these days were good, close enough to note that his eyes expressed some fierce and pained intelligence. Sometimes he ate at the Curlew Restaurant, to whom she'd

19

seen him deliver shellfish from the back of a green Renault 4. Occasionally he came into the shop and bought the odd thing, modern American fiction mainly. There was a certain swagger in his manner. As he browsed she was able to watch unseen his sullen eyes with the black brows running together above, his strong nose and fleshy lips sulking against one another.

Coming out of the shop one day she smelt fish offloaded straight from the boats and fancied getting a couple of small dressed crabs to take home for supper. She took a walk down past the fish shacks and heaps of orange nets, cut through to where the boats were moored at the saltings and there he was, smoking in the cockpit of an old white and blue cruiser called *Ellen*. His little boy sat on the wooden gangplank with his legs dangling. She'd forgotten the boy. How strange, she thought, the boy led me to the father, that's why he was fascinating. Now I've forgotten him. She started taking the dog for walks that way now and again, just ambling along with her hands in her pockets and Basil trotting on ahead chewing a small stick, tossing it up over his head and catching it again like a baton twirler. She could keep a proper eye on the pair of them now. She saw Michael bashing away at something with a lump hammer, grunting and swearing under his breath, the boy lying on the roof of the boat reading a book. There were visitors to the boat, many of them women. She saw a skinny tanned one with very short shorts and a whisky-and-fags voice that carried into the clear air; a broad-bodied, tow-haired one with a sweet smile; a vivid girl with purple plaits and a big mouth. All these people know him, she thought. Lindsay knows him. Mona Foreman knows him. Why don't I know him?

If he noticed her, he never let on. He came in twice when she was in the shop alone and never said a word even when buying a book, even though she smiled and made small talk. When she handed him his change, the thank you seemed an effort.

The blue-eyed boy was tall and thin with jet-black hair, a beautiful gaunt face with an incredible Saracen nose, and eyes of a startling deep blue like the sky at twilight. He moved all the time, his nervous dirty hands playing with money, his feet, his wide thin lips. Like a young dog.

'Are we just supposed to take our stuff and go out without paying or what?' he said to her in a loud voice meant to be heard in the back of the shop. Irish.

21

She grinned, panic-stricken.

The miserable papershop man with the long droopy nose came out of the back. 'No need for that,' he said without a trace of a smile.

'Oh well,' said the lad, and winked at Anita. 'I thought maybe you'd got the Invisible Man on the job.'

They were calling out the next show from Pepino's Circus.

'Right, you lot, come on,' said Auntie Connie, 'you've seen your ma, and wasn't she a hoot. Let's go and see the bears.'

Anita grabbed Robin's hand.

'She's not real,' he said, 'but the others are.' His hair shone like a new copper penny.

Anita looked back. The blue-eyed boy was turning cartwheels between the Hall of Mirrors and the freak booth to pass the time.

———

Lauren Jarrett was babysitting. Lauren favoured a pale waif look and brought her navy blue eye make-up right down into the corners of her eyes. She was downstairs pouring herself a coffee while Anita dressed. It had been a mad dash as usual, but now the girls were actually in their pyjamas, though not in bed, or at least not their own. They were on Basil's, an old baby mattress in his

den, which was really a utility room between the hall and the kitchen, which everyone had to pass all the time; it was pleasant for the dog now he was old, watching the traffic, most of which had a word for him. The girls got down with him in his den, where he kept his stones and filthy old bones and revolting chewed things, and did all the things they weren't supposed to do, such as kissing him on his dry black nose and letting him lick their faces. They hadn't caught anything terrible yet. Sometimes Anita did it too, though not the licking and kissing. She'd just sit there while he gnawed a bone or showed her his latest stone. 'Hey up, Bas,' she'd say. 'How's things?'

She couldn't think what to put on. The floor in front of the mirror was obscured with toys, stupid pearly blue and pink bits of things that drove her mad. She'd bought this beautiful lacy body the last time she went to London, high-cut, ivory and black, and a red dress. She wanted to wear them but the red dress didn't seem right for the Wool House. She kicked the toys aside, thinking: they're taking over, and stood for a while before the full-length mirror in the body, checking herself. Her figure was firm, tending a little to heaviness on the hips. She pulled strands of hair down around her face. The pink sweater

23

again, I suppose, she thought. With leggings.

She got the girls off the dog and into their rooms and read them a story with actions and voices and walking up and down the room.

★ ★ ★

It's not that I want to get off with him or anything, she told herself as she opened the big iron gate for the car. The one true thing in my life is that I love Charley.

The lion rug hung on the line to be beaten. Anita's mother in her blue and green check dress was rubbing a yellow-brown stone on the back doorstep and Connie was wringing out the dishcloth over the sink, when the blue-eyed boy came into their yard, bold as brass, walking up the side passage and standing there in the bright sunshine.

'Glass o' water, missis?' he said, and they all laughed together.

'Jesus, we can run to a cup o' tea, wouldn't you say, Connie?' Anita's mother said, jumping up and smiling all over, pulling in her belt and fixing the buckle.

'Aye, we can.'

He looked from one to the other and his eyes were not shy like a young boy's but quick

24

and sharp and confident, though there was a nervousness in him, and it dawned on Anita that they all knew each other already without her knowing how, and she felt angry with them. He came in and sat down on the settee, crossing one leg over the other. She was at the table by the window doing a jigsaw. Robin hovered shyly in the kitchen doorway.

Her mother ran her fingers through her springy curls. 'So the slave drivers let you off for a little while?'

Connie lifted the kettle from its place on the hob next to a pot of simmering stock that filled the room with a savoury smell. Anita could see that she was grinning like a fool, her face turned away.

'They did,' he said softly. 'I've to be back at one.' Then he jumped up and crossed the room to look over Anita's shoulder. 'Aw, I love a jigsaw,' he said with great relish. There was a curious faint smell off him, like twigs and beer and clean babies all at once, and when his slim brown arm with its sinuous veins came down, and his brown hand shifted the pieces about on the red chenille table cloth as gently as if they were the skeletons of leaves that might crumble at a touch, a soft scared feeling shot through her like the Red Sea parting straight up her middle.

'That's my little girl,' her mother said, and

25

she sounded proud.

'Oh yeah? *Aha!*' he said, slotting in a piece of sky and retreating to his place on the settee. 'And what would her name be now?' Looking at her in a full, forthright way. She stared back, not smiling.

'Anita.'

He leaned forward and peered at her as if he was shortsighted. 'Wow,' he said in a low voice, 'she's a stunner.'

Anita smiled coolly.

'A stunner,' he repeated, smiling lopsidedly as he felt in his pocket.

Her mother and Connie laughed.

'And this is my little boy. Say hello, Robin.'

'Hello.'

'Hello, Robin.' He spoke softly, with twinkling eyes as if everything was a joke. He was very handsome, though his lips were so wide and thin.

'What's *your* name?' asked Robin.

'Paddy.'

'Paddy *Riley*, no less,' my mother added, and Connie laughed and sang:

'*Come back, Paddy Riley, to Ballyjames-duff.*'

'Ah, shut it, woman,' he said, smiling so as not to give offence, 'd'ye not think I'm sick to the teeth of that bloody song?' He leaned forward, nudging a cigarette out of a pack.

'Cigarette, Geraldine?'

Her mother took one, then Connie. Her mother sat down on the chair on the other side of the table, head thrown back and arm cocked up, smoking. Anita looked at her mother's profile and saw her as if she had never seen her before, as if she was not her mother but a woman on the cover of a paperback, with her wide ripe mouth and swelling bust. Her dress was a shirt-waister that showed off her long strong throat, hugging her close to the belt before swirling out in a full skirt. Her mother's looks were full of imperfections and exaggerations that came together in a harmonious whole, memorable, mobile and very attractive. Anita looked down at the lid of her jigsaw. It showed a country cottage with a thatched roof and clusters of flowers like the ones on the floral clock where the Buddha sat. Darby and Joan were dozing companionably on a bench outside the door.

'And what do you like doing, Robin?' Paddy Riley asked.

'Meccano,' said Robin at once.

Connie poured the tea. Paddy Riley took four sugars and slurped when he drank.

'God, aren't you terrible?' her mother scolded. 'Did your mother never teach you manners?'

27

'Ah sure,' he grinned, 'you can't take me anywhere.'

———————

She drove into town and met Charley in the bar of the Wool House, where, oblivious to the gabbling crowds waiting for the start of *The Alchemist*, he sat with his nose in a scientific journal. Charley was like a big boy. She'd seen pictures of him as a child and he hadn't really changed at all. He had the kind of look that managed to be plain while showing subtle touches of boxer, Roman statue, Elvis Presley and the occasional dash of Marlon Brando in *On the Waterfront*; a round flattish schoolboy look with sweet, slightly weak mouth, solid jaw and a small vulnerable pouch under his chin. Not my type at all, she'd thought the first time she saw him at a party up on Gibbet Hill, and yet she'd watched him all night.

They had a drink and went into the play, and later, because the bar was heaving, wandered down towards the Alleys and tried The Wild Boar. That was packed too. Smoke gathered in a dull blue pall beneath the old oak beams. They squeezed up to the bar and there, pulling pints with a distracted air, was Michael. He didn't see her. She had a nice high feeling from enjoying the play, it had taken her back to when she was living at her Auntie Connie's with all her cousins, doing A levels and walking round Cheetham Hill every weekend with Alison. 'The sickness hot, a master quit, for fear, his house in town, and left one servant there . . . ' Of course, she thought, he *would* be here. The play is unfolding. She leaned on Charley, solid, broad of back, big of shoulder and knuckle and wrist and fist.

'Where's that bit,' he said, a fiver curled between his fingers, 'you know where the tube dips down and you go under the plague pit. It's on the Bakerloo line. Is it?'

Michael worked side by side with a girl with a weird cat-like worried face and geranium-red lips.

'Somewhere near Baker Street, I think,' Anita replied.

Charley frowned. 'God, I should know.'

The barmaid tossed her orange hair and worked her way towards the fiver held out between his fingers.

'I remember it so clearly,' he said. His voice was deep with a touch of nasality. 'Down you go, and sometimes it stops and stands still, you know what it's like, everyone fed up and tired. I remember looking up and thinking all that darkness overhead, like it was miles to the top, and I'd imagine them all tangled up

29

together. Like those pictures you see of holocaust victims.'

The bar staff were rushed off their feet; Michael was down there at the wrong end of the bar taking money, a long rumpled blue shirt hanging outside his jeans. The girl came to serve them; Anita couldn't decide whether or not she was attractive.

'Pint of Adnam's,' Charley said. 'Nita?'

'Oh, red wine.'

'It was when I was out at Swiss Cottage,' he mused. 'This'll drive me mad now.'

They worked hard behind the bar, brushing by each other up and down the narrow space, close but apparently oblivious. Anita wondered if the barmaid went back with him to his boat and they got it together on the bunk. She wondered where the boy was. Michael came to their end of the bar, swooping down for a bottle of Spritzer. His hands were large but refined. His dark hair fell forward, his face came near. She'd never seen him this close before in full, harsh light. He was far uglier than she'd realised, full-cheeked, pouchy-mouthed, with blood-shot eyes. Relief swept over her. Thank God for that, she thought, it was all illusion. Now I can let it go. She smiled at him, though his eyes were programmed to avoid hers.

'Hi,' Charley said to him.

'Hi, Charley,' he replied and went away.

The red-haired girl plonked down the pint, frowning, adding up.

'Who was that?' Anita asked, amazed.

'I can't remember his name,' said Charley, drinking the top off his beer. 'He used to go out with Doon.'

The crowd pushed them close together. Oh, darling Doon, Anita thought, it would just be her, wouldn't it? She worked in that dear little sweet shop on Buttery Lane, selling peggy's legs and cough candy and humbugs and jelly beans in shiny glass jars. She was brown and smooth and willowy with pale floaty hair and a permanent effortless winsomeness. She'd been out with Charley too. Charley was easy with women, he was brought up in a house full of them. Sometimes it seemed to Anita that he'd had a million girlfriends before her: Doon, the barmaid from the Fox and Goose, the posh county type who sold gorgeous and ridiculously expensive handmade dresses from a stall on the Sunday market — all ex's.

She couldn't help it. 'Oh, darling Doon,' she sneered.

Charley laughed. 'You're such a jealous woman.'

Phil Wragge, who put her pictures in his gallery, waved to them from a table where he

31

sat with Sarah and Ronnie Mottram.

'You know, sometimes,' said Charley, 'stuck there in the tunnel with them all pressing down on top of me, I'd get the feeling it was me up there in that pit. Tangled up with all the rest.'

'Sweetheart,' Anita told him, smiling, 'even if you were up there in some other time, you'd be long gone now. There's nothing there any more.'

'Feelings is feelings,' he said.

They took their drinks over to the table where Phil Wragge sat with the Mottrams. They'd all been to the play too. Conversation stayed with the Plague. Charley knew all about it, that and the Fire, though he didn't go on about it. He must have read everything written on the subject.

'What a time to live,' Anita murmured, putting her fingers in his pocket for the programme and rubbing his stomach.

'What's she been in?' asked Sarah, leaning over to look at the programme. 'Dol Common. Great name. I've seen her in something on the telly. I thought she was quite good.'

'She was, wasn't she?'

Perhaps, Anita thought, glancing at the bar, if I wore a kind of contact lens to blur him a little, just enough, then we could sort of conduct a whole relationship, sex and all, from a distance. In half light.

Paddy was full of talk. He said he'd shaken the hand of Yuri Gagarin when Gagarin visited Manchester. 'That's for me,' he said, 'I'd volunteer. Can you picture it, shooting away into outer space like a bullet from a gun. Looking down on the earth. I'd like to get right out of this world and be looking down on it all.'

'Did you?' Robin stared. 'Did you really shake Gagarin's hand?'

'I did.'

'Wouldn't you be scared?' Connie asked.

'No! Well, yes, but even if it all blew up, wouldn't it be worth it just for one second looking down?'

'It would not indeed.'

'Would you? Would you, really?' her mother asked in an incredulous tone.

'Oh sure, I'd go like a shot. Sure, you only live once.'

'I'd go,' said Robin.

'Of course you would!'

'You wouldn't get me up there.' Connie folded her arms.

'How about you, Geraldine?' he asked. 'You'd go up, wouldn't you? You'd be game.'

Anita's mother was preening her curls. 'I just might at that,' she said lightly.

'There's only one real sin in this life,' Paddy Riley said seriously, 'never mind what they tell you. There's only one real sin in this life and that sin is turning down a God-given opportunity.'

'There's truth in that somewhere,' her mother said, setting down her cup. 'Nita, go and get those nice butter biscuits out.'

Paddy caught Anita's eye as she got up from the table. 'Remember that,' he told her, smiling his long, crooked, lopsided smile, 'remember that.'

When she came back with the biscuits he was talking about his big plans. After the summer he was going in with his uncles in the painting and decorating line. There was money to be made. He was going to get a van and branch out on his own but he wouldn't stay in this country. Oh no. America, America was the place.

'Where the streets are paved with gold,' Connie laughed.

'Oh indeed, they are, they are.' He squinted through the smoke that curled up from the tip of the cigarette clamped between his joky lips, now V-shaped and as insolent as a pup. 'Any rate — ' he coughed, removing the cigarette, 'that's where I'm heading. Give it five years, I'd say. Before I'm too old.'

'Listen to the child,' said Connie. 'How old would you say he was, Geraldine?'

'I'm twenty years old,' Paddy Riley replied with dignity, looking at Anita's mother.

There was a silence.

'Just,' said her mother in a tender voice.

When tea was finished he offered to beat the rug on the line. 'It's a nice rug all right,' he said, nodding. It was old and worn and patchy, and the two great lions padding through the bush against a deep red background seemed to be coming through a dark mist. He took off his jacket and set his feet apart and whacked the lions again and again, and the dust came off in fantastic clouds that made her mother and Auntie Connie squeal.

'The energy of the boy,' said Connie warmly.

Oh yes. The energy of the boy.

She was drinking her coffee, smoking a cigarette in the front shop in defiance of all the rules, just going through the *Bookdealer* and making a mark here and there with her pencil; she was after a particular book that never turned up, a history of fairs in the Middle Ages. The Jarretts were coming over

35

tonight, she had to get wine, white cooking chocolate, strawberries. Her roots needed doing, God knows when she'd get time for that. She was getting irritated by the Edith Piaf Alison had left on the CD, wondering whether the man in the leather coat would buy the handsome Van Eyck book he'd had his nose in for the past half hour, when the bell rang and in walked Michael, ignoring her completely and browsing in twentieth-century writers by the door. A little pouch of skin appeared under his chin when he hung his head to read the spines of the books on the lower shelves.

From the lists her eyes kept wandering, slyly taking him in. She twiddled the cigarette. They could cast him as a werewolf, she thought, mentally crayoning his dark brows darker, sprouting hairs from his cheeks. He came closer, his foot kicked against a cardboard box full of books that had not yet been sorted and he dropped into a loose squat to take a look. Anita changed the CD. Elvis Presley, the Sun recordings, 1956. 'Blue Moon of Kentucky'. Outside on the estuary the gulls began to argue.

He looked up at her, suddenly surprised.

'I had this book,' he said. 'When I was a kid.'

He stood up, a very battered paperback in

36

his hands. They'd have put it in one of the 10p bins outside. She leaned forward to see. On the jacket was a faded Edward Ardizzone drawing. 'The Little Bookroom,' she read from the cover he held up. She had no belief in fate, yet she sensed a click in time, an odd rush of certainty, and suddenly knew that she had always known the time would come when one of them would speak.

He looked down at the scruffy old book. 'Hm.' A small shrug, a twitch of the lips. His nostrils were large and sensitive.

'Think,' she said, 'it might be the very book.'

'I doubt it.' He turned the pages slowly. 'It was a long way from here.'

'Well, books get around.'

'You know,' he said, 'I've never seen this anywhere.'

Then he continued browsing down the other side of the shop. A woman came in. Anita let the tip of her pencil skim down the margin. A soft tickle of excitement teased her stomach. He wasn't ugly now, he had a certain beauty, a strength and intelligence in his face, as if, she decided, he'd suffered hard times and come through. I want him for a friend, she thought, just that. Why can't he be my friend? What's wrong with it?

When he came to the table to pay for his

book she asked him, 'What happened to the original?'

'What?'

'The original book. The one you had.'

'Oh. God knows.' He looked down. 'Chucked out, I suppose. It was a long time ago.' It seemed he wouldn't say any more, but as she handed him the bag he suddenly continued: 'It wasn't like this, of course, the one I had. Different cover. Hardback. We had it in Hong Kong years ago. Couldn't read it then, of course.'

'Oh! You were in Hong Kong?'

'Oh, many, many, many years ago.' He grinned quickly, his teeth flashing white and crooked, his face suddenly quite ordinary, then nodded, dipping his head in a curious, old-fashioned gesture as he left. He stood on the Quay for a while, taking out his book and looking down at the cover several times before turning to the left, towards the Curlew Restaurant. Maybe he'd be there when she got off, sitting at one of the outside tables. It was twenty to one.

'This one, please.'

The man in the leather coat was buying the Van Eyck. She flashed him her brightest smile. 'Thank you,' she said. Already she was plotting. She had a sinking, soaring feeling. She used to not care, she'd have gone for

38

anything her pants itched at, but then she'd been a solipsist, there was no one else out there but her. Now there was Charley and the girls. But she wasn't going to do anything, she told herself. She was only playing in her mind. Step by step. Move by move. Next time she saw him he'd have to acknowledge her. She'd prepare an opening gambit. Something was there already anyway, some bit of her stuck in his head, though he'd shown no sign. She always knew.

'Thank you!' she said again, dazzlingly gay, and the man left. A minute later the woman went out without buying anything. 'Yes!' Anita cried, punching the air, as she went into the back and put the kettle on and smoked another cigarette. It only takes one, she thought, looking at herself in the curved chrome of the kettle. Her haughty aquiline nose looked enormous in the spout, her eyes small and far away. She was Alice, a dream creature; when she moved she elongated, chin stretching down to her feet. She was reminded of the Hall of Mirrors in Belle Vue. Only one, she thought, pouring boiling water on a tea bag, to be that bit more revealed suddenly by circumstance. That's what attraction was, the revelation of one to another in a sea of indifference. That, and opportunity. She got out her sketchpad and started sketching the kettle with all its reflections, including her own.

Alison came in at one to take over.

'Ali,' she said, 'do you ever have rape fantasies?' She had to say these things. Their friendship went back so many years it was grounded more on long service than shared interests, but Alison never gave herself away. She'd always had a formal manner, even as a girl. Dispensing peppermint teabags into her little caddy, she smiled indulgently.

'Do you?' she returned.

'Yes, I do.' Anita was getting into her jacket, all ready to go, but she leaned against the wall for a while and talked. 'Doesn't everyone? Really? Admit it. Don't you, Ali? Really? Ever? Surely it can't be just me that's weird.'

'I can honestly say,' Alison replied, looking amused and sounding slightly smug, 'that I have never had a rape fantasy. It's supposed to be a sign of guilt.'

Anita shrieked.

'It is really. Supposed to mean you feel guilty about sex so you can only enjoy it if you're being forced.'

'*That* hoary old chestnut,' Anita said, pushing herself away from the wall and striding down the shop. 'You want to try it, sometimes, Ali. It's good fun.'

'I don't think I'd force it, Anita,' Alison chuckled, smoothing her short brown hair and pulling down her jumper. Her ear-rings were shiny parrots.

Anita got as far as the door and turned back. Clearly she still wanted to talk. 'Nostrils are interesting,' she said. 'Do you ever notice people's nostrils, Ali? Yours are funny ones.' She knew because she'd drawn them. They were sharp and tight and asymmetrical.

'Nostrils,' murmured Alison in a thoughtful voice, gazing into the distance, 'nostrils. Do I notice? Hmm.'

'Have you noticed that man that comes in with the amazing nostrils? You gave him a credit note once.'

She thought.

'I fancy him like mad,' Anita said, and as she said it it became fact.

'Really? You must point him out.'

'Oh, you must know who I mean. He's got a really weird face. Looks a bit like the Missing Link or something.'

Alison looked worried. It must have been something in Anita's manner.

'Don't worry, my dear.' Anita walked to the door. 'It's quite natural.' Her voice grew defiant. 'Just because you're with someone, you know, it doesn't mean the rest of the world ceases to exist, does it? I mean, if

41

people were honest.' She turned again, scrabbled a cigarette out of her bag and waved it. 'It's just someone I see, he's really ugly and all, but it's OK, it's just nice really, gives me something to think about. It's OK, I have no intention of actually *doing* anything.'

Alison wedged herself in behind the table ponderously, uncapping her fountain pen and gazing thoughtfully at the jagged skyscrapers of books on either side of her.

'It's just really good fun,' Anita said.

'Well.' Alison applied herself briskly to the books. 'I only hope you know what you're doing. A sense of perspective always helps with these things.'

'Of course.'

The bell rang. Two schoolgirls in short skirts and clumpy shoes came in.

'You know, Ali — ' Anita took out her car keys and matches, 'you don't want to take me too seriously.'

'Take you seriously, Anita?' Alison lightened up. 'Would I be so foolish?'

———

When Anita was upstairs laying out her new school uniform on the bed and looking at it, her mother came and stood holding on to the door.

'Look,' she said, 'don't say anything to your

42

dad about that boy coming in here. I've told Robin.'

'OK,' said Anita. There was nothing unusual about this. She said the same thing whenever any of the Deasys came, because her father didn't like them. Grandma O'Leary was one but she'd married a settled man in Mullingar, and ended up here. The Deasys all seemed to be over in England too now; they used to camp sometimes on Melland's playing fields or over on Jackson's brickworks, and her mother told and endlessly retold the story of how she'd travelled with them as a child during the war, how she'd been evacuated with Connie to Ambleside when she was eleven but hated the old couple they'd ended up with, who pinched their evaporated milk and corned beef and made them do housework and run errands all the time. Slave labour, she called it. So she ran away and lived with the Deasys in one of their caravans and went round with them selling pegs and bunches of heather.

'Not that there's anything wrong with it but you know what he's like,' she said.

'OK.'

Her mother came in and sat down on the bed. 'He's from Tipperary,' she said, smiling. Her make-up had worn off and her eyes were big and staring. She leaned back against the bedhead and put her arm up over her head. Its underside was bluey-white and a few dark hairs peeped out from under her arm. She sang 'Eileen Aroon'. Closed her eyes and put her head back and oh! it poured, it poured, when like the early rose, Eileen Aroon, yearning and aching, bittersweet, Eileen Aroon, the lost, beloved. And all out of tune.

———————

A week later she took the dog and walked to the place on the cliffs where the samphire grew. Samphire impressed people not of those parts, and provided a little talking point at dinner. 'What's this?' they'd ask enthusiastically when it appeared, green and fleshy, dripping butter. 'Samphire,' she'd say casually, 'I picked it on the rocks.' Her mother hadn't taken to it when she'd come down from Crosby at Christmas.

Charley showed her the place where the samphire grew the morning after the night they met, after the fireworks for the opening of the New Imperial Hotel. She'd never seen such fireworks before or since, flowerheads exploding out of space, one following another so fast the sky was always full of colours: purple-pink, gold, silver, acid green, spangly red. Above in the cold black air, they had a sharp quality as if they'd cut your eye, like the sparkle of Waterford glass or the sequins on a woman's dress. On the smooth sea below, their reflections were soft and sinuous, twinkling kindly like eyes. A blue cascade descended like the glitter on her royal blue Alice band, the one Paddy Riley found in the Hall of Mirrors; it opened a door and the past rode out: the firework lake at Belle Vue, the cold stand where she sat to watch *The Storming of Quebec* with her father, the first time she ever saw anything on a real stage with him, the Hippodrome auditorium so dark and the stage so bright and the costumes of the dancers brilliant and shimmering; then the crowd with its collective voice brought back Quack Fair, and she saw flattened grass going yellow in a tent, a wire slung between trees, a fire of massive logs burning fierce at night through total country darkness; and the cosy little pin-pricks of cigarettes and joints moving about in some friendly farmer's field in the far west.

Sometimes still she woke up and thought she was there.

The prom and all the steps down to the beach were full of people watching the fireworks. She was down near the bottom and when it was all over and she turned round, Charley was standing there a couple of steps away, smiling up at the sky. He wore a big bottle-green coat with the collar up and his breath hung in a cloud in front of his face so that he looked like someone from a Russian classic. His hair was short and came down over his brow, fitting close to his head. She knew him, of course, though they'd never spoken. She'd seen him at a party she'd gone to on Gibbet Hill with Alison and Doug. He'd been on the other side of the room, drinking wine out of a plastic cup, smiling dreamily to himself as he looked into the tropical fish tank, his face illuminated by it. He had a self-contained look, she'd thought. His body was big and strong and solid, but there was a gentleness about him, a softness in the eyes, a roundedness to the shoulders. All the people were between them. She'd thought: I could hurt that man. Terrible, but there you are. She'd seen him in Kokoschka's many a time; he used to sit alone in the corner with a pint of beer in the early evenings, reading a book or sifting through sheaves of important-looking papers that he took out of a smart tan briefcase. He wore hound's tooth jackets, open-necked shirts, sometimes a pale suit. A breed she knew nothing of, a safe man, she thought, who'd never broken a rule in his life. She could not for the life of her imagine why she should have noticed him. She'd seen him coming out of the vet's with a sandy-haired mongrel in his arms, a small face with short hair and little prettifying twiddly bits round the ears. They'd started acknowledging one another in the street in a minimal sort of way: just a nod, a quick flick of the eyes. Once or twice she patted his dog.

Now, on the steps, they suddenly smiled broadly at each other.

'I didn't mean to stay and watch it all,' he said, 'but once I was here I got stuck on the steps and couldn't get out.'

'You could have gone down along the beach.'

'Well.' He glanced away, his eyes wandering. 'I suppose I didn't really want to.'

'Where's your dog?' Stupid question. Who'd bring a dog to a firework display?

'At home,' he said. 'He wouldn't appreciate this kind of thing.'

They walked up the fifty-three steps together at the heel of the crowd. A dark party was in swing all along the prom and a full moon sat shining vulgarly over the headland. He wandered away with his hand lightly touching the rail. She'd come up from London a few months ago. She knew only a few of Alison and Doug's friends, school-teachers mostly, and Phil Wragge, who ran the gallery and was interested in her drawings; they'd never got past small talk. She couldn't let him go. She wanted a friend. She followed, walking along beside him bold as brass, as her mother would have said, head held high, tossing her scarf back over her shoulder. They looked sideways at each other and laughed for some reason. 'Are you going in here?' he asked when they drew level with the thronging front porch of the New Imperial.

'Why not?' She smiled.

They were doing cheap drinks. All along the bar and on the tables were bowls filled with peanuts and pretzels and crisps. They couldn't get a seat so they stood in the crowd with their drinks. She asked about his dog. 'He's a rescue dog,' he said, 'I'm trying to civilise him.' She told him she'd come up from London; he'd been there too for a while, he said, and smiled. He had a sweet smile, she thought. He said he'd done a postgrad at City University but now worked at the Laing Institute. Laing was a marine research place eight miles up the coast. He'd done a degree in Oceanography. Anita just didn't meet people who'd done that sort of thing.

'And do you like your work?' she asked, sounding like the Queen, and he waxed lyrical about coastal erosion and wave power and currents and continental shelves.

48

She felt as if she were quivering with excitement inside. He said he'd come out tonight to get away from the people who were staying at his house, friends from the University. They were OK but it was a very small house and he'd be glad when they'd gone. His hair was flat and mousy, and he was, she supposed, plain, but his face was very pleasant to look at, dark-browed, the nose straight and pretty but big. He said he had a beach hut. He'd lived in it before he got his house, it was the size of a shoe box. She didn't know what it was about him. She kept thinking: I do not fancy him one bit but I could sleep with him. It might be nice. I could make him want me. I could fascinate him.

She drank fast. He watched her with careful eyes.

When they left, their paths lay in the same direction so they walked along the prom together and the cold air went to her head along with the drink. The moon streamed all over the flat glimmering sand and the little black bobbing waves all tipped silver, and the row of beach huts pretty as toy town, blue and red and green and brown and white.

She took his arm. He didn't respond. Come on, she thought, look at the situation, we are going to do this so why beat about the bush? You are my new thing and there's nothing you can do about it. Drink made her strong.

'Which is your hut?' she asked.

'It's further along.'

They strolled, though the cold was making her teeth chatter. There was something large and warm and comforting about him, as if he were a bed all ready for climbing in, with a hot water bottle and the sheets turned back. She made him point out his hut to her. She had to see it. She didn't care about anything any more but keeping this fine balance of perfect drunkenness, keeping this night, getting him alone in a small space, so she climbed over the rail and ran down through the dunes so that he had to follow.

'Can I see it?' she said. 'I've always wondered what they were like inside.'

He had the key in his pocket. He hesitated before he opened the door, thinking for a moment, then looked at her and smiled.

'You take risks, don't you?' he said mildly.

It was everything she could have hoped for. She lived at the time in a horrible room over the launderette, adjoining a toilet used by the café next door. People from the street came in and used the toilet even though they weren't supposed to. All day long they traipsed up and down the stairs outside her door and pulled the chain.

She could live here, she thought. He would let her. She'd live here and be happy. Every night she'd look out at the moon and the mysterious shore. At that moment it seemed to her that she had never had a home, never a real home, so far away was that distant time when she'd lived with her mother and father and little brother next door to Belle Vue in Manchester. Her breast filled up with self-pity. This little hut would be her happy home. It had a tiny covered porch of sandy boards. Charley lit candles and made the musty interior cosy. Sometimes, he said, he came down with a sleeping bag and stayed the night, just for the fun of it, though not usually in winter. It was nice to be able to step straight out on to the beach in the morning. He'd got it all kitted out with a paraffin heater and camping Gaz cylinder, both of which he lit, and a mat of foam rubber on which they could sit. They kept their coats on. He poured water from a plastic container into a pan and spooned coffee from a jar on the narrow shelf into two chipped, stained mugs. There was no milk. Out there, the night of returning revellers and humming sea expanded into the vast dark of the womb.

Sanctuary.

She was sitting on something hard. Tucked under a corner of the foam rubber she

51

discovered a bottle half full of Irish whiskey.

He said he kept it there for warming up after a swim.

They poured some into their black coffee. Soon it grew warm in the tiny space, full of their breathing and the hissing of the gas. Their faces glowed.

They talked all night, or she talked and he listened. She told him everything recklessly, hot from the whiskey which she kept pouring and pouring without permission, little nips that kept her going, paring her brain like a knife. She told him all about Quack Fair so that he would see what a strange and remarkable person she was, just like Sally Bowles: she talked of the swingboats going up into the sky, the hard, deep voice of the barker, the try-your-strength machine, and Tom Shafto going on ahead to cry the Fair on the village green in his silk cape that was the colour of mulberries. We should touch, she thought. Soon. Charley sat as far away from her as it was possible to get, which was not far, leaning into the corner with an easy slouch. We should kiss, she thought, the two of us in this little box all pushed together like this, all suddenly intimate in the night. But he was so strange with his deep amused eyes that she didn't know what to do, and none of her old tricks seemed right. Somehow, some time towards morning, she lost her grip. She ran out of cigarettes. The room grew bright and starry and unreal. She could hear her own voice babbling on but she seemed to be disassociated from it. Her fingers picked at things, flew about, shredded the empty cigarette packet up very fine using a trick she knew for making it into a kind of necklace, which she draped around his neck as a means of getting close to his mouth, close enough to kiss. Their lips came within inches. He gave a little outward sniff of laughter. His eyes were soft and vulnerable. He doesn't want to, she thought, that's all it is. He just doesn't want to. Poor man, I'm an awful pain.

She sat back. He leaned across and pushed open the door with his big slow hand and said, 'Look. Morning,' and the light came in cold and tired and the sea was a long grey line very very far away.

They walked along the beach in the icy morning. They were the only people about. He talked about sonar buoys and mountain ranges under the sea, and a remote control thing that could bore holes in the ocean bed. She went off along the cliff path and he followed, saying, 'Anita, you don't have to do this,' but she didn't know why he was saying that.

And at some point, he looked up and said,

'There, that's where the samphire grows,' and she tried to climb up but he pulled her down and she fell over on the path and lay there with the mashed potato sky whirling round and round her head and little daggers of light piercing her brain, thinking, done it again, done it again, oh God, I've done it again.

He gave her his hand.

'I think I'd better get you home,' he said.

She could never remember getting there, but she remembered her door looming, its satellite position beside the launderette reminding her of Paddy Riley's dusty black door so long ago. She remembered how squalid her room looked with Charley standing there in the middle of it, his eyelids soft and heavy as he looked round at all her things. She remembered how very gently he laid her down on the bed, took off her shoes, covered her up and left, closing the door without a sound.

Then she died of shame.

★   ★   ★

The cliff path met the prom at the seedy end of town, by the amusement arcade and Mr Magic's Merry Maze, where she habitually spent what seemed like hours sitting and reading a book or sketching, waiting for the

54

girls to finish sliding down chutes and wallowing about in ball pools. She was carrying her basket with the samphire, Basil trotting neatly alongside, the sun in her eyes so that at first she did not see who it was coming towards her carrying a fishing rod.

'Hello,' he said.

She shielded her eyes. The incident in the shop had taken on a kind of *Brief Encounter* haze over the past week; his sudden appearance called up an instant surge, a heady mixture of repulsion and desire.

' 'Going fishing?' she smiled.

He held the rod at arm's length and shook it. 'For Luke,' he said, as if it was assumed she knew who he meant. Luke. A name at last for the solitary child going home past her shop to the boat on the saltings.

'Your little boy has the most beautiful face,' she told him. 'I'd die for bones like that.'

He grinned. There was a very old scar on the end of his chin, a faint white thread. 'Well, he certainly doesn't take after me.'

'How old is he?'

'Ten.'

Then he said, 'Was it you with Charley Lamb the other night?'

'Yes,' she replied, 'he's my husband.'

He nodded.

'I didn't know you knew Charley,' she said.

'Only slightly. We were at the University about the same time. We overlapped.' He looked away over the sea, raising his bushy brows. His eyes were blue, deep and dishevelled. 'He was a grafter, Charley, wasn't he?'

'Still is.'

That was all. He went on his way.

She floated round to Lindsay's, Lindsay was always good for a quick gossip, she hadn't time but to hell with it, there was never time. Lindsay made coffee while she moaned. She had to frame up some more stuff for the Wragge Gallery, and, oh my God, start thinking about Sid's birthday party. What on earth had they been thinking, making it into some big garden affair, why couldn't they just have had six kids and jelly and ice cream and Pass the Parcel? Party bags! 'We never used to have party bags when I was a kid,' she said. 'I don't think we did, anyway. Not like now anyway. My mum didn't spend a bloody fortune every time one of us had a birthday.'

'Don't do it,' said Lindsay. 'I never did.' Her kids were long gone.

'Oh no!' Anita was shocked. 'I mean, you have to make it nice for them really, little things! I couldn't not do it.'

'S'posing it rains?'

'It won't. It's going to be nice at the weekend, Charley said.' Charley always got the weather right.

Anita recounted in detail the meeting by Mr Magic's Merry Maze. 'I don't know what it is, he's just so — you know — you just get the impression he's like, he's, you know, oh I don't know, like there's such a lot going on in him, he looks so — *deep* somehow . . . ' She rambled on in this vein for ten minutes or so, then leapt up in panic, glaring at her watch as if it had stung her. 'The girls!' she cried, scrabbling about for her things.

'You wanna watch it,' said Lindsay, grinning, 'you wanna be very, very careful. You know these *deeeep* types.'

★   ★   ★

'There's this bloke,' she said to Charley that night, as he shook risotto in a pan, the sleeves of his blue check shirt pushed up his arms, 'comes in the shop sometimes, says he knows you. The one that works behind the bar in the Wild Boar. Dark hair, odd sort of face.'

At first, with all the sizzling, he didn't hear. She sat down, pushing the stuff on the table with her elbow. Something fell off at the other side. His face was droopy and

57

there were two deep lines between his eyes as he shoved the rice about with a spatula, scraping the bottom of the pan; washing up after him was a nightmare. Steam gushed. She repeated her words. Charley thought for a while. 'I know who you mean but his name escapes me,' he said.

'Nice bloke,' she remarked.

'Yeah,' replied Charley, 'I think he was OK,' then he yelled out of the back door for the girls to stop pulling the wall down and come in and set the table.

Going into town on the bus, the one her father waited for every morning on Stockport Road, you could see from the top deck the words Blood Bank on a shabby old building down at the end of a side street. That was where her father worked. She'd never been inside but imagined it like a real bank, had visions of people going in and out and queuing up in front of glass partitions and paying in and taking away little bags of blood. He was going to be a chemist, her mother had told her, he was very clever; he'd been at the University and lived in a house with three storeys and a garden front and back when she met him, but he'd given it all up for love of her, the beautiful Geraldine O'Leary, and

58

now he worked in the Blood Bank in town and wore a white coat.

'I was a bit wild, you know,' her mother was always pleased to say, 'in my younger days.'

Anita's father was a distant, vague man with a long pale bony face, weary eyes with thick, heavy lids and an expression that was mournful in repose but lit gently into kindness when he smiled. He was a Jewish atheist, whose strictly orthodox family in Cheetham Hill had cut him off without a penny and observed a week of mourning as for a bereavement when he married out of the faith. Every night he came home and sat in his chair in front of the range with the big wireless on the little bamboo table beside him.

'Where's the *Chron*?' he'd say, and Anita's mother would lay aside her embroidery and hand him the *Evening Chronicle*. Her mother could do beautiful embroidery, crinoline ladies and trees and gardens full of flowers with the sun rising full of beams.

Her father always drank a cup of lemon tea made with water ladled from a pot that simmered continuously next to the stockpot, before her mother brought out the meal, meat and gravy and roast potatoes and cabbage, which he ate without a word, sitting at the table and forking away methodically, staring dreamily before him from time to time into something unseen. 'Your father's tired when he gets home. Don't make a noise,' her mother would say. Later he'd fall asleep in his chair with the *Chron* on top of his face.

Sid's birthday was on Thursday and they were having the party at the weekend. It had blown itself up into a do for adults as well, partly because they hadn't had people round for ages, partly because it was such a beautiful spring and it would be so nice to drink wine in the garden and pick party food from a table under the apple trees, which were full of blossom.

They'd invited her mother, of course. Charley was all for finding out about temporary oxygen supplies, said he'd go up to Crosby and fetch her if Clive couldn't bring her down, but after all the effort of Christmas her mother just wasn't up to it. Her mother lived with cousin Judith and her husband and old Auntie Bernie up on Merseyside, and Anita went up four or five times a year and felt guilty all the time. But, as Robin said, safely out of it in Toronto, what can you do? She won't move and you can't just pack up and move; move countries, move *continents*, by God, just like that, can you? Anita couldn't have lived with her mother anyway, no way. You could always hear her wheezing away, her whole great chest heaving up and down like a breathing bag. And the way she rambled, endlessly, about her childhood and how her sister Mary died, and the war when she travelled about the Lake District in a caravan with the Deasys. She went over and over her family history, contradicting herself, getting it wrong, telling the same tales over and over again incoherently till Anita's eyelids drooped.

And sometimes she talked about Paddy Riley to her, as if she were a total stranger and knew nothing about him.

———

'There was this young boy once, Anita, had a real crush on me, he did. Young Irish lad called Paddy, Paddy Riley, like in the song, you know that song, I like that song:

'*Come back, Paddy Riley, to Bally-
        jamesduff
Come back, Paddy Riley, to me . . .*

'Well, I used to sing it to him sometimes, just to annoy him, you know, I *was* awful. It was when I was the mermaid. Do you remember that? When I was the mermaid, Anita? Do you remember that wig I had? And sitting there showing all I'd got! Which believe you me was worth seeing in those days! Blow me, when I think of it all now, blow me, I think, the things you do. Mind you, you wouldn't believe this now, of course, but I had a lovely figure back then, people used to compliment me on my figure. And my hair was very nice in those days too. You wouldn't believe it, would you? You know, you young people, you don't believe you'll ever get old. You wait. I don't believe these people who say they wouldn't want to be young again, that's a load of old rubbish, everybody would be young again if they had the chance, I know I would. This little Paddy, I say little but he wasn't really, only he was very young to me, I was a married woman, of course, and he was only this young lad really, but he had such a big crush on me. It quite went to my head.'

Alison had gone off to a book auction. There was nothing doing in the shop, nothing doing at all. She'd taken in her sketch pad but the light was all wrong and her eyes were sleepy when she tried to read. She kept yawning and yawning, walking round the empty shop.

Nothing needed shelving, nothing needed dusting. All she had to do was wait for Charley to come and get her because he had the car. Quite late she strolled out front to breathe the air. Old wooden boats lay about at odd angles like seals basking in the mud. Thirty or forty swans preened their feathers and the slatey water gleamed beneath a still bright light. Turning to look inland the first thing she saw was the back of a man sitting at one of the outside tables in front of the Curlew Restaurant next door. It was Michael, she could tell by the set of his shoulders and the way his hair sat on his collar. He was drinking a beer, his head bent over a book, a smoking cigarette held by his right ear.

She didn't even think, she moved on tracks, impelled like a tram. Sometimes, she thought, a thing is just thrown in your path. You can't move for falling over. She locked up and went next door, gliding past his table without disturbing him, bought a glass of red wine and sat down at the table nearest the door. She lit a cigarette and spread out her book.

He did not raise his head until she had almost drained the glass, and then he did not smile, though she did; his eyes were hard, his lower lip thick and sensual. His forehead was extremely high, scored with wavy lines. He put down his book and pushed back his chair.

'Want another?' he murmured like a conspirator, looking over her head and reaching for her glass without waiting for an answer as he passed her table.

She curled her fingers together in front of her lips, resting her face on her hands and smiling as she looked out across the estuary. The brown sail of a barge lay furled in the air like a pupa. It was something to do with the weather, this feeling of childlike perception, as if everything was brand new, the fishy tang of the Quay in her throat and chest as she waited for him to return, the voices of the men calling to one another across the decks of boats in the harbour, dropping on her brain like raindrops on sand. The air was fine and nourishing, time stretchy and languid; there was purity, and exaltation: anything was possible. She stretched her arms above her head and yawned with pleasure. It was OK. Soon Charley would come strolling down the Quay, and nothing would be wrong and nothing would be hidden.

He placed a full glass of red wine in front of her and sat down with his beer. There was a very slight aggression in his manner.

'You bring them shellfish, don't you?' she said.

'Now and then. Me and the boy. We go

64

cockling and musselling alive alive-o.' What steady eyes. What nostrils! I cannot help but stare, she thought, I have an artist's eye.

'You know Charley.'

'A bit.'

'He'll be along in a little while,' she said, 'he's picking me up.'

The wine was bitter. She couldn't think of anything more pleasant than sitting drinking wine on the Quay in the late afternoon with a newly fancied man.

'So how *is* Charley?' he asked, leaning back and squaring his shoulders. 'What's he doing with himself these days?'

'He's at Laing, he's an information scientist.'

'Always a grafter, Charley, that's what I remember about him. He used to go out with Doon, didn't he?'

'Yes, he did.'

'Likes it, does he? At Laing?'

'Oh yeah. Oh yeah, Charley loves his work.' She smiled, thinking of him at home with the dog leaning up against his legs, his papers furled about him and a mug of coffee going cold at his side. 'He's like a hound dog,' she said, 'sniffing things out. Endlessly trawling through words. Documents. He'd have made a terrific historian, Charley would.'

Michael said he just did this and that. He'd studied Law but he'd never done anything with it. She asked him about Hong Kong and he looked surprised.

'How did you know about Hong Kong?' he asked.

'You told me. The *Little Bookroom*. You said you had it out in Hong Kong. Remember?'

He grinned and his face was normalised. He was born in Hong Kong, he said, but he couldn't remember much about it. His dad imported carpets. Quite posh obviously, she thought, though he's managed to expunge most of it from his voice. He offered her a cigarette and struck a match, and she moved towards his hands cupped round the little flame and thanked God for cigarettes, leaning right into his hands like the dewy heroine in an old black and white film, all gaslight and smoke and Vaseline on the lens. When he sat back the outer corners of his eyebrows were lifted. God, I'd love to draw him, she thought.

Charley came walking down by the old wool warehouse at the end of the Quay, looking out over the rail towards the other side of the estuary, over the crabbers and shrimpers and fishing smacks with big white numbers painted on their prows. She saw him as a stranger would; she liked the way he walked in his suit, nice long straight legs and his arms swinging, heavy, a little round-shouldered but not too much. His mouth drooped at the corners. He was wearing the faraway look he sometimes had, puzzled and worried. It seemed to her that he had an open, boyish, touching quality that set him apart from her and Michael, the dark ones, sitting there at their devious table. She stood up and waved to him.

'It was such a beautiful day,' she said, 'I just *had* to sit outside.'

Charley smiled. 'Michael Bastian,' he said. 'That's it, isn't it? I couldn't for the life of me remember but it's just come back.'

'That's me,' said Michael, lighting up another cigarette. Charley sat down and pulled off his tie and drank from her glass, touching her raised left knee which was hooked over the right one. They talked about people she didn't know, things from years before she came on the scene; they laughed and said times had certainly changed and look at them now, hey, fathers, no less. Charley got a round in. Anita and Michael did not speak while he was at the bar. Seven wild ducks flew over, an undulous V, and a spritsail barge glided seaward. When Charley returned with the drinks they talked about her drawings. Michael had seen the one in the window of the Wragge Gallery — the one of books lying scattered about on the stairs in a

67

random kicked-about fashion.

'How much would something like that be?' he asked.

'She said she wanted sixty pounds for it.'

'That's ridiculous,' he said, 'you'll never make a living like that. You've got to charge.'

'I can't.' She laughed. 'He hasn't sold one of mine for ages as it is.'

'Ah, that's not a brilliant gallery,' said Charley, 'you know, you really must see about making some other kind of contacts.'

'Oh, I suppose so.'

'You whack the price up and they'll sell,' said Michael. 'That's the way it goes. People see a piffling price tag and they think, oh that can't be much cop.'

'That's right,' Charley agreed.

Michael talked about his boat on the saltings. He said his boy didn't make friends easily, he thought it must be because they'd moved around such a lot, always changing schools. However, he said, they'd stay put for a while now. 'I always seem to keep ending up back around here,' he said, 'so when the boat turned up it seemed like a good idea. I like it. Kid likes it. We can get up and go whenever we want.' He shrugged.

Luke, it turned out, was at Jasmine's school.

'Why don't you bring him to Sid's birthday

68

party?' Charley suggested.

'Sid?'

'Our littlest. Short for Sadie,' he explained.

Anita looked away. None of this is my doing, she told herself.

Charley said it wasn't just a kids' thing, quite a few people were coming. Doon would be there, he said, you know Doon. And Phil Wragge and Mona and Rich Foreman, and some other people. And he started explaining how to get there.

★   ★   ★

She woke around six the morning of the party and got up and went down before anyone else was abroad and set about clearing up toys, picking bits of plastic jewellery out of squashed Plasticine. Basil lurched about the room in a kind of slow ricochet, a ridiculous parody of a young dog. She let him out and walked about on the lawn for a while with her first cigarette, sniffing at the coming day, lovely, fresh and cool. The apple trees made a dim green grotto. She followed the paths that the badgers used. The tops of the woods were swaying ever so gently with the movements of birds. Anita climbed over the wall at the back, dislodging a few more rocks, and wandered through the early wood with Basil trotting on ahead cocking his leg up at this tree and that. He used to have such an efficient gait, she thought, look at him, old thing. She came out on the edge of the big cornfield and lay down and closed her eyes against the bright sky and thought about Michael Bastian. She didn't want anything from him. If he had gone away tomorrow and never reappeared she might have felt a fleeting mild regret at the passing of some inessential pleasure. It was just that his strange intense face kept coming into her mind. It was newness, the thrill of conquest, the fascination of being fascinating that she wanted. She didn't want anything to change, she loved this house and all she had, and it wasn't sex either, she had Charley for that. Charley's passion was a shark under a reef. That day in the wood coming back from the library she'd known. What times those were! That dreadful morning ten years ago when she woke with a vicious hangover and cried because she'd blown it. She thought he'd never come back, walked about in a daze for a week, avoiding Kokoschka's, bought herself a fancy jewelled belt and strode about practising catwalk walks in her room defiantly. She'd grown so thin and her hair was still short. She'd grow it, she decided. This was terrible, she'd thought she could down him in one gulp and look at her, look, tossing and turning and pacing the floor at four in the morning with her umpteenth fag, and over what? What? Such a very ordinary man.

Then one day he caught up with her in the street, smiled and asked her where she'd been. 'I think you need to learn caution, Anita,' he said. Whenever she met a man she fancied they were in bed straight away, but not Charley. It took weeks. They just talked endlessly, she told him everything about herself, even the bad things.

Nearly everything.

They went for long walks along the shore, sat in his little house on Wool Street, saw films at The Wool House and drank at the Dun Cow. He pointed out to her all the places where the sea was taking the land. She tried to draw him but could never get him right. A few of the Quack Fair drawings had survived, the sword-swallower, Tom Shafto's wagon, Pantaloon, Punchinello and the Doctor, and, of course, the Great Candini. She thought they were alike in some ways, Candy and Charley, but Candy never had Charley's hard edge. There was a rock seam going right through Charley, where Candy was all water and had nearly drowned her. It showed in the poster she did of him, where she'd placed him against the background of

71

the great waterfall at Poulaphuca. Charley loved the pictures so she gave them to him and he had them framed and hung up in his hall. But never a kiss, scarcely a touch. She saw through his open collar that there were hairs on his chest, couldn't stop drawing his mouth in her mind. I wanted a friend, she reminded herself. Now I've got one. Well, I don't want anything else if he doesn't. But I want *him*. I don't care. He liked sprawling on the floor. Once in her room he leaned close and her insides convulsed like a dying fish. She couldn't remember anyone else ever having had this effect on her.

They drove out into the country to an old house he knew about where they had an archive of documents relating to the Civil War. The house stood in a grand formal garden and was open to the public, with a tea shop and folk museum and a lake with a Grecian temple where you could sit and feed the ducks. They had lunch there. That was when he described in great detail his memories of lying in the plague pit with the bodies of the people he knew falling like leaves upon him, obscuring the sun. He remembered a small dark place in a narrow lane, a terrible smell and a black pall of smoke. He still woke up with it sometimes, he said, wondering where he would run, and how he would run, and whether anyone would go with him. Anita thought he got it from the double page spread about the Plague and the Great Fire in the ancient children's encyclopedia he still had high up on a shelf in the study, away from the girls. It stemmed from when he was eight and staying with his auntie near Bath, the summer his father left, and he'd stumbled with his dog (he always had a dog) into Sleeping Beauty's forest, the garden of a grand house gone to ruin. He remembered the orchids, he said, small ones growing wild underfoot. Anita saw him as a child, all summer climbing trees, making dens, running through the jungle making the noises boys make when they play, alone. Not knowing about her waiting for him in the future. His aunt told him the people had come out from London to get away from the Plague, but they'd all died of it anyway. His aunt had shown him their fading names on stones in the village churchyard: Maria and Isaac, Elizabeth and Charity.

The archive was in a small library at the back of the house, a beautiful room full of brown leather and polished oak and hundreds and hundreds of very old books that made her feel faint with desire. He spoke to the keeper, a wonderful old lady with shiny brown hair done up in a bun, and got her to open up some special cases and show them the old documents. They must be very cautiously handled, the old lady said. Charley made careful notes, sitting at a long polished oak table. The sun came in through a high window and touched his hair as he wrote, striking gold from his mousy locks. His face was still, frowning slightly, his lips red, small but sweet. She felt she knew him well by now. When he looked up and caught her watching, he smiled.

She came and leaned on his shoulder, looking down.

'You may be very clever,' she said, 'but you can't spell for toffee.'

On the way back they stopped the car by a tract of ancient woodland he said was worth seeing and went for a walk. Far into its dark rampant green they penetrated, holly and mistletoe, ivy like veins running amok, strange bugle-shaped fungi, wetness under-foot, moss, lichen, tendrils, things rotting, rioting, bursting. Charley was a lover of wild places, of forests dank and deep. He spoke of the primeval forest this had once been, the hart and the hind, the wild boar, bears, wolves. They stood in a dim thin cleft in the wild silence whispering round them like the sound of a shell. She saw his trembling, touched his arm, he clamped her head between his big splayed hands and kissed her, his open mouth so warm and gentle yet so passionate that she felt something go, like waters breaking. They stood in the primeval forest, and she put her ear against his check shirt and listened to his heart pounding away in there, and it felt like all the world, everything, beating away like mad, and she knew then that all these years she'd been going wrong.

She went to Bluebell Wood with her father and mother and Robin. It was Easter, and her mother started prattling on to Robin about how you always got fairies in a bluebell wood. Robin said there was no such thing as fairies although there was Coleman Grey, of course, he was real.

Her mother sat by the picnic hamper slotting forks into the little holders in the lid. 'There are fairies though,' she said, 'they're not silly tiny little things like you see in books. They're like proper people only there's always something funny about them, not quite human. Sometimes, if you wait for the last bus, you can get on and find you've got on a goblin bus. I did that once. It was the 53 going down Kirkhamshulme Lane. I went and sat at the back and when I looked up from getting my money out of my purse the whole bus had turned their heads and was looking at me, and every face was the face of a goblin.'

There was a short silence.

Anita's father was slowly chewing a mouthful of tongue and mustard sandwich. He finished it and swallowed. 'Have you no more sense than you were born with?' he asked incredulously.

'It's true,' she said, biffing him with a rolled-up cloth. 'You go and boil your head.'

He lay back with the sun on his face, his long bony nose casting a shadow. Across his forehead he laid his thin white wrist. 'I'll have twenty minutes,' he said.

Her mother was in a playful mood. She went on talking, saying you could always tell a fairy by the telltale sign. Pointed ears some had. Eyes that glowed in the dark like a cat's. Webbed fingers. 'But one thing they all have,' she said, 'is a mark like a diamond on the back. That's the giveaway.'

———

They had a fine show of daffodils that year, all round the side of the house and spraying out from the bank outside the front gate. Under the trees was the table, the shade of apple blossom over the old white cloth with

76

lacy edges that used to belong to Charley's mum, the little bright dishes, the big glass punch bowl full of pink lemonade with fruit floating on top. The kids ran about in the glade at the back, the rest roamed around or sat on blankets drinking wine and eating food from little plates. Everyone was there. Doon, so beautifully thin and free and single, Lindsay, Philip Wragge loud in a long velvet shirt of canary yellow, Jane and Scott Jarrett with Lauren and her pretty little boyfriend, Alison and Doug and so on, and Charley's sister Joanne from Chelmsford with her three big boys.

She got so bored with them all.

Michael came late. He stood at the big iron gate looking about shortsightedly, a bottle of wine and a cigarette in one hand, a small wrapped present in the other. Standing behind his father was Luke, his profile still and serene as he gazed backwards dreamily down the lane, the long planes of his milk-white face remarkable as some natural phenomenon, Giants' Causeway or Table Mountain. She had the same feeling she got in old shops when she came across some appealing old thing that no one else had, some treasure that had lain in shadow for aeons waiting for no one else but her to connect with it; when even though there was

77

no money to spare and the whole thing was out of the question she knew it must be hers because it just must. She wanted them, wanted to own them in that same way. She was drawn across the lawn with her glass and a tipsy smile, as if by a rope.

'You made it.'

'Yeah,' he said. 'Luke, this is . . . this is . . . '

'Anita.'

Didn't even know my name, she thought.

'Come on,' she said, 'come on and get something to eat,' leading them to the table, proud of her apple trees in blossom. 'Luke, I think you must know some of these children. Bobby there, I think he's in your year.'

Luke raised an eyebrow and twitched a corner of his mouth.

Michael looked round. 'Which one of these midgets is Sid?' He waved the tiny package. 'Who do I give this to?'

Anita poured drinks. 'Sid!' she called as Sid went plodding by. 'Come here, Sid, come and see this.'

Sid stopped, frowning.

'Sid, this is Michael, and this is Luke.'

Sid looked odd in her red and white party dress, such a feminine little rag on her short stocky body, as if someone had dressed a teddy bear in a doll's frock. The front of it was higher than the back because her big

78

belly stuck out. Michael went down on one knee to her. 'Sid,' he said very graciously, giving her all his attention, 'happy birthday, Sid,' holding out the yellow package on his palm. She smirked a little, looking down.

'You open it,' she said, so he did, carefully and showily, like a magician revealing a great trick. The sun shone brightly on his eyelids and the smoke from the cigarette that drooped easily from his lips slid upwards across his face, though he showed no sign of noticing it. He chainsmokes, Anita thought. He's much worse than me. It was a little box with a smiley moon's face on it, from one of the craft shops in the High Street. He flicked it open to reveal pink and white sugar bon-bons covered with a fine white powder. That's nice, she thought. He's gone to some trouble there. He's gone out and bought those sweets and put them in the box and wrapped it up, all for a little girl he's never met.

'I'm going to put it with the others,' Sid said, scuttling away, never even saying thank you.

'Sid!' bawled Anita. 'Sid! What do you say!' He laughed.

'No really, I'm old fashioned, I think politeness matters.' She looked at Luke poking at the grass with the toe of his trainer.

79

'I bet you always remember your p's and q's, don't you?'

Luke's eyebrows shot up as his head dipped. 'Who? Me?' he murmured in a rough and curiously adult voice.

Those Quack Fair kids, they were tough little adults. They had no childish airs, and their faces were grave and knowing. Like everyone else, they worked and fished and hauled and hammered and hunted. Even the toddlers had that air, pottering about on their hard bare feet.

Luke had it, she thought.

The world divided into Quack Fair and non-Quack Fair types. Luke and Michael were Quack Fair types, and so was Paddy Riley. Charley and the girls weren't. Neither, looking round, was anyone else here.

She wanted to tell Michael, look, in spite of all this you must believe that I am not ordinary. I mean, I didn't grow up with all this. If you knew the things I've done, the things I've seen, Quack Fair and the band playing on grass, great steaming pots of curried goat and chickpeas, the smell of oil and grass and vinegar and spun sugar, red meat turning on a spit and the smell of toffee apples, and the tightrope stretched between

80

trees, and the sword-swallower bent back like a bow, and the sinews standing out on the neck of the Great Candini above his red and white striped longjohns, and all the characters of the commedia dell'arte mingling with the crowd.

Remembering Quack Fair was a way of life.

★ ★ ★

Doon came tripping across the lawn, tall and slender in a long black skirt and white blouse. 'Michael! Hel*lo*, Michael!' Her hair, the colour of milky tea, tumbled and bounced and flowed about her like a separate creature. 'What are you doing here?'

'Hello, Doon,' he said.

She was all lovely browns, the perfect tan on her face and throat, the length of her throat, the bones showing through her delicate feet, the long hand she put on his arm, the other holding a plate containing a salad of alfalfa and grated carrot. She had perfect lips and eyelids, perfection in the quirks of her brows and the upturn of her mouth.

'Hey,' she said, 'did you get your letters?'

He rubbed his nose and narrowed his eyes. 'They were at Heather's.'

'This man moves around so much.' Doon

flashed her big smile at Anita. In the loose V of her collar a little blue tattoo of a rose could be half seen on the rise of one breast. 'I didn't know you two knew each other.'

'We don't,' Anita murmured, drifting backwards.

★   ★   ★

Charley carried somebody's baby; a stain of sick or dribble had darkened the front of his blue check shirt. Blue was Charley's colour. How banal all their friends seemed; how easy Charley was with them. Lauren Jarrett went by, her eyes adorned with the kind of stark lines that only look good on the young and flawless, a small tasteful stud in her nose and big chunky shoes on her little filly legs. Phil Wragge was leading the games, tall and beaky, all wild exuberance and idiotic abandon like someone from kids' TV, flashing about in his hectic yellow shirt like some loud and gaudy bird. She took the punch bowl into the kitchen for a refill of the pink lemonade she'd learned to make at Quack Fair. Well, she thought, getting the stuff out of the fridge, I have resisted fridge magnets. Give in to fridge magnets, she always felt, and you might as well buy a loo roll cosy.

The phone rang.

'Hello, love.'

'Hello, Mum.'

Her mother wheezed.

'How you doing?' Anita asked.

'Not so bad, you know. Are you having a nice party?'

'Oh, it's lovely. Gorgeous weather. Thanks very much for the little iron, she's mad about it.'

'I thought she would be. I thought about getting the little laundry basket only it seemed such a rip-off for what you get, a few daft little bits of cloth, I mean I could cut a few old squares myself, they do charge a lot, and I resent paying over the odds, so I thought well if I get the iron and ironing board and a couple of nice little pictures to go on the walls, I know you said she hasn't got many, so I thought that one of the apples would be nice for the kitchen.'

'That's right. She's put it over the dresser and it looks lovely.'

Sarah Mottram was talking about her counselling course to Mona Foreman in the hall; she wore very bright leggings. They smiled at her through the door, their faces shiny with afternoon wine.

'Look, I'll get Sid, shall I? Mona, can you give Sid a shout for me, please?'

Anita checked her hair in the mirror, pulling down strands of hair around her ears and twisting them, saying, yes, she was fine, Charley was fine, the girls were fine, everything was fine, gazing into her own eyes while her mother told her the latest about Bernie's angina, till Sid ran up and grabbed the phone.

'Hello! Thank you for my doll's house stuff!'

'Don't shout! Say thank you to Auntie Judith and Uncle Clive for the Hungry Hippos too.'

'Thank you!' she bawled.

'That your mum? How is your mum?' Lindsay asked, coming downstairs.

'Still getting about. I'm going up next month. The oxygen's only really in the evenings.'

Sometimes, when she felt guilty about her mother living with Judith and Clive instead of her, she made herself think callously of her as just an old woman fate had thrown in her way. After all, some accident of birth that put us in the same house, she'd think, what's that? Then she'd flush with bitter guilt, looking down at her hands like Lady Macbeth. Thirty years ago she'd done things, such terrible things, and now she had to believe that nothing mattered. Guilt's only a thing in the mind, she told herself. Get back out there, be reckless, what point drinking all this wine if not to have a little flutter. Yes, yes! She knocked back another glass of wine quickly and carried the brimming bowl back out to the long table under the trees. The last words of the great clown Joseph Grimaldi ran through her mind: *Tonight I assumed the motley for the last time. It clung to my skin as I took it off, and the old cap and bells rang mournfully as I quitted them for ever.* Tom Shafto had been fond of those lines. She'd spoken them herself after leaving Quack Fair. If you knew where I came from, she said silently across the wide garden to Michael, oh yes, I've knocked about a bit. It took a long time getting here, I can tell you, I came the scenic route. It must be in my blood. Like my mum, she was a mermaid, you know. I could tell you some stories, maybe I will.

'Anita,' said Charley, passing by with Jane Jarrett's fat baby in his arms, 'I told you it was daft putting fruit in the lemonade. They're all moaning about the bits.'

'You should have done it then,' she smiled, patting his cheek.

She set down the bowl.

'Any more white?' asked Lindsay.

'God, has it all gone already? I'll bring some more.'

* * *

She was near her limit. Careful.

Smiling, she flitted from group to group. Lauren Jarrett and her boyfriend were snogging hungrily by the rainbarrel. Charley was talking to Doon. Sometimes they looked so nice together; she knew they still liked each other. Doon's nose wrinkled a lot when she talked to Charley, like an excited dog. Who left who? she'd asked him once. She left me, he said, and Anita hated her for that.

Michael hovered in a corner of the garden alone, drinking a lot.

'Could you go to sea in your boat?' she enquired, placing herself, breathless, by his side.

He laughed. 'Not a good idea.'

Her hand was twiddling the cigarette too much.

'Which is your other daughter?' he asked.

'There. Long fair hair. Blue dress. Playing Tig.'

'Ah,' he said, 'the fairy princess.'

The fairy princess looked a little awkward at the moment, trying to run about playing Tig without losing the rhythm of her nailbiting. Poor old Jas. She was so pretty and such a loser.

'She ought to have wings,' he said.

She worried about Jasmine. Not Sid, Sid would be all right.

'Jasmine's my nervous one,' she explained, 'and Sid's my sensible one.'

'And which takes after you?'

'Both of them.'

Luke was kicking a football about in the glade with some of the bigger kids. He was not well co-ordinated and his face, in all the hurly-burly, remained impassive, like the drawn face of a paper puppet, fixed for all time no matter what the action.

'It's unusual to come across a single father,' Anita said sympathetically. 'What happened to his mother?'

His eyes had been following the movements of the ball, but now he turned his face and looked at her with a steady intensity that reminded her of his son, smiling slightly. 'She's in Spain,' he said. An interval for effect. 'She's mad.'

In the course of a brief unsettling pause she saw that he was serious.

'Mad?'

'Barking,' he said, and took a long drag on his cigarette, still looking at her.

She returned to the kitchen and uncorked another bottle. There was a time, she thought, when I could uncork and pour in absolute silence. Her hand shook a little. One day, she thought, one day will I fall from grace?

Lindsay appeared in the doorway. 'Fancy a smoke?' she said. 'Where could we go?'

They went up to the study, the only room in the house where any kind of smoking was allowed because of Jasmine's asthma, and played about in the executive chairs, tipping them backwards and forwards and swivelling round while they passed the pipe.

'Lindsay,' Anita said, 'he is *gorgeous*, he is just *gorgeous*.'

'Do you think so?'

She laughed. 'It's the nostrils! Oh my God, those nostrils!'

Lindsay snorted, choking on the smoke.

'He just fascinates me. I'd love to draw him.'

'Aha!' said Lindsay. 'A purely academic interest.'

'They're sort of flat. You know, sort of like you know those little round sticky bits kids have, you know, for collages and things . . . '

'God help us.'

' . . . as if someone's just stuck them on.'

They shook with laughter.

'I never thought of nostrils as an erogenous zone before,' Lindsay said.

★   ★   ★

In the dark garden, she threw Basil's latest favourite stone for him. He was a devil for the things. When he was younger he'd go out collecting them, bring them home to his den and line them up and look at them. He preferred scratty, gritty-looking things to the nice smooth round ones, though now and then he'd adopt one of those as well, and he'd plague you to throw them endlessly.

She tossed the stone, a rough grey one; he dashed and brought it back. So that's it then, she thought, he's a friend now. Official. What will be will be. They were playing guitars in the living room, Charley and Michael, who'd stayed on after the others had gone, sitting in the corner of the living room in the green basket chair and talking very seriously about criminal law. The guitars were mellow through the window, Charley on the old Spanish one he'd had since he was fifteen. He'd taken off his soiled shirt and put on his favourite old blue thing with the ripped sleeves and underarms. Once upon a time, she thought, picking up the stone dropped gallantly at her feet and warm from the dog's mouth, show me a fucked-up loser and if he was halfway decent I'd have him. Rory Gotch, Mad John, Candy. All the fine young rebels. We thought only people like us could really feel.

But then she'd met Charley and found him deeper than anything she'd ever encountered in the world of the weird. Besides, she reflected, tossing the stone not too far down the lawn, all those intense, romantic, interesting lads, most of them were crap at sex.

Basil's heyday was past. Once she could have hurled the stone as high and as hard as she could into the depths of the wood and he'd have brought it back. Wouldn't have mattered how long it took.

* * *

The children, even Luke, were wordless in a darkened room in front of a Pingu video. The kitchen was piled with mess.

Later when the girls had gone to bed and Michael had disappeared down the long bat-haunted lane with Luke, heading for the big road and the evening bus, she went into the kitchen and found Charley, who was supposed to be doing the washing-up, gazing out of the back door, drinking wine and listening to his old records; Woody Guthrie,

Jackson C. Frank, Davy Graham, Rambling Jack Elliott, all crackly. She came behind him and put her arms round his waist.

'They don't have a bath on that boat,' he said, turning to her, 'only a shower. I said they could come round sometime for a bath.'

'Fine,' she said.

There was a kind of Kerouac seam somewhere in Charley. That's why he'd first gone for her, because she'd knocked about, because of Quack Fair and the streets and the track-mark.

'You know, I think I'll make a proper stile over into the woods,' he said. 'State of that wall.'

She put her hand on the back of his thick neck and kissed him, deep and full. Oh God, she thought, not the Madame Bovary syndrome. Not that old thing. She couldn't count the lads she'd had. Well, life was short and she didn't believe anything came after; dead was dead; it seemed like a sin to miss anything. But not this time. Not this time, she thought, this time it's just a game in my mind. This time I stick.

She started touching him up for sex. An owl called.

Ah, but, said a little voice, what are you going to do about Paddy Riley?

And she thought about her mother and

father and was certain she would not weaken; she knew all there was to know about the sort of messes people made when they did.

★ ★ ★

She kissed him, and there in her mind, clear as day, was Paddy Riley in his bath, his dark head lolling backwards on the white curved rim.

She always saw him through a mist because he liked his baths very hot, Paddy Riley, he liked his baths so hot that sometimes you had to peer through a cloud of white steam, and everything was wet, the walls and the mirror and the sides of the toilet and sink, and even the floor. And the radio played: *Bye bye, love, bye bye, happiness*, the Everly Brothers singing stridently through the steam.

But it wasn't that, it was Woody Guthrie singing *So long, it's been good to know you*, and she was here, now.

★ ★ ★

On certain random afternoons, while he worked at one of his many odd jobs, Michael left Luke with Anita and the girls. Luke, who totally ignored the girls if he ever encountered them outside the environs of their own house, led them about like the Pied Piper all afternoon, showing off his advanced years and maleness, and when Michael came to pick him up they would drink coffee in the kitchen and talk, or they'd walk in the glade while the children ran through the wood, cracking the branches and rustling the leaves, their high voices hollow. If it was very hot, they drank iced lemonade and wine outside the back door, in the shade from the big trees on the edge of the wood. Once, a weasel appeared on the ivy-covered wall right in front of them and they sat very still and watched the way it moved, like water. He told her about his boarding school, where the other kids had taken his pants down and forced him to sit on a red-hot radiator. She told him about Quack Fair and Belle Vue, how when she thought of it there was a sweet, sad seediness in the memory, a tarnished romance, a trace of carnival nightmare.

'I can't think of anything like it nowadays,' she said, 'not these slick plastic places, these theme parks we take the girls to. It was pretty shabby really. There's nothing there now, just a housing estate and a car auction.'

He sat straight-backed, smoking, after his bath. Both he and Luke took advantage of the odd bath now and then. He's a bit of a mess, she thought, I can see that, but he's a dignified mess.

Then Charley arrived and poured himself some wine, took off his tie and kissed her.

★ ★ ★

She met him in the launderette, he leaned over her shoulder. She'd gone in there to draw and sat with her legs up on the long bench. She drew girls deep in conversation with their long bare legs crossed, a kid asleep in its push-chair, bottle clutched in its cute fat hand, a woman getting her sheets out of the dryer. These were the kinds of mundane subjects she always did, like her friends' kids on their Playstations and people watching TV and eating their dinner and queuing up in Tesco's, or waiting in the playground for the bell to go. She drew the chip restaurant (exterior) and Kokoschka's (interior) and the paper shop with its cards for cleaners and bikes and kittens free to good homes.

'Did you go to art school?' he asked.

She shook her head. 'Completely self-taught.'

He was waiting for a dryer. He came round to sit next to her.

They'd been in Scotland for a week at Charley's sister's cottage near Inverness, and

94

she started telling him about it, what a wreck it was but how beautiful, with its corrugated roof and the little stream running by. 'It's wonderful,' she said, 'no phone, no TV. The deer come right down into the garden.'

He said her work was Hopperesque.

She watched the whirling colours of someone else's wash and asked him, 'How did you get that scar on the end of your chin?'

He rubbed it. 'Fell down the cellar steps. When I was about eight or nine. Knocked my chin on the handle bars of my dad's bike.'

'Did it bleed a lot?'

'Oh yes.' He spoke low, and it was hard to hear him in the din of the machines, even though he inclined his head towards hers when he spoke. 'Buckets and buckets of blood. That's why I'm so pale. Drained, you see.'

They discovered they'd both been strung out on drugs in London at the same time, he twenty-four, she twenty-nine, breaking up with Candy and down on her luck. She'd have gone for him then, she knew. What a team they would have made! What a glorious descent, holding hands and burning like Icarus in their screaming plummet to the depths!

Live hard, die young. And here they were, middle-aged. Strange days indeed.

The night after Paddy Riley came to their house and talked with her mother and Auntie Connie and called her a stunner, Robin sleepwalked down into the front hall and woke there screaming. Anita wasn't asleep. It was only about half past ten but he'd been well away for a couple of hours; she'd heard him brewing up for a storm in the next bed, tossing and mumbling and making sharp little mewing sounds in his throat. Dreaming of horrors, she supposed. Robin believed in everything, ghosts and bogeymen, Father Christmas, the Tooth Fairy, God. He swore there was a goblin called Coleman Grey that lived out there in the dark bit under the bush, where the drain always got blocked and the fat green caterpillars humped about. 'Coleman Grey! Coleman Grey!' he would call in a ridiculous solemn voice. Anita used to look out at the darkness in the small yard at the back of their house, knowing it was all a load of rubbish, like her father said. But she'd call out anyway sometimes: 'Coleman Grey! Coleman Grey!' and only the cold darkness hummed back at her.

She had her torch on, reading *There Is A*

Happy Land by Keith Waterhouse in the tent of the bedclothes, when Robin suddenly got up out of bed with a deep sigh and walked out on to the landing. She thought he was going to the toilet, but instead he glided downstairs like a little white ghost. There was a long silence, then a scream, another scream, scream upon scream, and a door bursting open, the sound of the TV, a long gurgling moan and her mother's voice: 'It's all right, Robbie-boo, Robbie-baby-boo, Mummy's here, my pet, my baby-baby, Mummy's here.'

After that there was lots of mumbling muttering talk, and footsteps. Anita switched the torch off and lay still, pulling the covers up over her head and pretending to be asleep. After a while her father carried Robin in and put him back to bed, and her mother soothed his brow. They whispered by his bed, then her mother retreated, her footsteps slowly dying away as she went softly downstairs. Anita lay rigid, listening, the book digging into her side. Her father sat by Robin's bed for a long time, silent and still, nothing but the occasional rustle, till at last she heard him rise and quietly leave when Robin's breathing was smooth again.

She couldn't sleep. She could hear their voices. They were downstairs by the range, talking. On and on and on, a long low rumbling, on and on and on. Anita rose out of her warm bed and drifted to the top of the stairs.

'I hear them,' her mother said.

'You hear nothing.'

'I hear them.'

Carefully, soundlessly, Anita stepped down to the foot of the stairs and sat leaning against the wall. Her small white feet huddled together before her.

'I do,' her mother said. 'I hear them. And when I open the door, there's no one there.'

Her mother heard voices in the house. No one else did. Mumbo jumbo, her father said. Rubbish. Her father was right. He must be. He was doing his competitions, she could hear the occasional flick of paper as he put something in an envelope. He'd leave them for her mother to post, a little pile of letters done up with an elastic band. 'It's always me, of course,' she'd moan, 'always me that has to post the damn things. And he never wins any bloody thing.'

Anita could picture him looking down his nose at her mother the way he did, literally, taking sights down the long bony ridge. A Jewish nose, her mother said. Anita had it too, though hers was less spectacular. She loved it. There used to be a photograph, very old and faded, of an ancient wrinkled woman with a stern face and no lips, wearing a shawl and bonnet. She had that nose too. Anita had asked who it was and her mother had just looked at it for a while and said, 'I don't know, I think that might have been his grandmother.' It gave Anita a funny feeling to look at the old woman's face with her nose, her father's old old Russian grandmother in her peasant shawl and bonnet. He never talked about his family, no one did. Anita knew she had an Uncle Louis and an Uncle David somewhere, but she'd never seen them, and cousins too, Sylvia and Adrian and Jessie. She had toyed with the idea of finding them. What would they think of her, their Shiksah cousin? That's the word they used, her mother said. Shiksah.

Not that she needed any more cousins. She'd counted them up once on her mother's side and it had come to twenty-one.

She'd been buying things for the new school term, socks and knickers and scrunchies for Jasmine, and a Winnie the Pooh lunch box for Sid, who was starting in September. Charley had taken the girls to Joanne's in Cheltenham. Sitting on the floor with her coffee, surrounded by toys and thinking of the first

99

time she ever left Sid at nursery, the time the tough little boot cried and held on to her leg. Anita grew sentimental, Sid, my little Sid, she thought, she's too young. The world is too hard.

Car wheels crunched on the gravel. Basil huffed and woofed, there was a ring on the bell. She thought it might be the woman from down the lane who'd promised to pop by with some eggs, but somehow when she opened the door and it was Michael it was not a surprise.

'Are you busy?' he asked, sweaty and dirty with a carrier bag under his arm. 'Any chance of a bath? Charley around?'

She was barefoot in all her scruffs. 'He's gone to his sister's with the girls. Come in.' She stood back, waving a hand. 'The bathroom's free.'

'Thank God,' he said. 'I stink to high heaven. I've been working like a dog all morning. Shifting stuff up four flights of stairs. Jesus.' As he passed her a sweaty miasma arose like dust from a footstep. 'I brought a change of clothing,' he said, grinning.

She waited for him nervously. Charley and the girls would not be back till late tonight. God knows where Luke was. She went into the wood and gazed at the sky through the high tree tops. There was no doubt in her mind that she could have him now, this very day if she really wanted to. She'd cracked the carapace.

But nothing would happen, nothing that the world could see. There's a kind of sex without touching, she thought. We're doing it now. It's love like the ancient troubadours sang, Courtly Love, that's what we'll have, yes, not some dirty, furtive little thing but the revival of an ancient tradition. I'll be the noble lady, Charley the husband, Michael the lover. He'll wear my token on his lance. We'll walk in glades and now and then, an accidental touch like fire. It's the Lancelot-Guinevere-Arthur set-up, though that's not right because Lancelot and Guinevere actually did it, didn't they? But we won't. No: Dante and Beatrice, Petrarch and Laura, always pure, always burning. Oh, yes! I will love him and he will love me but we'll never do it. Only in the mind.

In the mind we'll have sex to make angels weep.

She went back inside and put some coffee on. The smell of the coffee and the warm green wood through the open back door was intoxicating. Life was a pink house, a good man, two little girls, one fair, one dark. And now this. She tiptoed upstairs and listened to

101

him whistling in the bath and thought of him there with his head on the little pillow that sticks on the side, and considered men in baths, how raw and peeled they were, how like mandrakes, pluckable, fuckable, defenceless. Paddy Riley loved his baths. Red hot, unbearable. In like a lobster.

They'd never understand, she thought. No one, not Alison, not even Lindsay who'd been chaste for many a year. Nobody believed in that kind of sex now. The twentieth century thought sex was flesh and fluids, it didn't believe in Dante and Beatrice, Petrarch and Laura. Go scratch, it said. Grab a big handful. Get yours.

She knew. She'd swallowed the lot.

Michael came down fresh and clean with his old things in a bag and they drank coffee at the kitchen table. A machine buzzed somewhere. She talked about her children, how Sid seemed too little for school and Jas was ashamed of her poor dry little hands. 'All their problems,' she said, 'I think they've inherited them from me. Isn't that funny? I never think it might be Charley, always me.'

He leaned back, rocking on his chair. 'I never know with Luke,' he said, 'his mother being mad.'

'Where *is* Luke?'

'Sherborne. He's gone down to my parents.'

102

'When you said she was mad — Luke's mother — what did you mean?'

'Mad Marion.' He smiled gently. 'Mad Marion.' He looked into his coffee. 'Mad covers a lot of things.'

From among the jumble on the kitchen table between them, the phone rang. It was Anita's mother. There's a lot to be said, she thought, for the olden days when phones were always out in the hall. Her mother always talked very loudly on the phone as if she couldn't quite believe that she could be heard properly. Anita was sure Michael could catch every word, because he swivelled away discreetly in his chair and started reading the bits and pieces pinned all over the walls, the dates for the new school term and the Jade Garden menu and the invitation to the next opening at the Wragge Gallery. Her mother coughed constantly. She hadn't rung for anything in particular, just a chat. Have you heard from Robin? He's got this new girlfriend: Flossie. She's . . . she's . . . you know, obstreperous. What does Jasmine want for her birthday? Well it's not *that* far off. It is eight, isn't it?

'Mum,' said Anita, 'your cough sounds awful. Is Judith there?'

'She's in the garden.' Hack hack hack hack hack.

'When are you on your machine?'

'Not till four.' Hack hack. 'Well, I can go on it sooner if I — ' hack hack hack hack hack.

'Are you getting plenty to drink?'

Hack hack hack. 'I dread the winter. It's worse in — ' WHEE-eeee-ee-ee-eeeeeeze, hack hack hack hack hack hack hack hack —

After the goodbyes there was a silence.

'My mum,' Anita said quietly.

'Isn't she well?'

'She has bronchiectasis.'

He pulled a face. 'What's that?'

'What it sounds like. Bronchitis only worse.' She jumped up and poured more coffee. 'She lives with her sister and my cousin Judith and I feel terrible about it. I ought to have her down here.'

'Hum,' he said, 'well, sometimes these things can be complicated.'

'I know but — well, we did ask her to come down here but she wouldn't. So you feel like you should move up there. But you can't just — ' she gestured with her shoulders ' — I go to see her and she insists on getting up and going into the kitchen to make a cup of tea and it wears her out like she's just climbed the Himalayas.'

'Where does she live?' he said and touched her, just the tip of one finger very lightly on the back of her wrist for a second.

'Crosby. On Merseyside.'

'What about your dad? Is he dead?'

'No,' she said. 'Well maybe, I don't know. I don't know where he is.'

———————

She jerked awake on the stairs. She'd been dreaming about a giant caterpillar marching down one of the alleys across the road. For a moment she didn't know where she was and her heart fluttered; but then came clear the familiar sound of her mother and father arguing. They often had these rows late at night, sneakily, after she and Robin had gone to bed. Next day, though, her mother would tell her all about them, word for word. 'You know what he said, Anita? You'll never guess. Stupid fool! Sitting up there, he says, making an exhibition of yourself in front of all those people. Showing yourself off. They don't see nothing, I says. What do they see? And you know what he says? Your shoulders, he says. They see your shoulders. I laughed. What do I care, says I, they don't know it's me, do they? Walk past 'em in the street, they wouldn't know. Who cares? *I* care, says he, *I* care. Well, says I, you know what you can do, don't you? You can kiss my sweet — '

Then she'd blow a raspberry.

'I wouldn't have to do it anyway,' Anita heard her mother say, 'if you gave me more money.'

Silence.

'You don't give me enough.'

Silence.

'And why is that?' he asked. 'Why is that, may I ask? Why is that? WHY — IS — THAT?'

'You could ask *them* for some.'

He laughed then, but not as if anything was funny. By 'them' she meant his family.

'Well, you should. Particularly now your father's gone. You're due some.'

Long silence.

Her mother sometimes steamed open her father's letters, thinking he might be getting money from them that he was keeping from her. She'd shown Anita how to do it, how to let the flap come up all by itself and never try and force it, otherwise it would tear and crinkle up; how to reseal it without a trace. Her mother could read them after a fashion too, though reading didn't come easy, and writing not at all. But it wasn't the reading she was after, it was the money.

Anita heard the sound of the kettle going on the hob.

'I know better than to ask,' her mother's voice said. 'Oh yes, I know what they're like.

Oh, I know, I know, I know.'

'Oh,' said my father, 'you know them, do you? You know them?'

'I know *you*.'

'What's that supposed to mean?'

'Ha.'

'I said what's that supposed to mean?'

Anita had a strange place inside her head where she sometimes went. In it there was an earth turning in space, pitted and vast, rumbling. It balanced on something infinitesimally small, a thing she couldn't name. She thought it was where her earliest dreams came from. There was an abyss, black and bottomless. She was standing steeling herself to jump over to where her mother and father and Grandma and Grandad O'Leary stood on a green cliff top beneath, calling to her. Robin wasn't there. He hadn't been born yet.

She jumped when she heard the click of the door, and dashed soundlessly, still half sleeping, up to her bed. Her cold feet tingled as warmth returned. Her mother was coming upstairs, sighing outside her door. She went into the bathroom and ran water for a while then walked heavily along the landing and closed her door with a sound of gruff finality.

Silence set in like rain.

———

She had all sorts of things to do, she was supposed to be using her day alone to get on with useful pursuits, such as framing and gardening and organising the rubbish on the hall table into some more approachable chaos.

But when they'd drunk their coffee and talked for a while and he suggested driving out to see a friend of his who made things out of matchsticks, she agreed. It was such a lovely day.

She leaned towards him and smiled her best, most wide and warm and welcoming smile, almost a kiss, then jumped up and left him with that to think of while she dashed upstairs and flung off her old scruffs, everything, the smell of her own fragrant sweat flying from her in the armpits of the blue shirt. She hummed, sang, 'Hey where did we go, days when the rains came . . . ' A song of youth. This is pathetic, she thought. Women aged better these days. Her mother had been old at forty. She touched up her hair, looked at the heat shimmering outside the window, slipped on her pink sandals and long cool dove-grey dress, the one the sun shone through, the one with the slit revealing her bare brown leg; and nothing underneath, nothing at all between her and the muslin. She ran down to where he waited in his shabby green van with the engine running and slid in beside him.

They took off with a jerk. He was a mad driver but who cared? That was how she felt. She remembered a time when no risk mattered, when she would drink cider and drive fast over mountains with desperate young men, set off from Somerset to London in a car held together with string and putty and a driver who'd just ingested fourteen hash cookies and a soupçon of magic mushrooms. Because she'd been immortal then, and even if she wasn't, who cared? And there were no kids in the back taking off their seat belts and kicking each other and being sick, no dog sticking his big wet nose in her ear, no stupid map to read, no route bickerings.

They hurtled and roared to a beautiful village, all roses and thatch and timbered walls, with a wide green where ducks napped in the shade under a spreading oak. A pretty river, willow-fringed, flowed under an old stone bridge and spilled into a pond where a few fisherboys hunched peacefully. Michael parked the van by the church and they got out.

'You must see this,' he said, opening the creaky wooden gate and leading her through a shady bird-melodious graveyard to the church porch. The door was old and very beautiful. It was not dark inside the church, as she expected, but white and bright and airy with lots of space, and absolutely empty. They walked down the wide aisle and sat in a pew near the front, he with his hands linked loosely between his knees. She had never noticed before how knobbly and knuckly they were.

'Look up,' he said.

The ceiling was full of angels, all in white robes, with big droopy Renaissance eyes and hair of fine-spun sugared gold and chestnut-brown, blowing trumpets, singing orisons, floating barefoot in the clouds like fairies, massively silver-winged like Pegasus.

She gasped. He leaned back and put his hands behind his head.

'Sometimes,' he said, 'I just drive out here and look at them for a while then go home again. What's nice is that they're so predictable.'

She hoped he was not going to go weird and religious on her. Perhaps it was just the artwork he was getting excited about. After all, they were very beautiful.

'Angels shouldn't be predictable,' she remarked. They made her uneasy.

'Oh, they should. They absolutely should. If you can't count on an angel, what on earth *can* you count on?'

110

She gave a little snigger. Shoulder to shoulder they contemplated the heavenly host; till he stood, beckoning with his head, and led her out through the side door of the church. A path led down, through another, smaller gate and onwards, descending steadily by rough and rocky steps into a dim ferny copse resounding with water. They jumped a small stream, went through a kissing gate and emerged at the back of a low ramshackle cottage which gave the impression of a tree stump obscured by extravagant fungi, so thoroughly were its peeling walls encroached upon by all kinds of barrels and wheels and bits of wood and iron and rusty old machines. As they came round the front an outraged gaggle of geese, honking, necks outstretched, came running across a garden of weeds from a dirt track beyond a sagging barbed-wire fence. She clapped her hands at them and they stalled, complaining loudly.

'Call off your dogs,' Michael said.

A man, tall and grizzled with a brown leathery face and clothes so old and faded they lacked all shape, emerged from the gloom of a doorway. 'Shut up, you mad fuckers,' he said in a mild, vaguely Cockney voice, and started herding the geese efficiently back the way they'd come. 'They'll calm down in a minute.'

'We've come to see your models,' Michael said.

The man's eyes wore a permanent weeping expression. 'Well, come in then,' he said, not even looking at Anita.

His house was sparse and dark. The only chair was an ornate rocker, weeks of washing-up stood underneath the sink, and the stairs ascending into darkness were steep and grim and had no rail but cast a long black shadow backwards like a wing. They were papered with Esher's optical riddles of strange dreamlike figures going up and down impossible stairs and she was reminded of the House of Nonsense at Belle Vue, where people slept in a bed on the ceiling and doors opened on to nothing. On a bench that ran along the back wall were the matchstick models, the odd boat and van and some tiny musical instruments, cellos and guitars and mandolins, but mostly churches, some tiny, the size of a pat of butter, some a foot tall.

'Oh, these are beautiful!' she said quite sincerely, going over to look.

'Each one,' said Michael, 'is an absolute replica of a real church. Look.' He picked one up and opened the miniature door. 'Look in,' he told her. She did. She saw nothing but dark. Then he lifted the roof and she saw tiny pews and choir stalls and a high altar, and laughed with delight. She felt like Alice looking through the little door into the beautiful garden.

'I've done just about every damn church in the county,' the man said in a clipped voice. 'Dream about the damn things.'

'Now,' said Michael, 'just look at this.'

It was the church they had left not ten minutes ago, eight inches high.

'Oh,' she cried, 'it's perfect! You'd need a magnifying glass to do the detail on the windows.'

Michael lifted the roof and she looked in. There on the ceiling of the little church were the angels, the very same but reduced, as if seen through the wrong end of a telescope. It was all so carefully done.

She looked at the man. 'These are beautiful,' she said again. 'You must work so hard.'

He shrugged and walked out.

'I'd love to buy something,' she said to Michael. 'How much are they?'

'Dear.'

'I don't care.'

She stroked the curve of a matchstick mandolin.

'Ask him.'

'He's a bit odd, isn't he?'

'Yeah. Whole family is.'

113

'I'd like this one.' She held on to the angel church.

He walked to the door. 'Hey, Jeremy!'

She could give it to Jasmine for her birthday, she thought. That's what she'd do. Justify spending the money. She didn't care.

Her father used to play the mandolin sometimes, very late at night after everyone else had gone to bed and he thought they were all asleep. But she was always a bad sleeper. Wide awake in the small hours with Robin's long breaths loud in the darkness, she would find herself praying: let him play, let him play, please let him play. And after a while, when she had strained her ears for too long and was about to give up, the sound of his mandolin would creep into the silence like a cautious cat, probing this way and that with its sensitive whiskers, till it sensed all clear and grew bold and proud.

Late at night he would play like this, alone downstairs, his long delicate fingers drawing forth the little tunes she would remember all her life but never know the names of.

'Any tea?' asked Michael, a dark silhouette in the window, the sun streaming over his

114

shoulders. 'Any tea or coffee or anything?'

Jeremy sat motionless. 'Now you're asking,' he said, and lit an old cigarette.

The geese were gathering by the door. Anita sat holding her angel church. Dear, she was thinking. I undersell myself.

'Whole family's mad,' Michael said later as they set off back and left him driving his savage geese before him down the dirt track to God knows where. 'You know who he is?'

'No.'

'Luke's uncle.'

She looked blank.

'Marion's brother.'

'Really! Marion!'

'Madness runs in the family,' he repeated.

They were on the stone steps, walking back the way they'd come. She felt high and slightly dizzy. 'I wonder if I should have got the mandolin,' she murmured, holding out the church on her palms in front of her.

'The instruments are even dearer.'

'Really? Still, don't suppose he sells much.'

'Doesn't need to, he's rolling in it. Got more than you and me put together. Owns a place in Yorkshire and one in the South of France.'

'You're joking.'

'Things,' said Michael, 'are not always what they seem.'

115

They sat on a bench on the village green.

'They used to swim witches in this pond,' he said.

'Did they? How terrible.'

On this very spot she might have stood, Anita thought, some poor woman about to go under the duckweed.

'What was Marion like?' she asked.

He put back his head and looked at the sky, his legs stretched straight out in front of him, crossed at the ankles. 'I met her in the clinic,' he said, 'we were both doing the cure.'

She nodded.

He laughed. 'I remember waking up one day and finding myself vomiting into an empty Kentucky Fried Chicken box in an empty room with a needle hanging out of my arm.' He laughed again, a quick mirthless breath. 'And I just thought: if this is it — if — this — is — it — '

'Yes,' she said, 'yes, I know, I know, I do know.'

He turned his head and looked at her for a long time. His eyes were very blue and pale. The white scar upon his chin was changeable, sinking in or lying flat on the surface, depending on the set of his chin. If we were free, she thought, this would be the moment for the first kiss. They would move carefully together, savouring the foreplay of diminishing space. But they didn't.

★ ★ ★

Of course she'd told him about Summer Court. Three or four other people lived in the flat but there were always far more than that hanging around at any one time. A bag full of dead kittens hung from a nail on the wall. On the first day, Quack Fair still so recent that it ran constantly in her head like a TV in the corner with the sound turned down, she disturbed a large colony of dark brown maggotty things when she tentatively lifted a corner of loose oil-cloth on one of the kitchen surfaces. They humped themselves away from the light with remarkable speed. As for the toilet . . .

★ ★ ★

'She was nice,' he said. 'You know the way Luke is? Very frail. Those kind of slanted bones. She was very fair but she had a kind of a slightly Oriental look about her, and very long wrists and neck and ankles, very graceful, very languid.' Another of those mirthless little laughs.

117

He looked away and said nothing for a while.

'What happened?' she asked.

He took the church from her, raised the roof and gently traced the angels' forms with the tip of one finger.

'Oh, she was a mess. Worse than me. She was using again before she had Luke. Everything. You name it. Once she found some red pills in the park under a bench, no idea what they were, she just takes them. Could have been anything, cyanide, Christ knows. Turns out to be laxatives, as it happens.'

He turned his head suddenly and smiled at her. 'I have a penchant for messy women unfortunately,' he said.

They got up and strolled around the pond.

'Where is she now?' she asked.

'She went to Spain and took up with a bunch of French junkies and ended up in an institution over there. Far as I know, she's still there.'

She thought about him then, a young man bringing up a baby on his own. Staying straight. If he drinks a little too much now and then, she thought, who can blame him?

'Doon isn't like that,' she said.

He frowned. 'Doon? What?'

'Like that. Messy. I would have thought

118

Doon was Miss Normal.'

'Yeah,' he said thoughtfully, 'but she's got a nice bum.'

Anita was pleased. The way he said it diminished her. They stood still in the long grass.

'Time we were going,' he said.

★　　★　　★

Charley's plague memories were just another of those peculiar mind things, Anita thought, like the way she remembered the war even though she hadn't been born till a few years later. Who knows where these things come from? Sniff around, you always find the source: Charley's children's encyclopedia; the reminiscences of her father, who'd been a boy of sixteen and carried a stretcher in the Blitz before he was old enough to volunteer.

She remembered the sirens, soulful and wolfish, not harsh and ridiculous like the siren that went off on the stairs of the House of Nonsense when the wind blew your skirt up, or the one on the Caterpillar. She remembered the incendiaries going off like firecrackers, the Luftwaffe overhead, endless nights in the shelter; she remembered standing with a huge crowd of people watching the centre of Manchester burn

119

bright as day, the big warehouses round Piccadilly collapsing like a vision of hell.

The war came back in her half-sleep one afternoon. The girls were at school, Charley due home early. She'd just planted a hundred crocus bulbs and more of camassia and grape hyacinth and was so tired that she gave in and lay down on the bed and drifted away. She wasn't dead to the world, the window was open and she could hear the sound of birds and the leaves shifting with a sound like many small voices whispering scurrilously. It was lovely to be tired from such work and she went into that strange space where time stops, and there found herself a very small child again being dragged by the hand down Stanley Grove by enormous Grandma O'Leary. It was going dark. There was a narrow alley, really just a flagstoned entry. As they passed she saw down at the end of it the silhouettes of soldiers wearing round helmets, their guns pointing upwards.

Next she was in the hall of their old house. Grandma O'Leary sat lumpily on the stairs, all in black like a witch with her great knees wide apart and the material of her dress making a hammock shape between them. Someone came to the door. Anita saw a shadow bob towards the frosted glass then withdraw, as if someone had put their face to it. Grandma O'Leary put one fat wrinkled finger to her pale lips and opened her watery eyes wide behind the lenses of her glasses. 'Sssssh!' she whispered, long and low. Anita was scared. Something came through the letterbox but as she looked to see, her eyes opened, the room jerked into focus, the birds chattered and the leaves went shush-shush-shush-shush.

She heard Basil's pattering feet welcoming Charley home downstairs. When she'd first gone to live with Charley, the dog had been used to being left alone for a lot of the time. He'd loved it when Anita came along. He used to follow her everywhere and always contrive to get his head on her knee at every possible moment, till Charley, his true love, returned, when he would go into this same ritual dance of joy.

She heard footsteps on the stairs.

'Sleeping, lazy cow,' said Charley gently.

She didn't know why but the dream had shaken her up. The girl was so real, yet she could never have existed. She was so real and so scared and couldn't possibly know that she did not exist.

Charley sat down on the bed and pulled off his tie.

'I was so tired,' she yawned, rubbing her eyes.

'*You're* tired?' There were shadows under his eyes. He lifted his legs on to the bed and subsided next to her with a stifled groan.

'So much to do,' she mumbled.

'Well,' he said, closing his eyes, 'why don't you just have a break? Go to London for a couple of days. You haven't been for a while. Or the cottage even. I don't think anyone's there at the moment. Get away from it all.'

She closed her eyes. 'Strange dreams you get in the afternoon,' she said, 'I was dreaming about the war again.'

'We could go to Scotland at half term,' he said.

She turned and looked at him. He was smiling. 'Shall I get the girls? I've got to go in anyway. Dreaming about the war?'

She tried to tell him about the girl, her now self and her then self, the soldiers, the thing coming through the letterbox. It was horrible, that thing through the letterbox. She didn't know what it was but it was horrible.

'Do you know what I mean?' she said. 'I don't know why, it just made me feel very sad, something about this girl in the dream being a sort of me that never existed, because I was never in the war; and the fact that she

122

didn't know she didn't exist. It's not making sense, is it?'

'A kind of sense.'

They turned and lay against each other, half sleeping.

'It's not really sad,' he said after a while. 'Not for her, anyway. Sad for you maybe.'

'Why for me?'

He yawned. 'Because you exist,' he said, 'and she doesn't.' Then he opened his eyes. 'That's just brought something into my mind, something I used to think was really funny. A line from an old song my gran used to sing, years ago, years and years and years, before my sister was born. God! I haven't thought of it for years either. Sitting on my old gran's knee and her singing 'Love's Old Sweet Song'. Do you know that one? It's something to do with what you just said, the feeling of it. Starts like this — *Once in the dear dead days beyond recall* — and it always stuck in my head because it seemed so sad.' He smiled. 'But then, when you think about that line it's not really sad at all, is it?'

'Isn't it?'

'No. Because if the dear dead days are beyond recall, how can they make you sad? You wouldn't know about them, would you?'

She laughed. 'What a funny little boy you must have been.'

'I suppose,' he said, putting his hand on her leg, 'it's just the idea of something being finally forgotten. Then it really does no longer exist.'

She laid her head against his chest and closed her eyes. Sweet songs. Love's old. Come back, Paddy Riley. Oh, will ye no' come back again?

'Is it sadder to have existed and now no longer exist, or never to have existed?' he asked.

'To exist,' she said, undoing the buttons of his shirt.

'That's a dark thought, Anita,' he murmured.

★ ★ ★

The occasional click of the keys was soothing. She loved to watch Charley work, relentless, full of patience and persistence. He would have made a good detective. Sometimes she wondered that he had not become a historian of the seventeenth century, but no, he said, he preferred it this way. Charley was so thorough. If ever she went mad, he'd use that same patience and persistence to do the very best he could for her, and never, never ever ever would he leave her in a million years.

'I'd better go and get the girls,' he muttered.

He sat naked in the study updating his database. He was beautiful naked, she thought. The leaves went shush-shush-shush outside the window. The study was calm and green, its walls covered in maps and charts. She'd put on her old green willows nightie, an indefinable secondhand garment, charmingly faded, that may once have been a dress; lolling on the leather armchair, she drew Basil, who lay curled up and conveniently still under the desk. I ought to go to London, she thought, hawk a few things round the galleries. Phil Wragge was the only one who'd ever really taken a commercial interest in her work, unless you counted Tom Shafto, for whom she'd done the Quack Fair posters of course, and the throwaways, but that was different. She could have stayed. Tom Shafto didn't want to let her go, no one could do posters like she could, he even used to talk about getting them made into a book. She should have stayed but Candy begged and she was soft, and anyway still loved him in a way, at least when she brought to mind the bashful, endearing quality about him that had made her want to leave John and stay at Quack Fair in the first place. She dreamed over her drawing: Quack Fair with its

125

stiltwalkers and contortionists and rope walkers, and him — the Great Candini, slow and gentle, who could put a paving stone on his chest and invite people to walk on it. He was a heavy-boned shambling junkie by the time they left, so sensitive he cried at the least little thing. The fingernails of his huge hands were bitten down to the quick and he could no longer lift but that's not why they had to leave Quack Fair, it was because he fell out with Tom Shafto on one side over the deeper meaning of Quack Fair as a cultural phenomenon (Candy thought there was none), and a man called Hug on the other over drugs. Hug was a moron but he could stand on one leg with the other wrapped round his neck so he was OK with Tom Shafto.

She went next door to fix her hair. Shame to disturb him, she was thinking, I'll go to get the girls myself, when the phone rang. He answered it in the study. She was combing her hair, gazing at her angel church, which stood in a little space on the bookshelf. She hadn't given it to Jasmine after all, she'd decided it was too good for kids. Charley didn't like it. Seemed to think it was a little bit gross. She'd been quite open about it. 'Michael ran me out to see this workshop,' she'd told him, 'I thought I might be able to get something for Jas's birthday, but now I really look at it I don't think it'll do.'

'It's for you,' he said, putting his head round the door. 'Judith. Your Auntie Bernie's had a fall.'

Actually Judith was ringing more to see if Jasmine had got her card and the postal order OK. Bernie was all right, just a sprained knee, but at that age, you know, she said, you have to be careful. She said Bernie was sitting out the back playing crib with Anita's mum: 'She's marvellous, your mam,' she said, 'she's just started a lovely sampler.' Bernie, the oldest surviving O'Leary sibling, was a poker-stiff, poker-faced tall old lady, who, as far as Anita could remember, had always looked the same and never smiled, not even on wedding photographs, done up like a death's head in a fancy hat. Family tradition had it that she'd never really got over her sister Mary's death. Mary, the family saint.

'Tell them I'll be up soon,' Anita said. 'Half-term probably.' If we don't go to Scotland, she added mentally.

Charley had gone by the time she put the phone down.

She got dressed and went downstairs and sought out the two big photograph albums with all the ancient stuff in: the giraffes in their paddock, one with its great soft-eyed

127

head snaking down over the barrier towards the crowd; herself and Robin on the elephant, their bony knees sticking out; Robin standing in Willie the Whale's mouth. There was the big group photograph of Auntie Anne's wedding in 1960 with herself and Judith as bridesmaids in their pink dresses with leg-of-mutton sleeves, Grandma and Grandad O'Leary resplendent in the seats of honour, Bernie like the queen of the undead, Anne and Nora and Connie and Dymphna all with their various menfolk and assorted children and babies, and her mum smiling a big smile with her hands on the shoulders of little Robin with his freckles and big jug ears. Her father wasn't there. There'd been a row about that. Look at them. Grandma and Grandad long gone, of course. Auntie Nora gone last year. Cancer. Uncle Kenny. Heart. Uncle Mike in Toronto. Heart again. Look at Mum then. The sparkle in her lips and eyes. Look at her now. Hack hack hack. Beautiful Geraldine O'Leary, who stole the heart of young Maurice Silver when they danced on the boards at Belle Vue. Where do things get to? Lost. The picture of her old Russian great grandma. Lost. The picture she took of Mary's grave in Mullingar, gentle legendary Mary who died at sixteen, the good sister, her aunt. Lost. The picture of her father in his first pair of long trousers at his Bar Mitzvah. Lost. Her blue Alice band. Lost lost lost.

————————

They had to meet her mother in the Chinese Café to get the bus to Ardwick for Robin's shoes. The Chinese Café was a great dingy barn of a place with an institutional feel and a school dinner smell, full of long tables and dusty floorboards that amplified the sound of your heels and the distant hollow clanging of gong-like pans from the kitchens. Anita's mother was sitting up in the corner playing draughts with Paddy Riley. Robin took off and flew down the long aisle between the tables to be swept up into her arms.

'Did you hold Nita's hand like a good boy?' she was saying, smoothing the top of his head with her chin as Anita approached.

Paddy Riley turned in his chair to smile at her. That was what was nice about him. Even though she was a child he treated her with respect. She was not invisible to him, she warranted hello, goodbye, what-do-you-think-of-that-Anita? He pulled out a chair for her next to him and she sat down.

'Now, Anita,' he said, 'what do you think of this? Your mother has been telling me that

129

never in all her life has anyone bought her flowers. Is that true?'

'No.'

'Aha!' He laughed.

'And how would you know?' her mother cried, opening her eyes very wide.

'Because me and Robin get you daffodils every birthday.'

Her mother and Paddy Riley burst out laughing, rocking towards each other across the table till their faces nearly touched. Anita couldn't see what was so funny.

'Well, we do,' she said. 'We do, don't we, Robin?'

'Yeah.' He was eating the sugar out of the sugar bowl with his fingers.

'Stop that!' Her mother tapped his hand.

'There, you see, Geraldine!' laughed Paddy, 'You see? You're well looked after with these two. I don't need to worry about you at all.'

She batted the air between them with her hand and he jerked back. 'Finish the game,' he said gaily, 'don't try and get out of it 'cos you know I'm winning.'

'You are not!'

'I am so!'

'You — are — not!' She dug one long red nail into his slim brown hand and it left a little mark like a crescent moon.

'Jesus, Mary and Joseph,' he said softly, 'I will treasure this.'

And then they were off laughing again, worse than a couple of infants. Anita decided to sulk. If Robin and she had acted like this, her mother would have snapped: Stop it, the pair of you! That's what happened when their games got noisy and silly. But this was a grown-up game and the rules were all different. She folded her arms and looked away.

'Don't forget,' said Paddy Riley, 'the tiara for the charming girl.'

'It's not a tiara, you klutz! It's an Alice band.'

Anita turned her head. She noted the very gentle touch of Paddy's hands on the draughtsmen. 'Tiara, whatever,' he murmured. She remembered a description she'd heard of a flamenco dancer, that her hands were like white doves. Paddy's were brown ones.

'Here, Nita,' her mother said, opening her bag and taking out a royal blue Alice band that glittered like a Christmas decoration. 'Paddy found it in the Hall of Mirrors.'

'Some little girl must have dropped it,' he said.

Turning it over in her fingers, sliding it through her hair and looking at it in the little round mirror in her mother's powder compact, she imagined him picking it up and thinking of her.

'There now,' he said softly, 'you're even lovelier than before.'

When they got outside, her mother and Paddy Riley leaned their heads together to light their cigarettes. His hair fell in curls down across his forehead and his nose was a crooked wedge. They walked together, chatting away like old friends, with Robin holding her mother's hand while Anita slouched along behind in a mood, despite the blue Alice band that glittered in her hair. Her chest was flat. Her sandals were stupid. The clown faces above the entrance to Pepino's Circus laughed at her. She heard the sound of a sea-lion calling, a crude, chest-scraping, sore-throated cry. It sounded like she felt.

He walked with them to the Belle Vue Street bus stop outside the swimming baths on Hyde Road and they stood waiting in the shelter with the traffic roaring by and grit flying. Her mother leaned against the glass and talked in her quick way, picking about in her purse for change for the bus. Paddy took little nervous runs at the concrete pole of the bus-stop sign, seeing how high he could kick with his long thin legs while holding forth all the time: 'He is not to be taken seriously,

Geraldine . . . ' They were talking about
Archie Bannister, 'Honestly, have you seen
him eat? Have you seen his *wife*? Just because
he . . . Honestly, he brought this plaque in
one time, big brass thing, the sun in
splendour . . . what do you think of this then,
Riley? Riley, he calls me . . . Riley! Drop that
now and kiss my arse!'

'Paddy!' she warned, glancing at Robin.

'Kiss my fat greasy arse. Yes, *mein Führer*!'
He clicked his heels and flung up his arm in a
Heil Hitler salute. Something had made him
very angry.

'Paddy!'

'At once, *mein Führer*!'

Three girls came walking by the shelter,
two dark, one fair, all with bare arms and
little handbags and short curly hair. 'You're
mad, you are,' said the fair one, laughing at
Paddy.

'Joan,' he said, 'wait on.' He sidled smiling
away from us.

'Not working?' asked the blonde girl.

'I'm through till the night.'

One of the dark girls brought out gum and
handed it to her friends.

'Dirty skiver,' said the blonde girl. Her
skirt, sprinkled with tiny blue and yellow
flowers, was very full and must have had three
or four stiff petticoats under it.

'Me? Not at all.'

In the distance a bus appeared. 'Anita!' her mother called in her stern voice. 'Robin!'

Paddy and the blonde girl moved away, chatting lightly. The girl folded her arms and rocked slightly on her nice white flatties.

'This is ours,' Anita's mother said. 'Anita!'

Paddy was joke boxing the girl. She ignored him, looking the other way to light a cigarette.

'Are you coming, Joan?' her friend asked.

'Are you, Joan?' said Paddy. 'Are you coming?'

'Come on,' said Anita's mother.

'Will she come?' called Paddy after the girls. 'Get on!'

Anita saw his smiling face turn towards them. 'See you later, alligator!' he called.

'In a while, crocodile!' she shouted back, and everybody laughed except her mother. Anita started dashing upstairs but her mother pulled her back. 'Downstairs. We're getting off in a minute.'

'What's the point of getting the bus then?'

'Don't be cheeky. Downstairs.'

They sat down. The bus puffed and gasped on for a little then stopped at the lights. 'Look!' Anita said. The little group of young people sauntered by, the dark girls linking arms, Paddy and Joan a few paces behind, talking. His hand was on her waist. Her retreating legs were slim and graceful in the white shoes, like the gazelles in Belle Vue.

Michael was pulling pints in the Wild Boar at lunch-time, so she'd thought she'd walk down to the Alleys after work, pop into Polly Oliver's and have a look on their sale rail, make an appointment to get her roots done, then maybe, when the rush had died down, drop in for a glass of wine. But by the time she'd got down there it was raining hard and she dashed into Kokoschka's, taking her old table and looking across at Charley's corner, where he used to sit with his briefcase and papers before she knew him. She used to stop off in here on the way back from his house after he'd gone to work. She'd sit and drink her morning coffee, smiling at the memory of him, her knickers wet. Sometimes she'd be walking home and a great warm gush of him would suddenly soak her knickers through, run down her legs and make her thighs clammy. She remembered finding something sticky and clear on the back of her middle finger, like egg white gone stiff and starting to crack. She'd licked it and it tasted salty. Come, his or hers. They were doing it all the time then, just about every spare moment. They used to do it all over the garden at the cottage in Scotland where Jasmine was conceived.

When the rain eased a little she nipped down to Polly Oliver's and of course found nothing on the sale rail, but the loveliest little pink and grey crocheted silk dress, new in for ninety-two pounds. She lifted it from the rail, stroking it, wondering if she could get into a twelve. There was a nice little green print dress too, £149.99. God, they're expensive, she thought, but they're nice. I shouldn't, I know I shouldn't, but if Phil manages to flog something next week . . .

Oh, she thought, before the mirror in the changing room, Oh, I look gorgeous!

She couldn't resist. She bought the pink and grey one. It would look nice with old-fashioned pearly pink nail varnish and pink lipstick. Well, she thought, at least it wasn't the green one, feeling in some obscure way as if she'd just saved £60. Well, why shouldn't I have nice things? Why shouldn't my girls have nice things? Spoiled rotten, they are. Well, why should they have to go through what I went through? She could get herself a glass of wine whenever she wanted to now. She had clothes hanging in her wardrobe. She ate out regularly. She felt angry, as if someone had challenged her, angry but slightly tearful too, thinking of her mother on the cobbles with white dirty legs and the hem of her coat coming down in one place, face stiff with fear: 'Little bunch o' heather, sweetheart. Give me your palm. You give your hand but not your heart.'

———————

She had no shame.

That terrible time when she'd caused a scene in the catalogue place, the time after they'd seen Paddy Riley with the blonde girl. Her mother was in a foul mood. When they got off at Ardwick Green her face was nowty, and they walked in a disagreeable silence to the big discount warehouse where she bought all their clothes on the weekly. With her in that mood, poor old Robin knew better than to argue for the shoes he really wanted and took what he was given. By the time they got to the cash desk, her mother was ready for a fight.

Anita's heart sank when she saw the jolly woman's smile turn fixed as she scrutinised her mother's account.

'Have you made a payment in the last fortnight, Mrs Silver?' she said in a hopeful tone.

'I always pay at the end of the month.'

The woman looked perplexed. 'I'm sorry, I can't really add any more on to this account until . . . '

'I pay at the end of the month. If it's always been good enough in the past, it's good enough now.'

'I'm sorry, Mrs Silver. It's not up to me. I'm not allowed to . . . '

'You two! Sit down! There! I'll see the manager then.' And she stood with her brazen look and her back ramrod stiff, staring down the queue that had gathered behind her.

She didn't care about scenes in public. Anita and Robin hated them. Anita seethed. Everything they had was on the weekly. Everything! They got stuff from catalogues and her mother fell behind with the payments. She ran up tick in two or three local shops and got behind with them too. Anita's father didn't even know about any of it. The clothes from the catalogues never looked as good when you actually got them on, because in the catalogues her mother used you had to choose from line drawings. Once Anita had chosen a pretty little greyish-blue bolero top and matching skirt that swirled out elegantly on the graceful smiling girl in the picture, but when it

138

arrived and she put it on it looked horrible. The shoulders sloped, the back stuck out all funny and the skirt hung limp and dowdy. But her mother would never let her change anything. She was always sending Anita to Marge's with a long list that she'd dictated: *quarter of tea, pound of rody bacon, tin of cream of chicken soup, packet of Oxo, gravy browning, small tin evaporated milk, small tin mandarin oranges, jar piccalilli, quarter of corned beef, sliced loaf. I would be obliged if you could put this on my account. Yours Faithfully, Geraldine M. Silver. (Mrs.)* Anita wrote it, she signed it. Old Marge in the shop would read it and show it to her big square husband who smoked sixty cigarettes a day; they would briefly shake their heads, and then one or other of them would raise their eyes to heaven and sigh, and as the ground showed no consideration by refusing to open and swallow her up, Anita took to standing there on one foot with her arms behind her back, looking at the fancy cakes on the sloping glass trays in the window, brazen as her mother. She'd never forgotten the time her mother pushed them behind the counter in Marge's. 'You feed my children then,' she'd said and walked out, and Robin had burst into tears, which, of course, was exactly what he was supposed to do.

————————

She sat at the bar in the Wild Boar.

'It always seemed to be January,' she said. 'It was dark all day.'

Michael leaned against the other side of the bar. He reached out and took hold of her arm, turning it to inspect the inside of the elbow.

'Ah, you won't find much there,' she smiled. 'I never shot up, I can't stand needles. Candy used to do it for me, I used to look the other way.'

A customer came to the other end of the bar, and when Michael returned from serving him she said: 'I've been drawing the sandings.'

She'd started a series of drawings of the sandings, boats and ropes and steps and dinghies. She went down several times and each time Michael's boat, the *Ellen*, was locked up and empty. She was, of course, just working, though in reality her mind had split in two; one part thought about interesting compositions and saleable pictures, the other plotted ways of getting on his boat. It would all be completely natural and casual and nothing would happen. She just wanted to see where he lived.

'Oh really? What, the boats?'

'Of course the boats. What else is there?'

She sipped her wine, lit a cigarette. She saw in the bar mirror that they looked like Beauty and the Beast.

'So have you done a drawing of my boat?'

'It's on one of them.'

'Yeah?'

'Yeah. I knocked on your door the last time. I was going to try and cadge a cup of tea but you weren't in.'

'When was this?'

'Oh, Tuesday I think. About one. Were you here?'

'I don't work Tuesdays.'

'I looked through the window. It's nice inside, isn't it?'

'Yes it is.'

'I'd like to do some interiors, I think, sometime. It's the clutter. I love clutter.' She drained her glass.

'Oh well, I have enough of that — ' He sniggered. 'I was going to say to sink a ship, but maybe that's not the best analogy under the circumstances.'

'Probably not. You've got all these old bottles, haven't you? I hope you don't mind me looking in your window.'

'Not at all.'

'Can I come and draw your bottles sometime?'

'Anytime,' he said. He got up and served another customer.

――――――――

'D'you think she's pretty?' her mother asked her later at home, sitting on the end of Anita's bed picking her toes. Robin was asleep, the floor around his bed strewn with bits of Meccano.

Anita thought of the fair-haired girl's legs going along next to Paddy Riley. 'She's quite pretty,' she said, swinging her new royal blue Alice band from the end of her finger and watching how it sparkled.

'She *looks* pretty from a distance,' her mother sniffed. 'But when you get close to she's got bad skin.'

'Oh, well I haven't seen her close to.'

'No, well.' Her mother sighed, straightened, lay at length resting on her elbow with her cheek on her hand. 'He grew up on a farm,' she said dreamily, 'with lots of brothers and sisters. Can you imagine, Anita? A farm in Ireland. Oh, we'll have to take you over there one day! You'll love it. It's your country really, you see. Yours and Robin's. What d'you think he'd want to come over here for? Give me a little farm in Ireland any day, it'd do me fine.' She raised herself with a long, lazy movement, raked her hair and strolled to the

142

dark window where the streetlamp glowed.

'I met him on the Bobs,' she said softly. 'It was his twentieth birthday.'

———

Anita was a little tipsy. She tossed her hair back with one hand. Was that stupid? she thought. Am I making myself too obvious? 'I'll have another glass,' she said when he returned.

'I can give you a key.' He reached for the wine bottle. 'You can just pop in when you want to then and do whatever you want. I never know when I'm going to be around.'

'Oh, are you sure? That would be really nice.'

He poured. Politely, she sipped her wine. Free with his key, she thought.

There was an awkward silence. He looked away, surveying the room from under his heavy brows, which had fallen abruptly, caving into the centre.

'I'm off to pick up my girls in a minute,' she said, 'and then — highlight of my week — take them to Mr Magic's Merry Maze.'

'Sounds like fun,' he said.

★ ★ ★

She sat on a bench on the green outside school. In a minute she'd get up and go over and join the other parents in the yard, but for now she just wanted to sit here and get her breath back. She'd run all along the prom, thinking: Why did I say that? Have I made an assignation? Surely not. Words spoke themselves, actions took themselves. Sometimes it was as if she had nothing to do with it. That's how she'd ended up on the streets, she just sleepwalked there and woke up suddenly, like Robin in the hall. Life, she used to think in the terrible days before she left Summer Court, is elsewhere. Funny the things you miss. Like the sound of the generator, and sitting on the caravan steps mending the Fool's costume. None of her old friends were around and Candy's face had turned the colour of chewing gum. The carpet was dark brown and covered in little hard sticky things like abandoned pupae squashed flat. They wouldn't come off. One night late she found a man asleep on the ground outside the flat in the freezing cold. He wore no coat, just jeans and an unravelling maroon jumper, and his body shivered in huge spasms.

'Who's that outside?' she asked.

They said he was bad news and wouldn't let him in, so she took a sleeping bag out to him and tucked it in around him. He woke briefly, smiling and murmuring and opening his arms to her like a child. 'It's OK, my

144

dear,' she said, 'go to sleep,' went back in and watched a horror film. Someone gave her a wad of speed wrapped up in a Rizla. It was mixed with blood and had gone into a soggy brownish lump. And in the morning she'd got up, walked from the flat, past the huddled form in the sleeping bag, and gone down the road as far as the lights. When the traffic stopped she couldn't cross. I can't, she thought, I just can't walk out there, it's so big, like a stage, so she'd gone down the hill instead and sat in a café. She had thirty pounds and some change in her pocket. It was all she had in the world.

And nowhere to go.

Anita's throat filled up with fear. It had got into her so deeply so long ago that it was always there on tap. She'd made a vow that day on the cobbles, like Scarlett O'Hara, I'll get out of this, she'd vowed, somehow, some way, I'll get out of this and I'll stay out and I'll never be poor again. So much for that. Even now sometimes, at three a.m. or so, she walked the dark streets in her dreams, and they were bitter cold. A nameless threat breathed from them. Waking in the dark, worry was an ache in the brain. She'd reach out and touch Charley till he half woke and turned, stroking her and mumbling: 'It's all right. It's all right.'

145

Anita strolled over to the playground and stood by the big gate. There they were: Jasmine pale as milk and very pretty with her thin fair hair and lower lip a fat pink bud; Sid with her scratched knees and blunt face frowning in deep concentration as she rubbed the toe of her shoe.

Unbelievable. I should fall down on my knees, she thought.

★　★　★

'I'm going to do some drawings on Michael's boat this afternoon,' she told Alison when she turned up to take over on Thursday.

Alison folded her arms and gave her a long look. 'Oh really?' she said. 'What does that mean?'

Anita smiled. 'It means I'm going to do some drawings on Michael's boat.'

Alison opened her mouth to speak but decided against it and turned away. 'Well now,' she said airily, lifting a parcel from the floor, 'what might this be?'

'There's something wrong with our world,' Anita said primly, sitting back in the chair with her hands behind her head. 'No one believes in friendship any more. Nothing's going to happen, Alison. Nothing has *ever* been going to happen.' She grew indignant. 'Why shouldn't it be possible for a man and a

146

woman to be friends, real friends, I mean, and not have sex? Do you really think it's impossible? Really? Are you that cynical? I just think that's so sad.'

Alison, who always did everything thoroughly, put her head on one side and thought for a long time, one hand fingering the string on the parcel, the other rubbing at the brown circle under one eye as if she were smoothing on make-up.

'No,' she said finally.

'No what?'

'No, I don't think it's impossible.'

'Well then.' Anita stood up, brushing crumbs from her clothes.

'*I* may not think so,' Alison persisted, following Anita into the back where her drawing gear was, 'and you may not think so. But I bet he does.'

Anita straightened the side bits of her hair in the mirror. She sighed and for a moment her eyes glazed over, sliding sideways as she bit her lip. 'You underestimate him,' she said, then focused. 'Oh, he may want to screw me,' she said plainly, 'being a man and all that. But he knows it's not going to happen.' She turned from the mirror, smiling. 'It's all right, Ali. I've never been anything other than totally straight with him.'

'Rubbish,' said Alison.

'Ali!'

'Rubbish,' she repeated in a deliberate way, cutting the string on the parcel and smiling to take out the sting. 'You're fooling yourself, Anita.' She tapped her on the wrist with the scissors. 'You watch out.'

The bell rang for a customer.

'Anyway,' Anita said as a parting shot, 'he won't be there. So there.'

She walked down past the whelks and winkles and mussels, the dressed crabs and prawns. The stallholders greeted her as a familiar face. On the saltings it was peaceful: ropes lay coiled like sleeping serpents, some creature blew bubbles in the mud; a gull crouched upon an old wooden hulk like a vulture on the picked bones of a great beast. She had two clear hours before she had to pick up the girls, so she took out her pad and pencil and knocked off three or four very quick sketches of the gull before it flew away, then another couple of the hulk. It looked like rain. She turned her attention to his boat. The *Ellen* was speckled all along the water line. She drew that, and the oily motion of the water gently slapping her sides, then, my God, nearly an hour had passed and she couldn't believe it.

She boarded the *Ellen*. She didn't need the

key because he was there, and he'd been drinking.

'I thought you were never coming,' he blurted accusingly, jumping up from the table. He looked bizarre, pale-faced and all in black. She felt like a colour intruder in an old black and white film, something rather arty, possibly foreign or British kitchen sink.

'You weren't waiting, were you?' she said coolly. 'I didn't know we had some definite arrangement, I thought I was just supposed to pop in whenever. I've got a key.'

He walked up to her in the little space and brought his face up close, staring her drunkenly straight in the eye. His own eyes were sleepy and serious and bloodshot, the lids hanging low as if they couldn't be bothered to open all the way. 'I know,' he said, 'but you said you'd come today.'

She dumped her things on the table. 'It's very kind of you to let me do this,' she said warmly.

'Feel free.' He leaned back against the sink with his shoulders hunched and his big knobbly hands poised upon the rim like spiders. 'You going to draw the bottles?'

She looked around. 'Hmmm. I don't know.'

They were just a bunch of old green glass

with lettering on, she didn't particularly want to do them.

'Well, just so's I don't plonk myself down in your way or something.'

'Put the kettle on,' she said. 'I need a coffee. And you certainly do. Plonk yourself down wherever you like, you can't possibly be in the way, it's your boat. I'll just draw you in like part of the furniture.'

He put the kettle on.

'Oh, I spent too much time out there,' she sighed, looking at her watch. 'I'd better get started.'

She settled on a pile of cushions with her pad, rubber and 4B pencil, and started sketching the bottles. Michael made the coffee then sat down and announced his intention of carrying on with his book while she worked. For a while they sat in companionable if slightly fraught silence. The bottles bored her, so she started on his face, the most interesting subject in the place. From perceiving him as ugly she had come full circle: now he was beautiful, his scar, his sunken eyes and black brows, his hunk of a nose, his thick lips. He was wonderful to draw.

After a while he cottoned on.

'Are you drawing me?' he asked, raising his eyes.

'I am.'

'You seem to be spending rather a long time on me.'

She glanced at her watch. Damn! Should have asked Jane Jarrett to have the girls for an hour.

'I am,' she repeated, gripped by her drawing. It flowed, more than anything had for ages. 'Don't worry, I'll give you the going rate.'

'What?'

'The going rate for an artist's model.'

He laughed. 'Well, that's one picture you certainly aren't going to be able to sell. I don't think Philip Wragge's particularly going to want my mug gazing down from his walls.'

'Tough. Your face . . .'

'Do you want me to keep it still?'

'No. Just stay where you are. Your face is incredible.'

His eyebrows shot up.

She laughed. 'That's what I mean, the way it moves. Your face is incredibly beautiful.'

He snorted. He was, she realised, actually embarrassed.

'It is,' she insisted. 'I'm just stating a fact.'

'Don't be ridiculous.' He looked out of the window. 'I'm ugly.'

'No.' She shook her head.

'Yes, I am. Look at my nostrils.'

'Oh yes!' She was working on them. They

were turning out like the horns of a ram encircling darkness.

'I'm like a monkey,' he said. 'I know.'

'Well, yes, you are a bit,' she conceded, 'but you're still beautiful. Turn your head back please.'

'OK for me to talk?' he asked a moment later.

'Of course. Unless I say so.'

'You have serious perception problems, Anita.' His voice was sleepy and sarcastic and slightly blurred. 'You are wrong. You are looking at an ugly, ugly man with no illusions. Although I grant you some women do find me attractive.'

'I'll tell you something honestly,' she said, worrying away at his right nostril, 'I did use to think you were ugly. But I don't any more. I've got to know your face, I suppose. It's an acquired taste.'

'Like oysters.' He turned his attention back to his book. 'You know what they used to call me at school? King Kong.'

'King Kong's sexy,' she said. 'Everyone's rooting for King Kong at the end. You know the way he goes around peeping into bedroom windows and looking up women's skirts? He's some sort of primal archetype. Unchained passion. Elemental and raw.'

Michael closed the book on his finger. 'I don't think,' he said, 'the third form at St

152

Salvius were really thinking along those lines.' He opened his book again. 'Bastards,' he added in a near-whisper.

★ ★ ★

They drove to Crosby at Christmas. The journey was hell. Sid was sick just as they were pulling out of their lane. Charley banged his head on the wheel. 'I don't believe it!' he cried. 'She's doing it on purpose. She must be.'

'Oh, don't be ridiculous!'

'I'm not!' Sid had time to say before spraying another throatful all over Anita's shoes as she hauled her out on to the verge.

'Pooh!' Jasmine sat with her hands clamped over her nose and mouth. 'It stinks.'

'Well, it's not the car,' said Charley, 'it can't be the car, she's only been in it two minutes.'

Sid started to cry. 'It's not my fault,' she sobbed. 'What have I done? I'm only five!'

'Didn't you give them travel pills?'

'No.'

'No?' He groaned. 'Anita!'

'It's excitement,' Anita said.

'You know they have to have travel pills!'

'Well, I just forgot, didn't I?'

'You forgot?'

'Oh, shut up. Why couldn't *you* have

153

remembered? Why is it *my* fault?'

'Because you always do it.'

'So? Charley, I have so much to do!'

'Well so do I.'

'Well, you're not doing much now, are you? You're just sitting there. Can't you sort the back out?'

He got out and walked round and started wiping sick out of the door pocket with toilet tissue. 'I do wish your mum'd come and live down here,' he muttered. 'It'd be a damn sight more practical than all this toing and froing. It's getting ridiculous.'

'Well, she won't. And she can't. And that's that. There.' And thank God, she added mentally, clapping Sid on the shoulder. 'You'll do fine now. We'll open the window.'

She started fishing in her bag for the travel pills.

'It's a bit late for that now,' he said, shoving the dripping ball of tissue under the hedge.

'Charley! Don't leave it there.'

'OK.' He turned and thrust it at her. 'You can sit with it on your knee for the journey.'

★ ★ ★

'You don't understand,' Anita said, when they were at last on the road again, 'how much I have to do.'

154

'You don't understand how much *I* have to do.'

'Well, we're quits then, aren't we?'

'Quits? What are you talking about? We're not in a game, are we? It's just something we've got to sort out.'

Anita sighed and looked out of the window. It had been like this lately. They bickered. It was no big thing, no central issue; more like an attack of midges. It was her mainly, she knew, but it wasn't just her. Charley was going through one of his thoughtful, morose patches, sitting for long periods at his desk, sideways in his chair with his face resting on one hand and his eyes fixed on a point on the carpet. The girls got on his nerves. He was tired but he'd wake in the middle of the night and prowl naked about the house. As for herself, she was preoccupied. At any point in the day, with or without him, she would find herself drifting into deeply adolescent fantasy, ardent and harrowing. In one, she comforted Michael after some terrible tragedy, possibly Luke's death. In another, Charley was dead and she was alone with the girls. Michael was there.

'Nita,' Charley would say, 'shall I go and get the girls or will you?'

The M6 through Birmingham was a nightmare, nose to tail. She took over the

155

driving after Hilton Park while the girls squabbled in the back.

'You're in a funny mood,' he said.

'No, I'm not.'

'You are. You seem to have been in a funny mood for ages. Oh for God's sake, shut up, you two, how d'you expect your mother to drive with all that going on? Jasmine. Give it back! Now!'

'I suppose I'm worried about my mother,' she said.

'Of course you are.'

They sat quietly for a while.

'These visits are always difficult,' he said.

'It's not so bad when I'm on my own but it's the girls. I'm always worried that they're making too much noise or getting on people's nerves or something.'

'Have you had a word with Sid?'

'What about?'

'About not touching things and not rooting around.'

'I'm always having words with Sid. It never makes any bloody difference.'

'I know but you have to have an extra special word when . . . '

'You tell her then! I'm always telling her.'

'What have I done?' asked Sid, outraged.

'I've got so much to do!' Anita wailed. 'I can't always be remembering everything.'

'It can't be that bad,' he said, 'now they're at school.'

'You don't know. Sometimes I just feel it's impossible to cope with it all.'

'Impossible to cope? What do you mean? My mother was left on her own with two kids when she was younger than you. *She* coped.'

'Bully for her!'

'I just mean you haven't got it that hard, that's all. You haven't. You haven't got it hard at all.'

'Oh, well you'd know, wouldn't you?'

Silence prevailed.

In the mirror Anita could see Jas in a sulk over something, nervous clickety hands shoved up to her mouth, small as a monkey's, rough with eczema. Charley had assumed his noble martyr persona, turning sideways and looking out of the window with folded arms.

Towards Crosby the air softened. Charley wound down the window and sniffed the air.

'Going to stay fine,' he said.

He could be such a smug bastard, that was his problem.

★   ★   ★

Thinking back on that Christmas later, Anita would remember the bickering of the two old sisters, more restrained than that of the

157

children. It was Bernie's last, though none of them knew it. Anita thought her mother would go first, seeing her there under the tinsel in the puce paper hat, with the tubes in her nose connecting her to the machine. Her mother seemed to have shrunk. Her voice was the same but reduced, like thinned-down gravy. Between the words were awful long whistles of breathing. How did she get like that? Cigarettes? Anita remembered her as a young woman always on her hands and knees with a dustpan and brush or pulling and pushing the old broom. Years of dust. Anita had never used a hoover till she went to live at Connie's. Same with a washing machine and fridge. She thought of what Charley said about having it easy.

No one could have dreamed it would be Bernie, so active and terrifying, at least to the girls, who thought she was a witch. She seemed to be in every room all over the house, still with her eternal crêpe bandage around her knee and a bit of a limp, poking into drawers and cupboards and ignoring you if you said anything to her, not because she was deaf but because she was rude.

In the evenings they'd start, her mother and Bernie, rambling about in the history of the O'Learys and the Deasys. Her mother would recount again the walk to the station

158

with Connie in a crocodile of evacuees with Grandma O'Leary standing at the side of the road and Connie saying, 'There's our ma, there,' and the girl in the carriage who kept picking her nose and wiping it on Connie's coat. She would recall the days towards the end of the war when she worked at Dunlop's making barrage balloons, and she would sing the songs of *Workers' Playtime*. Anita knew them all. But she gets so many things wrong, she thought. So many. It's all turned myth now, like Quack Fair had a tendency to turn if she didn't consciously make herself remember every now and again how sour it had become with everybody stabbing everybody else in the back and all the bitching.

'No, Geraldine, he did *not* say that, you're wrong there. He said straight out: Mammy, listen, I'm leaving next week and that's that.'

'He did not, I was there, I was standing right next to him at the time.'

'You were not, Geraldine, because you were not at home at the time. You were at work.'

'How could I have been at work, I didn't work on Sundays, did I?'

'Who said anything about Sunday? It was Friday because Connie'd just got in with her wages and she burst into tears and said:

'Here, Mike, you can have my wages,' and Dad told her not to be such a bloody fool.'

'No no no, you're thinking about the time our Nora said she was getting married.'

'No no no . . .'

Once in the dear dead days beyond recall . . .

Anita and Charley bickered too, on Christmas Eve as they filled the stockings and put out the presents. He drove her mad sometimes on these visits. Her mother thought he was gorgeous. At Judith's he always adopted an air of uneasy boyishness and civil deference that charmed them all, apart from Auntie Bernie, but then Prince Charming himself would have had a job with Bernie. It was when they were alone upstairs in the loft extension, with the girls asleep in their shiny pink and yellow pyjamas on their truckle beds, that he'd start on an endless stream of snide little put-downs about the decor or the things they'd said. Then he and she would argue lethargically in whispers so as not to wake the girls.

They got into Judith and Clive's bed and made love quietly so as not to wake the girls. He thinks he's better than my family, she thought, though God knows why, his mum

160

was only a hairdresser, and she bit him too hard. He was very sweet, didn't complain but kept rubbing the place on his shoulder afterwards while he was trying to get to sleep. She put her hand on his hip. 'Sorry,' she whispered, kissing his back, 'sorry, my love,' and his hand came round and caught hers and yanked it up to his lips so that she was pulled hard against his slippery skin. He fell asleep soon, as he always did after sex, but Anita lay awake for ages listening to the fragile breathing in the room, thinking how she couldn't bear to lose any of them. They were a job lot. As soon as she'd met him the girls were there too. The day after the party at Gibbet Hill, before a glance or a word had been exchanged, she'd had a picture in her head of him sitting by her bedside as she gave birth, and it came true.

She thought of Michael and how strong the compulsion to touch him was at certain moments. She felt as if her finger was on the trigger of an insanely sensitive gun, as if one little tremor could shift it. She thought of her mother, wizened and small about the shoulders, slack and round about the middle, loose wattles of thin skin pendent under her chin. Absurd. This ailing old woman had ridden the Wall of Death with Paddy Riley. Though she'd never seen them she knew, because her mother had told her. Her mother told her everything. They say mothers and daughters should be best friends but it isn't true, she thought. Her mother made a friend of her when she was only eleven. She shouldn't have had to know that her mother shuddered when her father got into bed beside her, that she couldn't imagine what she'd seen in him in the first place now, that she was bored stupid with the sight of his miserable face and bloody stupid competitions that *she* always had to post. That she was all of a flutter, just *wild* about Paddy Riley — so sweet! So young!

'He's taken the pledge, you know. He has never drink taken in his life. He's seen something, I fancy, of what it can do. Such a face! With the wee curls and those blue eyes. I bet there's broken hearts in Tipperary.'

Then her mother would drive herself mad trying to remember all the words of 'Off To Philadelphia In The Morning'.

Her mother told her things she should never have known. Because when she had to lie awake listening to the sad sweet whine of the mandolin, thinking of her father's long gentle fingers on the strings, she was obliged to know more about him than he knew himself: that his wife no longer loved him, that he'd left his family and friends and all his

162

past not for love but for nothing. The knowledge filled her with such obscure guilt that she would creep down in the dark to the foot of the stairs and listen to those sad little tunes he used to play.

She never mentions my father, Anita thought. You'd think he'd never existed. But him, Paddy Riley, that beautiful blue-eyed boy, him she still carries. She doesn't know what I know though. Nobody knows what I know.

★ ★ ★

When she finally drifted off she dreamed stupid dreams all night, irritating little comedies in which she was always discovered naked or inappropriately clad on public occasions.

She woke with a sense of aching sadness in her breast.

Charley was lying with his eyes open but asleep, Jas and Sid were pulling things out of their stockings, Jasmine tossing bits all over the place, spilling her chocolate fish, losing the top of her fancy pen, her mess like a lava flow around her. Sid was setting her things out in very neat rows.

'Can we ring Basil later?' Jasmine asked.

Basil was at Lindsay's.

'You're lovely little girls,' Anita told them, sitting up and drawing her willows nightie close. It was chilly in the room.

'Shut your chatter,' said Sid.

Charley rolled over against Anita and yawned.

★ ★ ★

Likenesses were not her forte. She never did do Michael justice, though he was a good sitter, patient and relaxed once he got settled with his book and a big mug of coffee and a bottle. Poor as he claimed to be he always managed to get hold of some good malt whisky. They'd sit for an hour or two, sometimes without speaking; outside, the gulls would cry and the ripples on the ceiling mingled with the sound of water. Sometimes he'd lift his eyes from the page he was reading and smile at her, and she would smile back quickly, fixed on his left ear or the space between his eyes or the scar on the end of his chin. She drew him many times, and she drew the dishes on the draining board, a bowl full of prawns, Luke doing his homework, bottles on a shelf, ripples of light on the ceiling, condensation dripping like rain down the insides of the windows.

When he woke up in the morning, he told

her, big drops dripped off the ceiling on to his head.

* * *

The girls had gone to Sarah Mottram's after school for tea. Anita had been to the vet's with Basil to get something for his gummy eyes. Poor thing was decaying before her eyes. His back legs knocked together in a funny way when he walked, and his breath was always bad. He walked so slowly back along the prom to the car park that once or twice she thought he would stop completely. Just after their own old beach hut, she saw Luke, a skinny lost little waif running up along the side of the breakwater as if the demons of the cold grey sea were after him.

'Luke!' she shouted.

He ran on for a bit then stopped, looked around, didn't see her and set off again. She came up with him at the top of the steps where she met Charley, but he still didn't see her. The wind was blowing tears back from his eyes. At first she thought it was just the cold, then realised he was crying.

'Luke!' she called. 'Luke! What is it?'

He looked shocked when he saw her and dithered, turning away then back again. She

165

thought he was embarrassed at being caught in tears.

She took hold of his arm. 'Luke! What is it, Luke? What's the matter?'

'Have you seen Dad?' he blurted.

'Your dad? No, not today.'

'I can't find him.' He looked around, bewildered, wiping his eyes impatiently with his sleeve. 'He's supposed to be at home. He's always at home now. I don't know where he is.'

'Oh, poor Luke! Can't you get in?'

'I can get in!' he snapped as if she was stupid. 'But I can't find Dad.'

'Well, he'll be all right, Luke. He's probably just popped out for a loaf of bread or something. Got talking, you know. I bet he's there now. Come on, I'll give you a lift.'

They drove to the sandings. The *Ellen* was cold and bleak and damp-smelling, uncleaned. An empty whisky bottle lay on its side in the middle of the floor. Luke's school bag had spilled its guts where it had been dropped.

'He's *always* here,' said Luke, obviously near to tears again. 'He's going to kill himself!'

'What do you mean? Your dad's all right.'

'He is not! He's drunk again.' He flung himself down with the weary air of one much older. Anita sat opposite him, the ash-smeared table with its dirty plates and debris between them. 'One of these days,' he said bleakly, 'I'll be fishing him out of the sea.'

'Oh, Luke!'

Not yet eleven, she thought. Jasmine in three years. Poor little Luke with his haunted eyes and the tiny pointed face of his mother who couldn't take motherhood, didn't want to know, wandered round all night prowling like a cat, while the kid's father shoved bottles in its mouth and hoped for the best. She threw him against the wall one night like a little rag doll, said Michael, and that was the end.

'He'll be back,' she promised, 'any minute, I bet you. Shall I make you a cup of tea? Are you hungry?'

But he leapt up and waved her down frantically with his hands. 'No no no no, I'll make *you* one, you're the guest.'

And he wouldn't hear of anything else, but made her sit there while he presented her with a mug of strong red tea and a little plate of Jammy Dodgers, then sat staring wistfully out of the window, cramming his mouth and fondling the ears of Basil, who leaned adoringly against him gazing at the biscuit.

'He's always getting drunk now,' he complained. 'He doesn't take any notice of anything I say.' His face changed. 'Oh, Luke,' he pronounced, a fair take-off of his father, 'I know what I'm doing. Trust me, Luke.'

'And do you?'

He looked at her, smiling his narrow smile. 'Would you?'

This boy is too old for his years, she thought. 'What were you doing on the beach, Luke?'

His eyebrows gave a little self-deprecatory twitch. 'I saw something floating,' he said. 'It was just some wood.'

'Oh, Luke!'

'Oh, Luke!' he mimicked. 'I know, I know, I'm a stupid bugger.'

'You are not.' She stood up. 'You are a very nice boy who's concerned about his father. Come on.'

'Come on where?'

'We're gonna hunt him down,' she said, trying to make him laugh. 'We're gonna scour every dive and gin joint in this town. Then we're going to stand outside and sing temperance songs in the snow.'

'It isn't snowing.'

'Details.'

They locked up.

'You're mad,' he said as they got back in the car. 'Anyway, what are temperance songs?'

'Temperance songs are like . . . ' She

168

thought, and couldn't actually bring one to mind. 'Oh, you know — ' looking back to reverse, 'like: Daddy, dear Daddy, please come home, the rats have eaten the baby and so on, and Daddy's in the pub boozing away all the money, you know how it is.'

'I certainly do,' he said dryly.

They drove along the Quay.

'I don't know what he'd do without me,' Luke said. 'If I wasn't here to nag him . . . there he is!'

Michael was just coming out of the Mustard Seed with a carrier bag held in front of his chest, a French stick poking out of the top. She pulled up. Luke jumped out and ran across to him and she followed. Michael grinned, rubbing Luke's hair.

'Where *were* you?' said Luke. 'It's nearly five o'clock!'

'I had some things to get, I just . . . '

'For an hour and a half?'

'Hey! Calm down.' Michael glanced at her, laughing. 'You're all right, Luke, you're a big boy now.'

'He's a child,' she said, suddenly angry, 'you should have been there.'

He put the bag down. 'What is this?' he said softly, his grin fading. 'The Spanish Inquisition?'

'Dad!' Luke punched him softly. 'Why

didn't you leave me a note?'

Michael spread his palms and raised his shoulders, a pained look on his face, saying nothing. Suddenly he reminded her of Candy. Poor me, poor me, how can you be nasty to me? Whatever I've done, it's never my fault. They're all the bloody same, she thought. Go to some tribe in Outer Wherever and they'd still be the same. Babies.

'He worries about you,' she said.

Michael laughed again and hugged Luke. 'You know I'm all right,' he said, 'I'm always all right. You should have got yourself something to eat. Here.' He put a hand in his pocket and brought out some change. 'Go and get yourself some chocolate. Go on. Anything you like.'

Luke took the money without a word and dashed inside the Mustard Seed.

'He was crying,' she said. 'He'd been looking all over for you. He thought you'd drowned.'

'Oh, Luke!' said Michael, sighing indulgently. She smelt the drink then, a sudden sour waft. Apart from that she wouldn't have known. Drink didn't show on him, apart from his eyes.

'Couldn't you tell him you're sorry?'

'I will. I will.' It was the way he said it, poor reasonable soul badgered by neurotics.

170

'You're in the wrong,' she said coldly. 'He's your child. *He* shouldn't have to worry about you, you should take care of him.'

'I *do* . . .'

'He shouldn't have to comb the sea-shore looking for your dead body. He shouldn't have to come home to an empty place that's filthy and stinks and it's full of empty booze bottles . . .'

Michael drew himself up to his full height, away from her, his face blank.

' . . . he shouldn't have to gaze out of the window wondering if you're coming home. It's not fair! He shouldn't have to walk about in the freezing cold and get his own tea. *He's* the child. *You're* the adult. *You're* responsible for *him*.'

'Who do you think you are?' he said, and she turned on her heel and walked to the car.

She'd got her hand on the door when he ran across and gripped her wrist.

'I *do* take care of him,' he said.

It hurt.

His face was deadly serious. He squeezed. Face to face, eye to eye, his hand squeezing. It hurt.

'I *do* take care of him.'

Tighter.

They just stared. Basil began to snarl.

For a second, less, Michael's eyes filled up

171

with tears. Then they were gone. He let go, ran back across the road and met Luke coming out of the Mustard Seed. Anita got into the car. Her wrist was cold and tingly; it hurt. She shook it, held it. It was white where he'd gripped, then red as the blood came back. Michael put his arm round Luke. They walked away. Luke turned his head and waved. She started the car, drove, scared, she didn't know why, crying a little even. She didn't know what had just happened.

It just felt as if everything had changed.

★ ★ ★

She tried to write it all down in a letter she had no intention of sending. She wrote that she loved him, that his face was always in her mind; how Dante's love for Beatrice and Petrarch's for Laura was chaste, and of the Arabian poets, and the troubadours who condemned jealousy, and Eros and Agape and *amor purus*, which permits everything short of the sexual act. How daring, she wrote, to take on the challenge, make the old thing new, here at the butt end of the crass twentieth century. We can do it. We can do the impossible. We can love and be chaste.

She stretched, then got up and stalked to the mirror, throwing back her shoulders and lifting her chin. Arthur, Guinevere, Lancelot. Agony. Tristan and Isolde. Oh hell!

She flopped back into the swivel chair, covered her face and pushed herself round with her toe. The Courtly Love thing did not tally in all respects because Charley was never your typical medieval husband and she was never his chattel. In fact, she would have gone so far as to say that at first, after she knew that he'd really fallen for her, she'd considered him *her* chattel. But of course that wasn't true either. She'd figured him out all wrong, thought of him as a quiet, unnoticed man, sitting lonely with his history books and journals in the little terraced house he'd bought with the money his grandmother left; dreaming of her, yearning for her, she, the unattainable. He was a mollusc waiting in his shell for her to spike him with her sharp little pin. But after they'd started going about together and she'd seen how many women, and even very young girls, made a point of crossing the road to say hello to him, she'd realised it was she who was spiked. For a very short time she'd made herself capricious and unavailable, but to no avail. There was a certain anguished, bemused look that always ended up in the eyes of the men she'd had, but Charley's wouldn't go like that. His had a wary intelligence, a watchfulness that turned more quickly to anger than sorrow. She remembered them huddling together in a shelter on the prom. The sea was muddy, the east wind bitter. He'd been unshaven, a constant scowl of worry lowering his brows. 'I don't know what you think you're playing at,' he'd told her, shoulders hunched, hands in pockets, 'but I'm not interested. We're either doing this seriously or we're not, and if you're not, then we might as well just stop because I can't be bothered. It's boring.'

His eyes were narrowed at the luminous light shining over the sea. She'd thought of how many times she'd fallen in love, and how it never lasted, thought of Rory Gotch and Mad John and Candy and all the other fucked-up losers and vowed never again. She'd kissed his serious mouth, thought of swans and other creatures that mate for life. It will be easy now, she'd thought, like when you've been trying to thread a needle for ages and it suddenly just slides through, effortless. She'd stick with this one and everything would be all right.

And it was. Oh, it was.

She swivelled back to the desk and the letter. Of course she'd never send it. It was just to get things clear in her own mind. She wrote it and read it and tore it up and

174

threw it away. Some letters were better left unsent.

Dear Miss Palmer,
   Anita was unable to attend school on Tuesday owing to a very bad headache.
   Yours Faithfully,
   M. Silver

After she went to the Grammar School she learnt how to forge. She didn't like the Grammar School. She had no friends. Sometimes she gave herself a day off and went and hung around on Jackson's where little wagons of brick dust rode up and down all day on tracks through rosebay-willow-herb and convolvulus.

Dear Mrs Rogerson,
   Please excuse Anita from Games this week. Her knee has been very painful over the weekend and the doctor has advised her to rest it as much as possible.
   Yours Faithfully,
   M. Silver

Her father wrote her school notes. Her mother, though she could read a bit, enough to get the gist of things anyway, never wrote anything

175

but her signature: Geraldine M. Silver, (Mrs.).

Anita could do both their signatures, her mother's tremulous and loopy, her father's neat and businesslike. She could sign her own reports if she needed to. She'd practised in her room, the little back room her mother had cleared out for her now that she was at the Grammar School. It was funny sleeping without Robin. She had a transistor radio. At night in the dark, very softly, it played *Runaway* by Del Shannon and *El Paso* by Marty Robbins.

She went down next day. She had to. It was not a working day, she dropped the girls at school and drove down to the saltings. She had nothing in her head of what she would say, just knew she had to sort it out.

What?

Something.

It was a terrible day, a bitter East wind blew in from Siberia and rain like tiny ice needles was on the air. Huddled in her big sleeves, she ran up the gang plank and knocked at the door. It opened immediately.

'I saw you coming,' he said.

They sat facing one another. It was warm and smoky; he'd cleaned up and instead of damp it smelled of coffee. He offered her a cigarette and they sat without saying anything for a while. Then, 'Sorry,' he said.

She watched a big spider walk across the rug.

'Michael?' she said softly. 'I think we're thinking a lot about each other and I thought we should get it out in the open and decide what we're going to do about it. If anything.'

It was an enormous spider with long graceful legs that tickled the air. She kept her eyes on it. She might be hugely wrong. Anita, he would say as gently as he could, Anita, I'm sorry, I don't really understand what you're saying. All she heard was the sighing of the wind, mournful, fretful, and the pretty patter of the rain setting in, hitting the fibreglass in sharp little bursts. Time passed. Smoke drifted across her vision. Time passed. She was aware that he leaned forward.

'Anita,' he said as gently as he could.

She smoked her cigarette, watched the spider run.

'Anita.'

'Anita.'

She looked up. His eyes were very steady. His elbows rested on his knees, his hands were linked together under his chin. He could have been praying. 'I think there might be something wrong with you,' he said, looking closely into her eyes. 'You're not normal, I saw that straight away.' He frowned. 'You seem so nice and sweet on the top, your smiling demeanour, your big brown eyes, your friendliness. But there's something else about you, isn't there?'

He didn't blink.

'You make me afraid,' he said.

'Afraid?' she whispered.

'I knew,' he said. 'I knew that time at the Curlew. Straight away when I saw you. You gave me this feeling, almost a horror, you made the hair at the back of my neck stand up.'

He waited. He didn't blink. She stared him out, her eyes stinging. She stared him out till things turned grey. She saw Harlequin dance with Columbine, a human pyramid tumble, a flyer strike out for the hoop of knives. What have I done, she said to herself.

What box have I opened?

'All I am doing,' she whispered, 'is trying to be honest.'

'Honest?' His forehead wrinkled, his voice thickened. '*Honest?*' He's angry, she thought, scared. 'You want honesty? You want honesty?' His eyes fell, the brows bunched over them. For a moment his long gnarled fingers covered his face; then, looking up at her through them, he laughed: 'You want honesty? *Honesty?*'

178

She couldn't speak. All she could think was that he was so beautiful.

He fell on his knees before her, took her hands in his and kissed them, pressing his face against her palms. 'You want honesty?' he said. 'Honesty?' Falling forward with his arms around her waist and his head heavy in her lap, pushing his face deep into her lap like a dog.

She put her arms round him. 'Ssh!' she whispered, stroking his hair, 'Ssh!'

If she was honest she had to admit she enjoyed this. Though she trembled with fear, though her stomach sickened and Charley and her babies rose up and shook their gory locks at her like Banquo's ghost, she enjoyed it. She had him now. He was hers. She knew exactly what to do. She took his face between her hands and lifted it and kissed him very gently, first upon the lips then once upon each eyelid, touched the little scar on the end of his chin. Her nail fitted it almost exactly.

He rested against her for a while.

'You've done this,' he said. 'You, Anita. You can't blame it on me.'

She smiled. She was in control. 'Ssh,' she said. 'Now don't worry. We'll work something out. Listen — ' kissing him again, 'listen — '

He pulled her down on the floor, pushed

her back and lay on top of her, heavy and hard.

'Listen, listen, *listen* to me, Michael.'

He groaned and reared up his head, holding her wrists and grinding his body into her, spreading her legs with his knees. 'I want to fuck you,' he said, 'I want to *fuck* you, I want to *fuck* you, I want to *fuck* you, I want to . . .'

She jerked her whole body up, grabbed his lower lip between her teeth and bit till he cried out. They rolled together. 'You wanted honesty,' he said. '*This* is honesty,' covering her mouth with his entirely and gagging her with his tongue.

Well, she thought, I can give as good as I get.

They came up for air.

'Now,' she said, hugging him close to her then pushing him off with all her strength, 'you *listen*!'

They sat panting, on their knees, face to face.

'We have to talk,' she said.

He burst out laughing.

'Michael, this is important!'

He leaned back against the sink. 'I know,' he laughed, 'I know.'

She took hold of his arms. 'I'll never do anything to hurt Charley,' she said, looking

180

him straight in the eyes. 'Never. And I'll never leave him. Ever. That's the truth.'

He turned his face sharply away but she still held him. The cords of his throat were stretched.

'Don't worry,' she said. 'It's OK. It's OK.'

He laughed again and buried his face in her neck. 'OK,' he mumbled. 'OK for who? OK for you, maybe.' He started kissing her again. It was as natural as rain. That being a fact, I have to make this work, she thought. It can't be impossible. We are all reasonable beings. She put her hands on either side of his face and made him look at her. His eyes were soft. 'We just have to work this out,' she said.

'We can't.' He shook his head. 'We can't work a thing like this out. You're mad if you can even think it.'

He put his face in her neck again and she put hers in his. It was warm with a little vein throbbing. They stood there for a time, till he put his leg between hers and pushed. They staggered and lurched, embracing blindly to his bed, and fell down upon it and lay as they had stood. Then they opened their eyes.

She shook her head slowly.

'What's that mean?' he asked.

'It means we're not going to do anything,' she replied.

He smiled then, a peculiar, malicious,

lop-sided grin. 'Really?' He feigned astonishment.

She had to get control. It was important that he understand from the start. 'Charley,' she said, 'we're going to be completely unique.'

'You called me Charley.'

'Oh, God!' Her hand flew to her mouth, she laughed and cried, pushed him aside and jumped from the bed and ran to the door. It was as if she'd suddenly woken from a dream to find it was real. The blood pounded in her head. 'What am I doing? What am I doing?' she cried.

'Anita!'

She stopped. Tears fell from her cheeks and the end of her chin. He came and took her by the arm and walked her back to the bed, held her against him and stroked her hair.

'You can't just run away from it now,' he said, 'it's not an option.'

'No!' she heard herself say, too loud. 'No, it's not, you're right.' She pulled away and stood up, wiping her cheeks with the flat of her hands and sniffing. In a moment she was back in control.

'Things are different now. Of course they are.' She sat down again and took his hands. 'I'm not going to sleep with you, Michael. It's not because I don't want to, it's because I'm just not going to. Then I won't have done anything wrong. I'm not going to fuck everything up because of sex. But I still feel the way I feel and we can still . . . '

He started shaking his head.

'Really,' she said urgently, 'you've got to take this seriously. I can't just do this!'

'Then why did you come here?'

His voice and face were clear. He stood up suddenly and started putting the kettle on. 'Perhaps you ought to go,' he said, 'because you know what we men are like, don't you? I only wanted a fuck.'

'OK,' she said, standing too, 'well, this isn't going to work then, is it?'

'Possibly not.'

He turned, leaning against the sink. For a moment they just stood there, till he smiled suddenly and held open his arms. She went to him and they kissed, long and gentle. He was a good intuitive kisser, and she felt the kiss in her toes. He moved his hips. 'I want to fuck you,' he whispered.

'No.' She kissed him.

He turned his face sideways, rocking his erection against her. 'You trying to drive me mad?' he breathed in her ear.

The rain poured down, streamed on the windows.

'No,' she said.

'Are you going to help me out here?'

'No.'

He pushed her away.

'You're dangerous,' he said. 'Go away.'

'I will.' Suddenly she was strangely elated. 'I'll go. But whatever's going to happen's going to happen. It's OK. I'm your best friend, Michael. Sex doesn't matter. This is much better, Michael. Friends go on for life. What more can I offer?'

By now he was far away.

'Go away,' he said, sitting at the table with his face blank, 'go away, Anita, go away.'

She was forging a letter when her mother called upstairs that she had an errand for her. When she went out on the landing her mother was standing in the hall looking up with an anxious expression on her face.

'You know that lad?' her mother said just above a whisper, 'that Paddy from Belle Vue?' The mermaid season had passed but she worked Friday and Sunday nights now at the Bingo in the King's Hall. 'Well, I'm going to tell you where he lives, and I want you to go and just knock on his door and tell him this: just that Geraldine has thought about what he said, and if he likes she could come and see him about it on a Friday morning. Just

184

that. And is there any reply. Tell him he can write it down. OK?'

It was Saturday. Her father was in the back room reading the newspaper with the TV sport on. Robin was round at his friend's.

'What is it?' Anita asked.

'Just something to do with work. Only I don't want your dad to know, because you know what he's like.' She stole a glance towards the back room. Her lips were pale and her face shiny. 'You've got to go down Clowes Street.'

She took Anita into the front room and, leaning on the windowsill, drew her a map with arrows on the back of a white envelope: 'Where it says 53A it means it's a little flat. It's over a hardware shop, you'll see, there's a little door at one side. Just ring the bell, it'll be all right.'

'Denise lives near there,' Anita said. Denise was her friend from the old school.

Her mother hustled her to the door. 'Go quick,' she whispered on the doorstep, patting her on the shoulder, 'go quick and get back quick. Watch yourself crossing those roads. Cross at the lights or with other people. If your dad asks you anything about where you've been, say you had to take some wool to your Auntie Anne's.'

Anita walked down the path in a state of

185

elation. She was going to cross Belle Vue all on her own, cross Hyde Road and walk through strange streets, alone, entrusted with an important message that made her cheeks burn because she knew that, however innocent it sounded, it was not. Her mother was making a fool of herself. Anita felt both shamed and protective. Her mother was much too old to be throwing herself at this boy. She had chosen Anita's father and she had to cook their teas and make them their hot water bottles. Thinking of her father made her scared, and yet she was elated too, and walked with a spring in her step because she was carrying an unwritten love letter across Belle Vue to blue-eyed Paddy Riley.

She had no money to spend. She just looked but that was OK, she loved just looking. She watched the green canopy unfurling itself over the rollicking caterpillar just before the siren wailed, and the carriages hurtling up and down the Bobs with all the people screaming their heads off. A fat man with a big red goitre was taking the money. Further on, the elephant walked back to the mounting steps with her sweet, sad-eyed head harnessed. The lake was dotted with boats, and the miniature railway loaded up with a party of serious little girls in coats.

The traffic was heavy and noisy on Hyde

Road. She walked up to the lights and waited to cross with all the people outside the hotel. What was the message? She couldn't remember all of it. Only that she would go and see him on Friday morning. Wasn't there something more than that? She realised suddenly that she could say anything. She was a talking letter. 'My mother says: *My darling Paddy, I long to see you. Your blue eyes are always in my heart.*'

She crossed importantly with all the other people and worked her way through smaller streets away from the big main road. His dusty black door marked 53A was easy enough to find. It was as her mother had said, next to a small hardware shop on a dilapidated row, the window hung with saws and spanners and shears. It made her think of Silver's Ironmongery in All Saints, founded in 1894 in Strangeways before it moved to Cheetham Hill. The All Saints' shop was the third. She herself had passed by on the other side of the road with her mother, had stood and looked in the window once and traced the gold curving letters that went in a rainbow curve across the glass of the door: *Silver.* Her name.

She'd never been in. She was going to though one day. Soon. She'd take the day off school and get the bus to All Saints and go in and walk up to the handsome, black-haired Jewish boy she knew would be behind the counter and say: 'I'm your cousin.' And he'd be shocked to know he had her because to them, her mother said, we simply don't exist.

In a funny sort of way, when she pressed the bell on Paddy Riley's dusty black door that day, she felt as if she were ringing at Silver's door. She almost expected that old, old Russian woman with her bonnet and shawl and suspicious bright eyes to answer to her. But it was Paddy Riley who appeared after the muffled thump of footsteps coming downstairs. Barefoot in a white vest and black trousers, his shoulders sharp and high.

'Anita!' He put out his arms and pulled her in through the door as if there were some danger on the street. 'Is she with you?'

'No.'

'Oh!'

He closed the door and they stood in gloom.

'Come on up, so.' He padded before her up the stairs and she followed to a tiny landing with brown oilcloth and two doors, one of which was open. They went into his room. It was very tidy. The window was open. Beneath it was a good solid table with a red checked cloth and a kitchen chair on either side. There were armchairs by an electric fire in a tiled grate, small framed photographs all along the mantelpiece, and a large wireless on a table with the voices of the Everly Brothers singing, *Bye bye, love, bye bye, happiness,* slightly muted from the round central speaker.

'I've got a message for you,' she said.

He stared at her like a hawk.

'Geraldine said she can come Friday morning and is there a reply?'

His face relaxed. 'And she sent *you*?' he said softly. 'She sent *you* to say that?'

'She said you could write a reply.'

'Jesus,' he whispered and looked away. A slow smile crept on to his face. 'No,' he said, smiling, 'no reply.'

'Oh.' Anita glanced quickly around at the plain, bare room. 'I'll go then.'

He watched her to the door then said, 'Have you walked all this way?'

'Yes.'

'On your own?'

'Yes.'

He shook his head, still smiling. 'She's a terrible woman, your mother, a terrible woman.'

'I'm all right,' she said bravely, 'what could happen?'

'It's a long walk.' He stood up straight with an air of sudden decision and turned towards the sink in one corner of the room. 'Come on

189

and have a cup of tea before you go back. I'll make a pot, will I?' He lifted a grimy, battered old kettle and swung it from his fingers. 'Sit down now.'

She sat in one of the armchairs looking at his photographs and the books he had on a small wooden bookshelf between the chair and the wall: *Fame Is The Spur* and *Shabby Tiger*. She'd read *Shabby Tiger* and thought it was fantastic. *Cannery Row* and *Another Country* and *Lolita* and *Tropic of Cancer* and *The Ragged-Trousered Philanthropist*. Books on bird-watching and angling, and a lot of old *Readers' Digests*.

'Do you read a lot?' she asked. 'I read a lot.'

'I like a good book,' he said, filling the kettle.

'I've read *Shabby Tiger*.'

'I'm reading *Dr Zhivago* at the minute,' he said. 'That's a very good book.' He pronounced it Zivago. 'You can borrow any of those if you want.' He nodded towards them with his head.

'Here.' Paddy offered her a digestive biscuit out of a packet. As she took it she touched his hand, which was warm and smooth like strange meat, eatable.

'Can I really?' she said. 'Can I borrow anything?'

'Certainly.'

She wanted *Tropic of Cancer* because she knew it was dirty but she couldn't imagine such a book in her own house, she'd have to hide it. Surely he'd say it was too old for her.

'This one?' She picked it up.

'Sure,' he replied, peering at it and lighting a cigarette. 'That one'll open up your eyes. How old are you now?'

'Nearly twelve.'

He smirked, the cigarette in his mouth. 'That's a very smutty book, that is. Your ma'll kill me, she'll say I'm a bad influence.'

'I'll hide it.'

He laughed.

The kettle started to shrill and he joined in with it, whistling thinly through his teeth as he crossed the room. As he poured the water into the pot she watched the muscles on his naked shoulders move, the sharp blades of them under the white vest, like the muscles in the legs and shoulders of a horse visible through their skin when they ran.

'And you're twenty,' she said.

He stirred the pot. 'That's not so much older than you. You may not think it now, but it's true.' He turned and smiled at her. 'Now, there's a thing. I'm closer in years to the daughter.'

'What?'

'Oh, to hell with it,' he said, opening a

191

drawer, 'I will send her a reply. You're a smart girl, Anita. You'll take it.'

He poured the tea and came and sat down on the floor at her feet with his hands wrapped around his cup, and talked to her. No one had ever talked to her like that before, as if she was a real person, a proper grown-up sort of person worth telling things to. He told her how he'd met her mother on the Bobs, not realising that she worked next door. She was sitting in the seat in front of him, he said, and her screams were penetrating, high enough to crack glass.

He said, 'Do you know why the Bobs is called the Bobs?'

Anita shook her head.

'Because you used to have to pay a bob to get on it,' he said, lighting up a cigarette and throwing back his head as he blew out the first jet of thick blue smoke. 'Your mother,' he said, 'is a lovely woman. Your mother is wild.' He laughed. 'There's one moment, you know, Anita, just when you reach the top of the climb, you know when the carriage is right at the top and it pauses just for a wee second before you go over? Well, it was just at that moment, just then when she turned around and smiled at me; and then we were over and we went *plunging* and she screamed all the way down.'

He shook his head. 'Your mother is an odd woman, Anita. Don't you think it's peculiar? She sends you?'

'But she tells me everything anyway.'

'Everything?' He looked at her very seriously. After a while, he asked: 'Do you not talk to your daddy then?'

'No,' she said, 'he doesn't talk. Not to us.'

Paddy's hands were shaking a little and his eyes had gone hooded and very far away. But then he jumped up. 'You like books?' he said, 'I'll tell you what's a good book,' and grabbed a fat paperback and flicked the well-thumbed pages and read to her, walking about the room. He held the book with one hand and used the other to make gestures with his half-smoked cigarette. His fingers made a long smooth curve. He read about a woman who was born with a bit missing in her mind so that she was a monster, even though her face and body were very pretty. Her nipples went in instead of out. Anita watched him, dazzled. He read a terrible thing about a horse being worked to death, and a bit about a man waking up as a beetle, and another about a man taking his wife a cup of tea in bed. And that, he said, was the immortal genius James Joyce, the greatest Irish writer, though some didn't think so.

Anita's heart was fluttery because of the nearness and attention of Paddy Riley, and because of all these books: so many, so many, she thought, so much to read. The wealth of it made her weak with a kind of desire.

'Now this, this is a nice kind of a book for a girl to read.' He gave her *To Kill A Mockingbird* by Harper Lee, putting *Tropic of Cancer* back.

An hour had passed. She had to go. 'My mother'll kill me,' she said.

'She won't.' He took a writing pad out of a drawer and a pen from the mantelpiece and sat down at the table, scribbling fast. 'I'm telling her,' he said, 'that it's all my fault for keeping you talking. Sure, she knows what a talker I am. You're not in trouble. Here.'

He licked the envelope and sealed it.

★　★　★

She walked back across Belle Vue with his letter in her pinafore and his books in her hand. She didn't know what was the matter with her, she hurt inside. She wanted to kiss Paddy Riley. She wanted him to send her a letter but he never would, and the knowledge made her more miserable than she could ever remember being in her whole life. It was like the moment when she was quite small and suddenly realised she really was going to die one day: total, paralysing fear. Knowing Paddy Riley would never kiss her or send her a letter was like that, aching all through her, deeper than tears. She didn't go straight home. She went to the elephant house for comfort. She liked the rank and lovely stink in there, and the echoing, shifting sounds, and the poor huge beasts slowly swinging their trunks. Anita stayed leaning on the rail in the elephant house for nearly half an hour, late as it was, and sometimes she cried in a forlorn and hopeless way.

———————

It was Paddy Riley who gave Anita her love of books. During the nearly two years she was a go-between, she worked her way through most of the stock on his shelves. She read Steinbeck and Salinger and Scott Fitzgerald and Anne Frank's diary and *Saturday Night and Sunday Morning* and *Dr Zhivago*.

It was a sad thing, but when she thought of Dr Zhivago now, it was the film she remembered rather than the book. The next time she saw Michael she felt like Julie Christie in the scene where she was doing the ironing and Omar Sharif was looking at her with his big googly brown eyes and she says:

so far we haven't done anything we need lie to Tonya about.

She'd met Michael on the Quay, gone for a long walk with him right up the estuary and they had talked and talked and agreed just to be friends. She would continue to come to the boat and they would talk and she would draw, and each would be the secret best friend of the other (secret only for appearances' sake) and their relationship would be unique.

'It's impossible,' he said, 'it's impossible but anyway,' and shrugged.

Not making love was erotic. They held hands across the table in the boat and trembled. Now and then they drove inland; as spring progressed, they lay down in wild grasses and flowers and kissed like a courting couple.

'I never thought I'd end up like this,' he said, lying on his bed with his head on her chest. 'Some woman's bit on the side.'

Mostly she just drew him. An hour at a time in silence.

★   ★   ★

Two or three months into their relationship she asked if he would take his clothes off. After all, she was an artist. His body was hers.

She did him all ways, sitting, reclining, standing, kneeling, front, back, sideways, making love to him with a 4B pencil. She knew as they flowed that they were the best pictures she'd ever do, but no one would see them. She'd keep them. When she was old and grey and full of sleep, she would have them still. He was beautiful. Softly shading the hard planes of his body, she explored every inch of him. Sometimes he had an erection. Sometimes he was in such a state of excitement that staying still was a torment, but she wouldn't let him move.

★   ★   ★

'This will last,' she promised sincerely, there on his bed with the rain sing-songing on the gang plank. 'This will. Because this is different. I'm your best friend.'

His hand was smoothing and smoothing the hairs on her mound through her skirt. She took a lot of care over her underwear these days, silk for the feel, so it would be nice for him, since touching through cloth had crept in as permissable. Not for him though her naked, loosening body. That was Charley's.

'I never get it right with women,' he said. 'Never. Go on then, you tell me. What do I do? What do I do wrong?'

'You're OK,' she said. 'You're OK, Michael. You've just been unlucky.'

'How come nothing ever lasts? I get older and still nothing lasts. So who cares? Who cares? But sometimes you do care. Know what I mean?'

She cradled his head.

She loved to catch sight of him in town with his swagger and hard looks and think: I have him. She loved him and would always be kind.

★   ★   ★

Auntie Bernie died in July just when they were getting ready to go to Scotland. Connie rang Anita with the news. It was a stroke, she said; poor old Bernie was never the same after she had that fall. Anita offered to ring Robin in Canada but Judith had already done it.

'Auntie Bernie's dead,' she told Charley, then went outside and stood in the garden in the thickening dusk and looked at her house and felt scared that she might lose all this from one second to the next. Soon we'll all be dead, she thought, what does it matter what we do? Get it while you can.

The only sin in life is a missed opportunity.

Charley opened the kitchen window and called out, 'Do you want a coffee, Anita? Are you OK, love?'

198

'I'd love one!' she called. 'I'm fine! I'll come in.'

I'm here, she thought, I've got all this. I've got all this.

★ ★ ★

She went up for Bernie's funeral. Travelling on her own on the train she started thinking what it would be like to be single again. No Charley, no Jas, no little Sid. Free. She closed her eyes. To be on her own. It hadn't really happened to her all that much, the last time was when she was on the streets, and every other time she was always working her way towards another man, even if he was only an idea in the back of her mind. She sat alone with her book and newspaper, undisturbed, bought a coffee from the trolley and drank it alone, looked out of the window, arrived, walked smartly down the platform with the heels of her shoes clicking, out of the station and into a black cab, where she pulled out a mirror from her bag, retouched her lipstick and worked at her hair with a tentative comb. This was how she must look whenever she returned home, as if she was doing well. Not that Crosby was home, of course, never was nor ever would be; Crosby was just the place her mum and Robin had moved to when everything broke up.

Judith opened the door to her, a soft, small, plump woman with a worn face both sweet and anxious. 'Ooh, Anita,' she said at once, smiling hysterically, 'I'm so glad you've arrived.'

Robin was in the hall behind her, paler and beakier than the last time she'd seen him about two years ago, his red hair tamer and greyer and thinner, northern accent undimmed by twenty years in Toronto; in fact, she got the impression he was laying it on a bit for effect. He kissed her gently and seriously. 'This is Floss,' he said, introducing a woman with a pretty but very ruddy face and a lumpy silver ring in one nostril. Flossie had a smile like a Jaffa orange in a sunshiny cartoon. She and Anita disliked each other on sight.

'It's nice that you could both make it,' Judith said. 'Your mam'll be glad to see you. She'll miss my mam.'

* * *

Anita stood with her mother in the church before they buried Auntie Bernie. Her mother looked horrible. She'd got smaller and her face had collapsed inwards and was very pink. She was sixty-five, Bernie seventy.

They're popping off regularly now, Anita thought, first Mike in Canada, then Nora, now her.

Everyone was there: Connie and Uncle Ian, Auntie Anne and Auntie Dymphna, loads of cousins, some with their partners, and grown-up kids that made Anita feel old. Robin stood with Judith. Anita had always wondered about those two; they'd grown up together side by side from twelve to eighteen, till he went to Canada. There were Deasys, of course, gruff men and sharp-faced women, and one young man who would have been quite gorgeous if it wasn't for his mixture of teeth, some of which were gold, some of which were thin and rotten and brown. They sang 'Come Down, O Love Divine'. Connie and Anne and Judith cried, but Anita's mother and Dymphna didn't. Anita was discomfited and slightly embarrassed by the peculiar rituals, the incantations in the gloomy church, the procession, the graveside tableau, the long cars leaving. Robin's face was set and stoical, the old twitch in his cheek ticcing away. She remembered him living at Auntie Bernie's dressed as a hippie in the old days, with a stupid girlfriend who fiddled about with tarot cards and wore crumpled brown Indian loincloths that looked like old parchment. He was in computers now, and

Anita had a niece and nephew she'd never seen.

This is how my family has evolved, she thought, this is what we do, we all meet up every now and then to see one of us off. Anne and Dymphna still looking pretty good. Connie stout. My mother. Fancy her outlasting old Bernie, she supposed everyone was thinking, she'll be the next. She looked at her mother, who was breathing visibly with her whole body:

Our Geraldine. Auntie Gerry. Mum. Beautiful Geraldine O'Leary. Mrs Silver. Geraldine M. Silver (Mrs.).

The Sunday in every week.

★ ★ ★

She still had the original, the very scrap of paper, so thin and frail now she thought it ought to have a glass case to preserve it like the precious manuscripts in the British Museum. It said: *You are the Sunday in every week* in Paddy Riley's peculiar stunted handwriting. She'd thought at the time it was more like an insult; after all, Sunday was the most boring day; it was only when she'd gone to Ireland with Quack Fair that she started to see the meaning of it, with the people all gathering in the villages, the pubs full, the young men and girls dressed up in their best and flirting with one another outside the stores.

It was the only writing she had of his, though she'd carried so many letters: *Geraldine, thy beauty is to me* . . . Such a flowery style he had. *From the time I was born to the time I saw you on the Bobs, I think I must have been lonely.* That was nice. *When you are old and grey and full of sleep,* a crib, of course, how many were cribs she didn't know, maybe all of them. *The Sunday in every week* she'd come across years later in a book of Irish poetry.

My love forever, Paddy.

She used to sneak into the kitchen while her mum was making the beds or downstairs over the mangle, and steam them open over the spout of the kettle or the steam rising from the constant pan of water. Half the time, after an initial cursory glance that picked up the main gist, her mother got her to read them for her anyway. To her mother it was a lovely game. She used to laugh about it: 'We don't do anything, you know, Anita. He's just a nice, lonely young boy and it's nice for him to see me. He likes talking to me.' The passing of notes was a little ritual, part of the whole thing: so was Anita's inclusion. She'd deliver to him at work, sometimes at the Hall of Mirrors, but also now on the Waltzer; and she would take them to his room, bring back her book and get another as if he were a lending library, and he would make a cup of strong red tea and ask her questions about what she was doing at school and which pop stars was she in love with, and what did she think of the death penalty. She was the kind of girl who roamed around a lot and stayed out, she could hang around as much as she wanted in the summer. She'd been talked to as if she was an adult by her mother for so long that she believed she was one. She even felt a little superior to them, important, as she wrote out something at her mother's request: *Dear Paddy, can't get away till Tuesday. See you by Waltzer? Geraldine, XXX.*

And of all that she carried, only *the Sunday in every week* had survived.

––––––––––

Her mother shook her arm. She looked down. Her mother's finger ends were spreading, flattening out under bulging nails. Anita supported her out of the church and they all went back to Judith's. The house filled up to bursting. Mum went back on her machine, a tube up each nostril. Anita was desperate for a fag but felt she ought to sit with her mother, and she wasn't allowed to smoke anywhere near her and the machine in case they blew the house up. Everyone except Judith and her mother started getting drunk and babbling, all catching up at once on what had been going on with everyone else since the last time. Now that she was a proper person with a house, and a husband and children whose pictures she could get out and flash around, Anita had been able to hold her head up more at these dos.

'Have you got a boyfriend now?' her mother asked her.

'What?' With all the talk and the engine of the machine, she thought she'd misheard.

'Whatever happened to that lovely chap, what was his name, the one with the really white-blond hair? Oh, he was nice!'

'Rory Gotch?'

'That's it! Rory! He was a nice lad!'

'Mum, that was ages ago. I'm with Charley now.'

'Isn't he here?'

'Who?'

'Your Charley.'

'No, he's with the girls.'

'I suppose so,' she sighed, 'I suppose it's a long way for the little ones.'

'Well, it is for something like this, I don't think it's the sort of thing for them.'

'You're bringing them up heathen, Anita.'

Anita smiled and looked away. 'It is a lot of

travelling,' she said patiently, 'and they were
up at Easter. And anyway we've got to go all
the way up to Scotland.'

'Oh, are you going to Scotland? That's
nice, whereabouts?'

'Joanne's cottage. You know.'

'Your Charley's a terrific bloke,' her mother
said heartily, 'a real nice type. He's got a face
like a little boy.'

'He's lovely,' she agreed.

'He is, he's lovely.'

Anne and Connie brought a bottle of
Cinzano over.

'I can remember our Bernie looking after
me in the war,' said Anne, her face shiny and
bright, eyes sparkling. 'I'd have been about
three, I suppose, I can remember it just like
that.' She snapped her thin ringed fingers.
'We used to go on Melland's with the dog
and our Mike. Dymphna was a baby. A right
scriky scraggy little thing. I remember our
Bernie and our Nora looking after us. I
remember she gave me her gas mask once
when I couldn't find mine, down in the
shelter. She was always like this, our
Bernie — ' pulling a serious face, 'you know
what she was like, but she gave me her gas
mask that time and she didn't even think
about it. Just think, if there'd been gas!'

'I had a great war,' Anita's mother said,

'well, the first bit anyway. I was up in the Lakes.'

'*You* missed it all.'

'I had a great war.'

'Do you remember when they bombed Rushford Street?' asked Connie, with the air of someone recalling a golden youth.

'Oh God, yes! I was six,' said Anne. 'It was freezing cold, I remember, it was January. January the ninth . . .'

'Your father's birthday,' Anita's mother said, turning to her and smiling.

The world stopped. Her mother had not mentioned her father for twenty-five years.

'No, it wasn't, Anne,' said Connie, 'it wasn't January. I was home by then and I remember, and I was older than you, so I remember. I was ten. It wasn't in January, it was March because it was coming up to Easter, I remember . . .'

'I had a great war,' Anita's mother said.

Anita sneaked out into the smokers' room and had a fag with her cousins. All these years I have not thought of my father's birthday, she thought. All these years. When she went back to her mother, Connie was singing in a cracked voice, 'The Snowy-breasted Pearl', then 'The Wind That Shakes The Barley'.

'We used to hear about the bombs in

207

Manchester,' her mother was saying, 'but I was having a great time. They brought in these Italian prisoners of war later, they were gorgeous, some of them. They used to work in the fields. They used to look at you as you went by, and some of them had such nice young faces. I like Italians. Don't you think Paddy Riley had a bit of an Italian look about him, Anita? Of course, I don't suppose you'll remember him. He was this young boy who had a big crush on me when I worked at Belle Vue.'

'I remember him.'

'Of course, Belle Vue was used as an internment camp in the war. For Jews.'

'That's right,' said Connie.

Anita hadn't known that.

'Do you remember Mr and Mrs Brisket?'

'And that dog!'

'It was so cold, that winter! Up in Ambleside. Do you remember that freezing cold bedroom?'

'Of course, you know, don't you, Anita, we were evacuated up there, me and Connie . . .'

'Yes, I know.'

'And that dog,' laughed Connie, 'used to go out the back door up to its neck in the snow, and it always looked surprised every time, a right comical dog that was . . .'

'Sammy.'

'Sammy.'

'Sammy. You was scared of him at first.'

'We both were. He was a big dog and he looked quite nasty really.'

'But we got really fond of old Sammy, didn't we?'

'Oh, we did.'

'Sammy.'

'Sammy.'

'He used to love bread dipped in dripping. Sometimes that was all he got for his dinner.'

'The Briskets were tight old sods,' Anita's mother said. 'We used to laugh about their name.'

'I had to do all the polishing,' said Connie.

'They used to make you knock before you went into the living room.'

'You used to have to go out in the dark with the coal scuttle. Do you remember that horrible tree? We called it the witch tree.'

'Mum,' Anita said, 'was my dad interned?'

'Your dad?'

'In the war? In Belle Vue?'

'Don't be daft,' her mother said.

'No,' Connie said, 'those were Germans and Austrians that had come over. I don't think they knew what to do with them so they put them in Belle Vue.'

'They weren't there for long.'

'Your father,' said Auntie Connie, 'was a bastard, Anita. A bastard of the first degree. He kept her right short of money. Anyone who'd do what he did and leave his wife and little kiddies just like that.'

'Your father's a jealous man,' her mother added. 'Don't ever live with a jealous man, Anita. Or a sulker. I can't abide a sulker.'

★ ★ ★

Anita went to bed in the loft conversion. Is that all my dad was after all, she thought, just a bastard? It's true. How could he do that, after our Hightown walk? How could he just leave without a word? They'd walked one day by the Old Shambles and the Cathedral, and then from there a long way down Cheetham Hill Road to what he said had been old Hightown, where he grew up. He got excited and pointed out to her a house that had been the premises of the first Silvers' Ironmonger's, and told her that his father and grandfather before him had both been ironmongers.

It was so clear.

She couldn't sleep.

She brought into her mind the playing of her father's mandolin at night, then the playing of a fiddle and bagpipe drifting out over the cliffs on the coast of Clare.

Charley would never do what my father did, she thought. Charley would never ever leave me and the girls, never in a million years.

———————————

Anita remembered her mother picking through the things on the rag and bone cart. She remembered standing by the horse's head and hearing one woman say to another: 'Irish as the pigs in Muck Alley, she is.' She hated those women.

She remembered the miserable-faced papershop man in his buff V-necked jumper:

'Mrs Silver, I'm not interested. You've got till Friday. I can't say fairer than that.'

'You'll have it by Friday. Haven't I just said?'

The papershop door was opening, people were coming in. Robin held her mother's coat by the pocket, staring at the man with his face full of hate and hurt.

'Friday then,' said the papershop man, straightening his magazines and papers with dainty little hands.

'Are you deaf, man? Or just daft? Haven't I already said Friday?'

A girl was looking at the chocolate bars and a man stood waiting, watching.

'If you're not settled by Friday noon,' said

the papershop man, looking straight at her mother with hard, mournful black eyes, 'I may have to have a word with your husband.'

In the awful silence that followed, Anita's face burned. Her mother held the man's eyes, her face a picture of lofty disgust.

'Yes,' she said at length. 'You'd enjoy that, wouldn't you?'

The Winter Solstice Festival happened every year at the harbour and was really just a standard old Christmas Fair, with Santa Claus and stalls selling candles and cakes and home-made decorations; only instead of just selling coffee and squash and so on like the Christmas Fairs at the primary school, for which Anita had made her old Quack Fair staples, ginger bread and toffee apples and pink lemonade (all declared authentic by Tom Shafto), this one always had a heavily besieged bar on a revamped spritsail barge.

Charley and Anita went down with the girls. Michael was there with a woman who looked familiar, one of those Anita remembered having seen occasionally in the cockpit of the *Ellen*: the vivid one with purple plaits, only now her hair was short, with a big floppy bit that was always falling in her face and demanding constant attention. She was twenty-three or twenty-four at a guess, with a large lively face and a nose stud, and she walked with such aplomb, such an air of slightly wacky confidence that Anita was immediately jealous. Michael and the woman stood by the silver jewellery stall, putting their heads together to count out money. A little boy of about three, hers presumably, prowled about in their wake. Proper little family group. Anita felt quite sick.

Michael saw her but at first pretended not to. He must have realised then how stupid that was, their eyes having quite clearly met, and he flashed her a sudden huge smile as if there were some private joke between them. She waved. The woman with him looked at her. They all met up as a group in the space in the centre of the stalls.

'This is Jessica,' Michael said.

Michael and Jessica, she thought. Jessica and Michael.

They all said hello. Jessica had a nasal, husky voice and rolled her eyes like a horse.

'Where's Luke?' asked Charley.

'Gone to my parents,' said Michael. 'I'm going down for him after Christmas.'

'What you doing for Christmas?'

'Not much. I'm working for most of it.'

213

'We're having this one at home, thank God,' Anita said.

'You'll have to come over for a drink if you're around.'

'Yeah.'

After that they kept bumping into each other. She kept glimpsing them here and there and couldn't help watching to see if they touched. They didn't. There was such a nice easy feel between them though that she was quickened with envy. Jessica had stylish hair and an interesting face, and she wore a beautiful but battered brown velvet coat, the kind of thing that looked good on the young, that looked good on Anita once, but now, she thought, if she wore something as picturesquely battered as that she'd feel like the bag lady she very nearly became. She would never be young again. She saw her reflection in a dark window: the softness of youth was gone, there was a stretched kind of look under her chin, a small pouchiness near the corners of her mouth. I suppose I could have something lifted if I was really desperate, she thought, and shuddered at the very idea. Maybe she ought to lose a few pounds. All these awful truths rushed in, like it got more stubborn to shift as you got older, like she was really going to die. As she walked around the fair she felt like a ripening cheese.

Michael and Jessica left. She ran into Jane and Sarah and stayed on and had a drink with them while Charley took the girls home. She started drinking hard, the way she used to, miles away from the other two though she didn't think they noticed; after all, she performed well enough. Of course she'd known that she was not the only one. What could she expect? Well, good, she thought, it's better like this, if he'd been alone and lonely as in courtly days I might have broken. But there were women on the boat sometimes at nights when she was not there. She knew because they left behind their scarves and pens and smells, their hairs in the sink.

How could she complain?

It was the last bottle of wine that was the killer. She found herself feeling terribly depressed by the weary little reminders of Quack Fair, the palmist, the popcorn, the slight, fair-haired juggler with the fashionable face. It was all bright and hilarious but somehow manically sad, so she decided to finish the bottle — waste not want not — even though Jane and Sarah both said they couldn't, but more than that, she felt as if she was on the brink of some profound insight into her life and the significance in it of all these recurring images.

She may have achieved it for all she knew.

She may have encountered a total understanding of the nature of reality in her deepest cups, but unfortunately she didn't remember any of it later. What she did remember was the lights swirling about in the harbour, smoking dope with Phil Wragge in the car park, being disgorged from Jane and Scott's car at her gate with the frosty stars above, reeling about the lawn feeling at one with Orion then going straight to the kitchen and eating nearly half a tub of toffee ripple ice cream with a broken Calpol spoon before bursting into tears and being sick in the sink.

Charley got her upstairs. She lay on the bed with her hand in her mouth, crying. Her nose ran and she felt sick again and the room was going round.

'It's all right,' Charley said comfortingly, taking off her clothes and wiping her face, 'you're just drunk, that's all. Everything'll be all right in the morning.'

'No, no!' she moaned. 'It won't!'

'It will.' He covered her up, put her nightie over her head and kissed her and went to clean his teeth. She cried more then, partly because she felt so ill and partly for him, because he was so good to her.

'Oh, Charley, Charley,' she wept when he came back and climbed in beside her, 'I'm getting old.'

216

'So you are,' he said. 'So am I. So, as we are . . . '

He lay there smiling in the dark, unfathomable.

'I'm scared!' she wailed. 'How can you be so calm? We're going to die, we're going to die, we're all going to die!'

'I know,' he said, 'didn't you realise?'

He put his arms round her but she started to feel so sick he had to run for the bowl.

★   ★   ★

Charley got worried that she was drinking too much again.

'You could get away with it for a while when you were young,' he said next day when she had such a terrible hangover, 'but you can't any more. Have you noticed how there's a tradition of elegant old male drunks that everybody sort of admires, but there isn't one of female drunks? Why do you think that is then?'

'I don't know,' she said sulkily, 'perhaps it's because women have more sense.'

'No. It's because women don't look so good when they're drunk. You're as vain as could be so you shouldn't drink so much for purely selfish reasons.'

'Oh,' she said, 'so a male beer belly and a

217

big red nose is elegant, is it?'

He shrugged. What he meant was that if she wasn't careful she'd end up as some silly old bag that got squiffy at parties. So she didn't drink till the afternoon of Christmas Eve, when Michael came over and spent most of the time talking with Charley about methods of tackling condensation on his boat. Whenever he looked at her he smiled. How can he do it, she thought, how can he come here and act as if everything was the same? Yet she too sat calmly drinking her wine with her legs drawn up underneath her, and a strange normality prevailed. Michael was drunk but did not show it. It was as if two separate realities rubbed alongside one another, like being half asleep and half awake; so when she opened her eyes there was the room as it always was, and when she closed them, the dream again, washing in like water. She was alone with him for about thirty seconds in the hall at one point. 'Come to me on Wednesday,' he whispered, and as his fingers brushed the back of her hand she shivered and felt it in her throat. But then when he'd gone she kept thinking: what if he talks about me to those other women? What if he tells people what we do? What if I'm just like all the rest? What if it's a joke? What if everybody

218

knows? What if Charley ever found out?

Unthinkable.

She decided not to go on Wednesday.

But when it came she kept wanting to. She couldn't get away easily anyway until four o'clock, when Charley suddenly decided to take the girls out on their bikes, and she found herself driving into town. The lanes were lovely, all crisp and bright and sparkling, and there was a smell in the air, a heady fragrance of clay and mist and distant sea. It all seemed very innocent, this thing she was driving to. We are coping, she thought, we are accommodating it and no one's getting hurt.

'I can't stay long,' she said, 'I have to get something in the oven by half five.'

He was playing his guitar.

'Ah,' he grinned, 'mustn't miss that.'

'I just came to say Happy New Year. When are you going to fetch Luke?'

'Tomorrow and tomorrow and tomorrow. Sit down. Have a cup of coffee.'

The boat always smelt damp in winter. The cushions had a clammy feel.

'I wonder if you'll develop chest conditions,' she mused, 'you and Luke, living here.'

'I know.' He spun the lid from a jar of coffee. 'Can't be good, can it?'

He came and sat down beside her and put his head down on her shoulder in a deliberate, unrelaxed way. 'If only you were free,' he said.

'Free,' she smiled. 'What does that mean?'

He looked up. 'You know this is quite impossible don't you?' His voice and eyes were steady. 'It isn't going to work, you know.'

'It will work,' she said, 'as long as we don't lose our nerve.'

'Yes.' He drew in a long breath through his nose, detached himself from her in the same peculiar and deliberate way, and went back to the coffee. The atmosphere was strained. When he came back with the mugs he sat down opposite her on the other side of the table.

'We're walking on a tightrope, aren't we?' she said. 'Is that how it feels to you?'

'You were jealous,' he said, 'you were jealous seeing me with Jessica. I saw it.'

'Oh God!' She groaned and put her face in her hands to hide a grin. 'Was it so obvious?'

'Only to me.'

'Of course I was jealous. I'm always jealous. I was probably born jealous.'

He put his hand out and closed it around her wrist and brought his face very close. He was exquisitely ugly, his eyes heavily shielded but with a lost look. Is he safe? she thought.

'You have absolutely no idea what you're

doing, do you?' he said. 'You have absolutely no idea how dangerous this is.'

She shook her head. 'Sometimes it just stops me in my tracks,' she said. 'In the middle of the day it stops me cold.'

'I'm jealous too,' he said, 'I'm jealous of your husband,' as if he'd never known Charley.

'We will feel like this,' she said, putting her other hand over his. 'We *will*. We can talk each other through it.'

He laughed, taking his hand away. 'You are really too much. You are insane. Honestly, I mean it, you make my blood run cold.'

'Please, Michael, we can stop this now if you want.'

They looked at one another wordlessly for a moment, their faces tight.

'We can't,' he said in a tone of mild despair, 'it's got its own momentum now. We're just going to roll right on down with it into the shit.'

'Do you sleep with her?' Anita asked.

'I did once. I don't now.'

'Oh.'

He stood and walked up and down the boat, then came back and leaned over her, speaking close to her ear: 'Don't think I go short though, Anita.'

She put her hands up and stroked his face. 'You're so beautiful,' she said, and they

221

started again, the kissing, as always, a slow descent.

★ ★ ★

In the New Year Michael went away and didn't come back until the end of January. While he was gone she pined luxuriously, spending ages gazing out of the window at the ivy on the back wall, while the tasks of the day piled up. The place started looking grubby, the washing got left, and she started getting angry with Charley for not noticing it and doing more to help. They bickered about stupid things. On a walk along the cliff road in a stiff East wind he kept saying she was going too fast; she got furious with him for dawdling about too close to the edge to get a look at some plant or another. It was a bad example to the girls. She could see them all falling off the cliff one by one, even Basil, and herself left alone at the top. He was so irritating, the way he smiled on the edge of the cliff, six inches away from death.

'Well, if you've gone down into the Plague pit and come up again, death's your mate,' he said, and she hated him for it.

'That's stupid and meaningless and trite,' she said. 'Come back from the edge at once!'

He cleaned up the garden and cleared all

the rubbish from the back of the house, then sulked because she did not wax lyrical enough about it. If he behaves like a child I'll treat him like one, she thought, and ignored him. The mood simmered all day and erupted in a horrible scene in the bathroom while he was cleaning his teeth. She accused him of being a prima donna. He rinsed his mouth out and said: 'Is your period due?' in a nasty way, which made her throw cold water down his naked back, so that he chased her down the landing and into the bedroom. She jumped into bed and pulled the duvet over her head but he pulled it back sharply and thrust his face into hers.

'You're a fucking nightmare lately,' he shouted. 'What's the matter with you?' and picked up a glass on the bedside table and flung some dregs of water into her face.

Next morning he ploughed through the snowy wood and brought her some holly berries and put them in a little jar on the bedside table. Jasmine came in and looked at her solemnly. 'Are you getting up, Mum?' she asked in a strange, anxious way. This isn't right, Anita thought, I'm ruining my life. I'll tell him as soon as he gets back. Michael, I'll say, this must stop before we go any further. He'll agree. He'll probably be relieved.

Her first sight of him was the night she went to the Dun Cow with Jane and Mona. He was with some people, taking photographs of them in the window alcove amid much camaraderie. She saw his back, long, wide at the top and narrowing, his hair just touching his shoulders. She was smitten anew.

'Hi, Michael,' she said, running into him at the bar, 'didn't know you were back.'

'No,' he said, 'I only got back last night.'

'Luke OK? Did he have a good Christmas?'

'Yeah, fine.' He brought his forehead suddenly close to hers and for a second she thought he was going to kiss her there in the bar in front of everyone. Did he want them to be seen? 'Let's go for a drive out in the country,' he said, 'tomorrow.'

'I can't.'

'When?'

'I'll let you know.'

★ ★ ★

Tuesday they couldn't drive too far because of the snow, so they ended up going for a freezing walk and a drink in a hotel.

'I want more,' he said bluntly.

'I have never been anything other than completely straight with you, Michael . . . '

224

'I want more, Anita.'

'What more, Michael? This is it.'

He was cold and sullen, saying nothing.

'Don't,' she said, 'don't let's quarrel. Don't let's ever quarrel. We're doing the impossible, of course it's hard.'

'Christ,' he said, 'who's that?'

'What?'

He sighed. 'Nothing. Nothing. Thought it was your friend Jane.'

'Oh Christ!'

'It's OK, it wasn't.'

But they became so paranoid about the possibility of being seen that they gave the whole thing up as a bad job and went back to the boat. This happened more and more now the weather was so bitter. They got it warm and cosy and the windows misted over, the condensation standing in big silver drops on their metal rims. Winter breathed outside like the great bear in the Snow Queen. He got out the whisky and boiled some water and made hot toddies, then came and lay down with his head in her lap, his face pressed into her stomach. He liked to lie like this, sometimes falling asleep with her rubbing his shoulder or stroking his hair.

'I've missed you,' he said.

'You haven't.'

He lifted his face. 'I have,' he said softly. He looked flushed, as if he might be coming down with something. 'I missed you all the time. I don't think I can go on with this, Anita.'

It was a little pang in the heart, a shot of cold dispersing.

'I know,' she said. 'It's getting worse, isn't it? It's getting worse for me. Is it getting worse for you? I get so scared. It's like a big black cloud sitting on top of my head. My teeth chatter.'

He sat up, bleary, his eyes bloodshot. 'It wouldn't matter,' he said, 'I could carry it on if I didn't care. But I do. And it's not good, Anita, it's not good, I can't carry it on any more.'

'I know.'

He poured out whisky for them both. 'Here's to us,' he said smiling, 'to what might have been.'

She lifted her glass. 'To us.'

They drank. It had got so that every scene with Michael was a drinking scene. They leaned companionably together and got tipsy. He put his arm round her and sang 'Go Now', and she started to snivel a bit. Then he kissed her and pulled her head down on to his shoulder. 'It doesn't matter,' he kept saying, 'it doesn't matter. In the grand

scheme of things it doesn't matter.'
    She laughed. 'A hill of beans.'

———————

The Deasys came to their house with heather,
the day Paddy Riley bought her a 99 and took
her to Pepino's Circus, the day she came
home with a letter, sealed with his sardonic
smiling kiss, in the pocket of her gingham
coat. The basket of heather sat upon the
table, and the Deasys covered the kitchen, all
around the fire and all over the settee and the
chairs and the table, overflowing out of the
open door and into the hall. There were lots
of little children younger than Robin, big
girls, a big boy in the yard, and Uncle Tommy
and Aunt Julia, who must have stood
somewhere in the relation of cousin to her
mother. Uncle Tommy was small and dark
and angry with a high-pitched, fretful voice.
Aunt Julia's hair was piled on top of her head.
Her mother was telling them that Dymphna's
intended was a bit of a chancer. Aunt Julia's
face was huge and hurt and perpetually
open-mouthed. Every now and then, deep
and distressed, a great bellow would sound
forth from it when she shouted at one of the
smaller children. Uncle Tommy picked up a
finger roll and stuffed the whole thing in his
mouth and ate it in one go. When they left,

Anita and her mother and Robin went out and stood on the front to wave them off. They were all stuffed in one big car and Uncle Tommy kept turning round to bash the people in the back as he drove.

The Deasys never came when her father was there. Robin and she knew not to mention them without needing to be told. They had so many secrets from their father.

★ ★ ★

'You mustn't ever mention anything,' her mother would whisper in the back kitchen. 'He's only a friend. There's no harm in it, only you know what people are like.'

'Poor Anita!' Paddy Riley would say. 'All this way in the rain? Your mother is a terrible woman. Come on, I'll take you to Sivori's.'

He was always asking her to go on the Bobs with him. 'Dare you,' he'd say, 'dare you.'

For a time had come, she was never sure afterwards thinking back how long it had lasted, but it did not matter, for it was a deep, rich time, when she was actually going about with Paddy Riley. He said he could get her on the Bobs with him for free, he knew the man with the goitre; but the Bobs had always terrified her, too big, too high, too fast. She would watch him on it sometimes, doing circuit after circuit to prove his mettle. He took her for ice cream and espresso coffee, he took her on the cakewalk, the Caterpillar, the Bug and the Big Wheel. 'Top o' the world, ma!' he'd cry when the Big Wheel stopped with them at the very top.

She was a very big girl. Her periods had come. Now, her mother said, you have to be careful. Now you must never let a boy just do what he wants with you. She was twelve. Two large breasts were growing on her chest. When she walked with Paddy Riley she came up to his shoulder. 'You're a nice girl, Anita,' he said frequently, 'a very intelligent girl.'

They walked across Jackson's because he had to go and see a man about a dog; he talked about getting into the painting and decorating line, she talked about *West Side Story*, which she'd just been to see. He was thinking of getting a whippet, he said, but when they got there there was no one in so they got a bus back to his place. He told her about his brothers and sisters in Tipperary and how his father used to line them all up in a row and slipper them, and she thought how beautiful he was with his fierce Saracen nose and thin lips.

When they got back he said he was going to have a bath.

'Carry on talking,' said Paddy, 'I'll leave the door open so I can hear you.'

She was in the middle of telling him about going for a walk around Piccadilly Gardens with her friend Denise and meeting an old tramp who told them his son was the man who banged the gong at the beginning of the J. Arthur Rank films. The door ajar, he ran his bath. The boiler went whoosh in a terrifying way; she could see the steam and the toilet and part of the wrinkled mat from where she stood. He came out stripped to the waist and went about the place, gathering things up. He was like meat, brown smooth meat you'd want to slice.

'Have you ever had a bath?' he asked.

'Of course I've had a bath.'

'No, a real bath,' he said, smiling through cigarette smoke. 'To a real bath there's an art.'

He cut cheese on to a plate, took a jar of Branston Pickle, a packet of cream crackers and a transistor radio with a long trailing flex, and bore them into the mist. There was a diamond-shaped birthmark on his left shoulder-blade, burgundy-red, that moved with the movement of his body.

'Why don't you make us a nice cup of tea, Anita?' he called back.

She did.

The door was still ajar when she brought the tea. The flex from the radio was plugged in in the corridor.

'Come in, Anita,' he called. 'Don't worry, I'm all decent yet awhile.'

She looked in. He was like a ghost in the grey. 'The secret is,' he said, 'to have it as hot as it's humanly possible to stand it. No no, hotter. And then . . . ah, thanks.' He took the tea and put it down on the ledge. The food was on a little bamboo table at the side of the bath, and next to it the radio.

'You shouldn't have the radio in the bathroom,' she said, 'it's dangerous, the electricity.'

'Only if you're stupid. Then,' he said, 'music,' passing her close, flicking on the switch. It was Billy Fury, but she didn't know the song. 'And food, and some tea. Or lemonade will do. That's how you have a real bath.'

'Is there a letter for her?' Anita asked. 'I suppose I'd better be going.'

He straightened his long angular body and looked at her. 'You're a nice girl, Anita,' he said. 'You're a very sensible girl.'

She blushed.

'Can I talk to you?'

'Of course you can, Paddy.' She was

growing her hair. She pushed it back from her neck.

'Lovely hair you have,' he murmured.

She smiled.

'Your mother,' he said intently, 'is driving me mad. Did you know that? Does she laugh at me? Does she laugh about me behind my back, Anita? Would you tell me that?'

Though he was not moving, he gave an impression of fine quivering.

'Oh no,' she cried, shocked, 'she never does that. She never laughs about you.'

'Sure? What does she say about me?'

What?

How could she repeat the things her mother had said?

But she did. How could she not?

'She says you're gorgeous. She says she has little dreams about you every night, not real dreams but like little daydreams in her head. She asks me what I think of you.'

He smiled slowly. 'And what do you say?'

'I say you're OK.'

He laughed, then came and stood very close. Anita smiled shakily.

'Have you ever seen a fellow naked, princess?' he asked.

'No.'

'Would you like to?'

She said nothing.

'A man naked is only a man naked, Anita. Would it scare you?'

'No.'

'Would you like to?'

Long pause.

'I don't mind.'

'Princess,' he said, 'you're a sensible girl. A very grown-up sort of a girl.'

He took his trousers down and his socks off and stood in his white Y-fronts. Anita looked at the bulge in front, she wasn't going to pretend. It looked softer than the ones on the men in her mother's catalogues.

'Go on.' She put her head back and folded her arms. 'Let me see, then.'

Suddenly he looked embarrassed. A silly little snigger escaped his nose as he turned sideways and took off his underpants and dropped them on the bathroom floor where they lay like a dish-cloth. His penis was a lot bigger and browner than the ones in pictures or on statues, and it had a strange, drooping, bashful quality she hadn't expected. Before this she'd only seen little boy's penises, and not even one of them for a long time as Robin had turned coy at the age of seven. How many people in her class had seen this? None, she thought, none.

This was life. Like in the books.

He stood facing her, naked in the fog.

'Now I'm going to have my bath,' he said softly.

She watched him ease himself down, slowly curling, so soft and peeled, a child. His buttocks were hard and muscled, dimpled above, the cleft stark and shaded. She'd had no idea that a man's bottom could be a thing of beauty. Inch by inch he lowered himself into the boiling water and settled back with a groan of pleasure and pain, his dark head lolling sideways on the hard white rim.

'A book's the thing at this stage,' he said, closing his eyes. 'But company's nicer.' His pointed red tongue came out and licked his lips. 'So talk to me, Anita. Talk to me while I have my bath.'

———————

Michael laughed and a tear ran down his nose. They kissed, wet-faced and sentimental.

'Do you ever wonder what our children would have been like?' he asked.

'No.'

'That's the difference between me and you.'

They kissed again. That was the trouble, they always ended up kissing again. Even if it was only goodbye, there had to be a kiss, and that kiss led them back each time to the centre of the maze.

'Come away with me,' he said, thrusting his whole hand up between her legs and grasping.

'No.'

'I could find a place. Just for a couple of days.'

'No.'

'We'll do everything.'

'No.'

'That cottage of yours in Scotland.'

'No. Absolutely no.'

There was a clattering on the gangplank. They sprang apart. The door flew open and Luke burst in and threw his bag down on the floor and stared at them suspiciously.

'What are you doing home?' asked Michael.

'Heating's buggered at school,' he replied.

'Oh Jesus! The girls!' Anita jumped up and her head swam.

'It's all right,' Luke said, looking at her sharply, 'they're all in the hall with their coats on.'

If she walked to the school now, she could pick them up and take them for a snack in Kokoschka's, drink a load of coffee and have time to sober up again before driving them home.

'At it again,' Luke said wearily, coming to the table, picking up his dad's glass and sniffing at it knowingly. But it was Anita that he looked at.

'Don't nag,' Michael said.

'Me? Nag? Never.' Luke shrugged off his coat and flounced over to the sink for a glass of lemon barley water. 'It's like an opium den in here,' he muttered.

Anita got up and pushed by Michael, who touched the backs of her knees as she passed. 'I'll pop back for the car,' she said.

'Yeah right, Anita.' Michael followed her to the door. 'Tell Charley I'll sort that out for him.'

'OK.'

'What?' said Luke.

She opened the door, let in a blast of winter.

'Take care,' said Michael, 'it's slippy underfoot.'

Luke sighed and opened the fridge. 'What do you know?' he said. 'Fish again.'

★   ★   ★

Why am I doing this? she thought. She wanted to run but couldn't. The ground was white-blue, smooth as satin. Why, when she knew how much it fucked you up? Don't tell me my dad going didn't fuck me up, she thought. If me and Charley split up. If me and Charley split up. She had to stop and stand gasping, gasping at the boats along the Quay, horrified that the words had even entered her mind. The girls would hate it. Her father should have stayed, he should have stayed. It was so bitterly cold along the Quay, the estuary will freeze over, she thought, if this goes on much longer. They should have been nicer to each other. He should have given her more money. Why did we always seem so poor? Why was she always scared? How did she get in such a mess? She was so heavy. You'd see her just sitting like a rock, glazed over staring at a spot on the carpet, frozen in time, a tableau: Worry. Misery. Ennui.

She took the girls to Kokoschka's. They were always excited in Kokoschka's, the bar, the picture tiles, the tank full of sea urchins and starfish. They wore their Christmas tams and ate their ice-cream dreams with total absorption. Anita's mind was fractured. Here she was, Mummy, talking to her children, buying them ice-cream dreams and telling them to wipe their mouths. There she was also with the head of a man in her lap, his mouth upon the covered place between her legs. And there she was too, watching her mother sell heather on the cobbles outside Exchange Station. A family story, one the girls loved.

Anita existed in a state of high excitement, a manic condition that persisted even in her endlessly streaming dreams. She felt she could no more stop the ball rolling than she could stop the rain. She talked a lot, cried a lot in the day alone, flew into rages with the girls, went frequently through the woods to stand on the edge of the cornfield and stand transfixed with terror at the situation she'd got herself into.

The long summer passed.

Alison said, 'Charley's going to find out, you know, he's not stupid.'

'Find out what?'

'You're fooling yourself. The fact that you're not going to bed with him is neither here nor there.'

'Everyone's doing it in their heads all the time with all kinds of people, and anyone who says they're not's a liar,' Anita replied.

'So?'

'So all we did was talk about it. We haven't *done* anything.'

Lindsay thought she was stupid. 'You may as well just screw him and have done with it.' She shrugged and grimaced, heaving up her shoulders. 'It's just ridiculous the way it is. It's a worse bloody hypocrisy than if you were fucking like rabbits.'

'You don't understand,' said Anita. That just about covered everything.

★ ★ ★

She was still drawing him. She was knocking off pictures of other things all the time now for the gallery, fast, pointless; some of them sold. The pictures of Michael though, the best she'd ever done, could never be shown. They had a special place in the plane-chest. She started leaving his face indistinct, morphing it, smearing it out with her thumbs. If she should die suddenly and they should go through her things, he must not be distinguishable. The later pictures were rampantly sexual: she laid him out how she wanted him, moved his limbs, moulded his flesh ungently with her hands as she positioned him. He would draw his breath in sharply, squirm, hold the position as long as she wanted, a thigh trembling occasionally, a sinew shifting. When she'd finished he'd put on his pants and jeans and loll on the bed with a cigarette and one arm hooked behind his head, watching her while she packed up her drawing things.

Sometimes they didn't do anything but drink coffee with whisky and talk.

'I think we need to get away,' he said. 'How can we ever work anything out in this situation? We're always on this boat. If we could just get away from everything for a while, just the two of us without any distractions . . . '

'No,' she said. Always no.

He was changing. His pale eyes were worried.

Once when Charley and she were down at the beach with the girls they saw him fishing off the pier. Charley and he sat and talked for a while with their legs dangling while she hunted through the shingle with the girls for shells to take back to the beach hut. Michael's eyes were on her the whole time.

'He likes you, you know,' Charley said as they walked on.

'That's sweet,' she said. 'He's nice.'

Charley looked sideways at her with a strange quick look, wary and amused.

★ ★ ★

There was a message from Judith on the answering machine when they got home. Just: could you call. Judith never said anything more than the minimum, she hated answering machines.

240

'Your mum's not so good,' she said when Anita returned the call.

'Bad?'

'Well . . . the doctor's been a little bit concerned, but it's a lot better now.'

'Shall I come up?'

'Oh, she's all right really, only, what I was wondering . . . it's more like I'm trying to sort out Christmas. What are you doing at Christmas?'

Oh Lord, thought Anita, one day we'll get a Christmas to ourselves.

'It's only September,' she said, irritated, 'of course we'll come up. Do you think I need to come sooner?'

'Well, she'd always be pleased to see you, of course.'

When she'd put the phone down Anita was stricken with a panic attack and had to get out of the house. She took Basil, lifted him over the wall and walked with him in the wood. Only September and already she was supposed to start thinking of Christmas. I can't do it, she thought. The poor old dog could hardly walk so she sat down with him under a beech tree and let him lean against her. He stank. What am I doing here? she thought. Why am I given all this responsibility? I can't bring up these children. I can't face my mother looking like

241

she does. I don't know what to do about Michael. I can't cope! 'Oh Basil!' she said, putting an arm around him. 'I never meant any harm!' He had a tic in his head. Sometimes his breathing when he slept sounded as if it was about to give out, like her mother's. I can't be in charge of this dog, she thought. He's a wreck. I can't cope with any of it, any of it, any of it!

I'll run away.

Charley called from the back of the house. He'd made coffee. She got up and roused the dog, who'd fallen into a trance while leaning against her. He walked into a tree on the way back because his eyesight was going, and she remembered his glory days, the jaunty little walk he had, the way he'd trot along with a stone in his mouth, flinging it in the air from time to time with a toss of the head and catching it again.

Then everything became clear. It was Charley she loved and she'd go mad if she lost him. She'd end the thing. Tomorrow. Again.

★   ★   ★

Her mother took a turn for the worse so she went up early on the train. Judith rang Robin, who got on a flight from Toronto with Flossie. Anita didn't want Flossie to be there,

242

she didn't see that she was family, but her mother, for all the snide things she'd said about her in the past, seemed delighted and talked to her more than she did Anita for the next few days.

Her mother had a bed in the front room. She actually looked a little bit better and had quite a high colour, but Anita didn't trust that. Her eyes were very bright and mischievous and she had a queer smile on her face all the time, but her breathing was terrible, like an engine dying very slowly, a rusty musical box running down, something terminal. It went on and on and on like a grey thread running through the house.

On Christmas Eve Charley and the girls arrived. Charley was always good with her mother. He sat and talked quietly with her about her early years, the history of the Deasys and the O'Learys, the war. She loved Charley. 'He's the one,' she'd say jokily, 'if I had my time again, he'd be the one.' She was the only one who thought his plague memories were real, and he'd sit patiently having his hand held while she studied his palm, or read his tea-leaves with a look of deep concentration, stumbling on about fortunate meetings and money in the post and friends who'll stab you in the back. One night, peering into her own cup, she jumped visibly. 'Now, I know who that is!' she cried, leaning forward in her clean pink nightie with the shiny ribbons. 'I know that face. It's Paddy Riley! You remember Paddy Riley, Anita. He was that lad that worked on the Hall of Mirrors when I was a mermaid.'

Charley knew about Paddy Riley but not the whole story. He knew about the letters and the meetings and even the baths, but not the whole story. Only Anita knew that. She leaned over and looked in her mother's cup. She couldn't see Paddy Riley there.

'Of course, I was quite pretty in those days,' her mother told Charley confidentially, drawing him closer by the hand.

'I know,' he said, looking at Anita and smiling.

'This boy had a big crush on me. He was a nice boy. Very attractive, but I was a married woman, of course.' She looked down into her cup, smiling in a wistful, satisfied way, as if at an old photograph.

★ ★ ★

Christmas Day was surprisingly enjoyable. On the photographs they all looked happy, with their party hats on and their faces flushed and smiley. Anita wore the pink and grey dress she got from Polly Oliver's. Flossie's face was a brighter pink, like a rose. Anita's mother played crib with Robin or sat quietly in bed embroidering a Scottie dog on to a little jacket for one of her nephews' children. Anita detected a certain sexual tension between Judith and Robin as they pulled a cracker. She tried out a scenario where they had a late affair, but couldn't see it. It just wasn't there, somehow, like sex with Charley just was there as soon as she saw him.

They went for a walk, hand in hand.

'Let's go back to France next year,' he said, 'let's get a little gîte somewhere nice. Perpignan maybe.'

'Champagne,' she said, 'Bordeaux.'

It was frosty and their breath made little clouds in front of their faces.

'Your dad,' Charley said, 'he shouldn't have left your mum just because of an affair.'

She couldn't look at him.

'I don't suppose it was *just* that,' she said.

'No, of course not. But that was the main thing. Sex. It always is.'

Grease was on the television when they got back, her mother sitting semi-comatose in front of it. Judith had made a pot of tea and there was a plate of mince pies on the coffee table. Anita waited for the bit where John

Travolta and Olivia Newton-John go on the cakewalk, knowing it would have her back as it always did on the cakewalk at Belle Vue with Paddy Riley, she in her black patent-leather shoes, he behind in a brown corduroy jacket. She could see those black patent-leather shoes so clearly, walking along on the grey cobbles of the alley. She yawned. The fire was hot. She wondered did Archie Bannister sleep with her mother? He was there once when she came home from school, and afterwards her mother bought them a big chocolate rabbit. Look at her now. Her mother didn't seem so bad. She has a year or two probably, Anita thought. A year or two! Sid will be ten. Jasmine at secondary school, twelve. The year she saw Paddy Riley in his bath. Her mother started rambling to Charley about being evacuated, name tapes on her clothes, her little duffle bag with the gas mask hanging down the back, and all the parents crying, but not Grandma O'Leary. Grandma O'Leary was a rock.

'I would have hated it,' Charley said. 'The idea of being evacuated used to fill me with terror.'

'You're a baby.' She patted his knee. 'You're not old enough to have been evacuated.'

'I know. I mean when I used to hear people talk about it.'

Anita turned her head and studied Charley with a detached eye. She'd never been able to draw him, couldn't catch him at all, he flew away as soon as she tried.

'My uncle was evacuated,' he said. 'It's the idea of being sent away from home.' He looked at her with a fragile smile. 'Like boarding school, I always hated the idea of boarding school. The idea of not being able to go home.'

'I wouldn't go,' said Jasmine loftily. 'I'd just refuse.'

'We wouldn't send you,' he said.

'So I never experienced the Blitz,' said Anita's mother. 'Your father now,' turning to Anita, 'now he remembers the Blitz. He loathed it. He carried a stretcher, you know. He was only sixteen. He was in the sixth form. It was when they bombed the Jewish Hospital.'

Anita knew all this.

'He was in Italy in the war, you know,' she told Charley, who, knowing already, nodded.

'A right religious Jew your father was at one time,' her mother went on. 'They blame me, you know. They think I lured him away from his religion. But it was the war. That's what did for him being a proper Jew. He saw things. And with it being his people, I suppose . . .'

Maurice Silver, apostate.

'Your father, you know,' she said, 'if he'd have dared to show his face again I'd have had him back.'

———————

Paddy's baths became a regular thing.

Nothing was ever said and he never came near her while he was naked. He would just run a bath as soon as she arrived, gather together his bits and pieces, undress and stand before her to be looked at before climbing in. She would sit on the closed lid of the toilet with her feet up on the sink, and they would talk about the Bomb, the films they'd seen, and the books she'd borrowed from him. When she was fully grown she would look back and still not understand. Was it sex? He just liked to be looked at and she liked looking. Later, he'd light a cigarette and walk about with a thin steaming towel round his waist, curly black locks dripping into his eyes.

★   ★   ★

She went to Bluebell Wood with her father and mother and Robin. It was Easter, and her mother started prattling on to Robin about how you always got fairies in a bluebell wood.

Robin said there was no such thing as fairies although there was Coleman Grey, of course, he was real.

Her mother sat by the picnic hamper slotting forks into the little holders in the lid. 'There are fairies though,' she said, 'they're not silly tiny little things like you see in books. They're like proper people only there's always something funny about them, not quite human. Sometimes, if you wait for the last bus, you can get on and find you've got on a goblin bus. I did that once. It was the 53 going down Kirkhamshulme Lane. I went and sat at the back and when I looked up from getting my money out of my purse the whole bus had turned their heads and was looking at me, and every face was the face of a goblin.'

There was a short silence.

Anita's father was slowly chewing a mouthful of tongue and mustard sandwich. He finished it and swallowed. 'Have you no more sense than you were born with?' he asked incredulously.

'It's true,' she said, biffing him with a rolled-up cloth. 'You go and boil your head.'

He lay back with the sun on his face, his long bony nose casting a shadow. Across his forehead he laid his thin white wrist. 'I'll have twenty minutes,' he said.

Her mother was in a playful mood. She went on talking, saying you could always tell a fairy by the telltale sign. Pointed ears some had. Eyes that glowed in the dark like a cat's. Webbed fingers. 'But one thing they all have,' she said, 'is a mark like a diamond on the back. That's the giveaway.'

Anita stared at her, feeling a blush creep up her neck. Her mother spent time with Paddy Riley while they were at school. It was their secret, she, her mother and Paddy Riley. Yet sometimes her mother acted as if she wasn't supposed to know anything. She grinned widely, all to herself, as she tidied the hamper. Robin picked bluebells, humming high-pitched. Her father put out his hand and punched her mother on the arm, not quite gently.

'If that child has nightmares tonight,' he said tightly, 'it'll be all your fault.'

'Away and boil your head,' she replied, 'if the world was all like you, there'd be no such thing as stories at all. You'd have us all as boring as yourself.'

His eyes shot open and stared furiously at the sky. He said nothing but went on blinking in a surprised and injured way for some moments before slowly sitting up, rubbing his face with his fingers and pulling up the knees of his trousers.

'I'll take the children for a walk,' he said gruffly.

Robin, who had always been a mother's boy, wanted to stay with his mum, so it was just Anita and her father who walked through Bluebell Wood towards the sudden grassy edge of a cliff that hung out over a leafy valley. Here they sat down. Her father told her how important it was that she try her hardest at the new school, that it was the trying that counted and that she must always work hard and listen to the teachers. 'They're there to help you,' he said.

'I know,' she replied. 'Some of them are OK. But some of them really are horrible, you know.'

Her father said teachers were much, much worse when he was a lad at school, and told her how terrified he used to be of one particular teacher called Mr Moss, who used to flick boys just behind the ear in a particularly painful way.

They sat in silence then for a while. They often sat together in silence.

'You know, Anita,' he said after a while, lighting a cigarette, 'this second sight of hers, and all her ghosts and muck like that, it's all a nothing at all. She's deluded, your mother is. A superstitious woman.' His smoke came out in a listless trickle in the still day. 'She'll have your brother as daft as she is, but you, you've got more sense. You've got brains.'

Smoke was rising in the valley.

On the way back they came upon something strange. A big rock had fallen on a fox and its baby. Part of them was crushed, but their perfect heads and front legs and chests stuck out from under the rock. Their fur was sticky and stiffening. The mother had her arms round the baby, as if she were protecting it, and their eyes were closed. The baby looked as if it were peacefully sleeping. The mother's mouth was drawn back in a snarl.

Anita started crying helplessly, big hot tears streaming down her face.

'No use getting upset,' her father said kindly.

She wanted to bury them but he said it was impossible, they hadn't got a spade, and it was nature for things to die, she mustn't get upset.

'Dead is dead, Anita,' he said, and they stood there looking down at the little tragedy.

———————

Anita started crying one day on the boat.

Michael had been drunk and morose when she arrived, sitting with his elbow on the table, looking out of the window with his face resting on his hand. She locked and bolted the door.

'Scared we'll be disturbed?' he said, not taking his eyes from the window. 'Scared we'll be discovered in the throes of our frantic sexual activity?'

'What's the matter, Michael?'

His eyes swivelled sideways on to her, hostile. 'We only exist in here,' he said. 'Outside of this we're nothing. You're a different person and so am I.'

They had these conversations all the time. Anita sat down beside him. 'It's true,' she agreed. 'There's real life and then there's this. This is in a space all its own.'

'Real life,' he repeated sadly. He reached out, picked up her hand and brought it to his lips, never taking his eyes off her. She thought he was going to kiss her hand but instead he turned it over and bit the inside of her wrist with a quick, snarling bite, hard enough to hurt. She gasped and pulled it away, staring at the marks of his teeth, blue on the vein.

'I'm leaving you,' he said. 'I'm leaving here. I've decided.'

She turned away, cradling her wrist. 'Whatever you want.' She closed her eyes, biting her lip hard.

'It won't matter so much to you,' he said.

'You've got your real life.'

She didn't trust herself to speak. Missing him began, a great dull ache bloating itself up like a rain cloud. He jumped up and pushed past her to unlock the door.

'Now go,' he said stiffly. 'This time I mean it.'

She stood up, gazing around blankly. He was facing away, eyes grim, lips tight. She stopped by him but he wouldn't meet her eyes. She had always loved the way he looked. He was like a favourite picture hanging on the wall, the kind you went back to again and again, in which you saw more and more each time. His eyes flickered. 'What are you waiting for?' he said gruffly.

She kissed his cheek and he flinched.

'It *will* matter to me, Michael,' she said. 'I don't want you to think . . . '

A strangled moan of exasperation escaped him and he pushed her backwards into the room. 'This isn't fair!' he cried. 'I'm just supposed to sit around here waiting for you! What do you think I am? I want to go away somewhere with you. I want to sleep all night with you. I want to see you naked. I want to fuck you, for Christ's sake! It's just a diversion for you but it's not for me. I'd go for the whole thing with you if I could. Children. Everything. But you'd never leave your cosy little nest for me, would you? You don't care enough. It's true, isn't it? It's true. You just don't care enough.'

'Michael . . . '

He dropped down on to the settle and let his arms hang limply between his legs. 'You know,' he said, 'I was OK really. I was OK till you started this.'

There was a silence.

'Go on,' he said wearily.

'Was it only me?' she asked him. 'Am I the only one to blame?'

He rubbed his face and looked up at her, his eyes guarded. 'I don't know,' he said, 'I don't know any more. I'm just sick of it.'

That's when she started to cry. It was all her fault, everything. A great wave of shame and self-loathing reared up and drenched her and she gave in and stood miserable and ugly with her head hanging and her face distorted, nose and eyes dripping. A moment later she felt him standing very close to her.

'It'd be all right if I didn't care,' he said, 'I'd be well up for it if I didn't care. But I just can't do this any more, Anita.'

She covered her face and her breath seized up.

He put his arms round her roughly and made her sit down with him on the settle, put her head on his shoulder and held it there firmly with his hand. 'Ssh,' he said impatiently, 'ssh!' but she couldn't stop. She was blind as he walked her to the bed and laid her down with his arms around her.

'I wanted to hurt you,' he whispered into her hair. 'Sssh!'

She thought he would try and make love to her then, and that if he did she didn't know what she would do, but nothing happened and she cried till she fell asleep.

He woke her just before three. 'You have to go and collect your children,' he said.

★ ★ ★

After a good cry she liked to spend money. She took the girls to town after school and bought them sundaes in Jak's, then they went down to Bobbie's Bazaar and got a little waistcoat for Jasmine and a performing wooden parrot for Sid. It was going dark when they got back to the car. There was a hotdog seller on the corner of Buttery Lane and the Prom. The smell of frying onions wafted out over the car park. The girls wanted one, of course. She should have said no, all the grease and artificial colouring, but what the hell. That smell revolted Charley, he couldn't sit within its range. She sighed, breathing it in like a Bisto kid, singing tunelessly under her breath as they ran with their money: '*Once in the dear dead days beyond recall . . .*'

The Italian man, small, mustachioed, fat, standing in his greasy white coat at his painted white stand at the Longsight entrance of Belle Vue. They used to run up from the house and buy, eat them walking home, dripping onion grease. The girls didn't go for onions, it had to be ketchup. They dripped it on the back seat of the car, smeared it on their school clothes.

'Look at the state of you,' she said, looking in the rearview mirror.

———

'Look at the state of you,' her mother said, straightening her shoulders. 'Look at your skirt. Run up and put something else on. I want you to take a message to you-know-who.'

Her mother was in an awful mood. She'd been peculiar for days, sitting brooding and gazing into the fire, all wrapped up in herself.

Anita ran and washed her face, looked at herself in the triple mirrors over the kidney-shaped dressing-table in her room, took off her skirt and top and put on her new suspender belt and sheer stockings. She was thirteen now, able to wear these things. Thirty-four inches already, her breasts swelled in a peach-coloured bra from a catalogue. She hated all her clothes apart from her black patent-leather shoes. All she had apart from her school uniform were a couple of dresses that were too young for her, her dirty skirt, a blue polo-necked jumper and a green embroidered blouse with puffy sleeves that used to belong to her cousin Diane. She put the blue polo-neck under a pleated pinafore dress, slid her feet proudly into her black patent-leather shoes and brushed her hair. Her blue Alice band matched the jumper.

'Write this,' her mother said, leaning forward and biting her thumb nail. She thought for a moment then cleared her throat: 'My dear Paddy, I will not be able to make it on Friday.' A long pause for serious thought, then: 'You must not send a reply, dear Paddy.'

She knitted her brow for a long time.

'Anything else?' Anita asked.

She blinked. 'What?'

'Anything else to write?'

'No,' she replied in a puzzled voice, 'nothing else. Just take it and give it to him.'

Anita folded the paper. Her mother went into the back kitchen and started sorting through the laundry basket. Anita thought for a moment. It seemed a bleak little note. She unfolded it and wrote quickly on to the end of it: 'I love you but we two must never meet again.'

She loved to watch her shoes as she was going down the alley, stepping out so bold and shiny.

He was standing in on the Bobs that day. She waved to him, showing the letter. A carriage was just rolling in. The people got off and more got on. He checked to see the carriages were secure. He came to the barrier, took the note and put it in his pocket. 'I'm off in half an hour,' he said, giving her three shillings. 'Go on and wander around for a bit and I'll see you back here.'

She bought some chips and ate them in the Great Apes house. When she got back he was waiting for her between the Bobs and the Water Chute, smoking a cigarette and pacing restlessly. He stood still as she approached and a bitter smile narrowed his lips.

'She said anything to you?'

She shook her head. They walked down to the floral clock and stood looking at the gibbons in their huge dome of a cage. She didn't know what to say to him. He turned and looked at her. 'She said anything to you?' he repeated.

She shook her head again.

He chewed his lip.

'What does she mean?' he asked. 'Does she mean there are to be no more letters?'

'She never said anything. She was in a lousy mood though.'

He shrugged and flicked his dimp at the Buddha. 'I am dismissed,' he said, flexing his shoulders, 'cast away like a smoked cigarette. But she's wrong, you know. She'll find out that she's wrong.'

They strolled on.

'Don't be sad, Paddy,' Anita said, touching his arm, 'it's not that she doesn't like you. It's just that she's married already. You always knew that.'

'Aye,' he smiled, 'I did indeed. Now isn't this a strange thing? She writes me that she loves me.' He stopped and wrote in the air, quoting grandly: ' 'I love you! I love you but we two must never meet again!' Fine turn of phrase. I'd say she'd been at the romances, your ma, wouldn't you?'

'Don't laugh at her! She's not happy.'

'Well, that makes two of us,' he cried harshly, stamping his foot like a child.

Anita jumped. 'Don't shout at me,' she shouted back, 'it's not my fault.'

'Anita, Anita,' he said, 'what am I to do?' He put his hands on her shoulders and it was as if his palms were charged with some force that changed her body inside in a deep, irreversible way.

'I don't know!'

He let go, walked a few paces backwards and forwards jerkily, then stopped all at once and seemed to go limp. 'Anyway,' he muttered sulkily, pronouncing it *annyway*. 'She's too old for me.'

'Yes, she is,' Anita agreed.

He swung about and looked at her. 'So,' he said, smiling, 'you won't be coming to see me any more.'

'Oh,' she babbled, wordless hope welling up inside, 'I can still come and see you. If you like.'

He went on looking at her closely but didn't reply. 'I have to be back soon,' he said. They walked on slowly. 'What can I treat you to before you go? What would you like to go on?'

They were passing the tiny round booth of the Flea Circus.

'I want to see the fleas,' she said.

He bowed. 'Your wish, oh little mistress of the universe, is my command.'

A show was about to begin, so they paid their money and went into the dark little booth with the light shining down on the baize table where the fleas performed. They took their places. Paddy was behind her.

261

'She'll find out,' he whispered on the back of her neck. The crowd, small like the show, leaned forward as the fleas lined up on the table with their paraphernalia, and the skinny little flea man talked. The human flea, he told them with a slight accent, can pull 360 times its own weight. 'Now,' he said, 'come on, my darling, come on, my good girl, good girl,' and one of the fleas pulling a tiny golden coach stepped out of line and circled the ring.

'I'll die without your mother,' whispered Paddy.

'Ssh.'

'The human flea,' said the flea man, 'is a very stubborn creature, very temperamental. Great skill is needed to train her. I say her, for all my artistes are ladies. The gentlemen are not so good for this kind of work . . . '

'I've not given up. You can tell her that from me.'

Paddy sighed on the back of her neck and his breath was warm. A whole procession of tiny coaches circled the ring slowly. 'She'll find she can't do it,' he said.

'Ssh.' She jabbed her elbow backwards into his chest.

'Can't give me up.'

If she can't give him up, Anita thought, what will she do? She'll leave my dad. What

262

about us? Me and Robin? Will she leave us too?

A flea walked a tightrope. The crowd gasped.

'Let her try,' said Paddy in Anita's ear.

My house, she thought, my mother and father sitting together by the fire after tea, the sound of the mandolin when I'm in bed, the four of us walking in the park, my father carrying Robin on Blackpool prom, my father walking with me through town, by the Cathedral, the Shambles, down Cheetham Hill Road —

The flea trapezes swung. Hup! Hup! Hup!

— gone, all gone.

Two more fleas fought a duel, backwards and forwards across the baize, and Anita was afraid, deep down scared, deeper than she'd ever been. His lips, close to her ear, gave off heat and breath and a sweet smell that tickled her insides.

'Tell her,' whispered Paddy, 'no no, don't tell her, I'll tell her so myself . . . '

It was her father who first brought her to see the fleas. He held her against his chest, her arm around his neck. He smelled of tobacco and freshly ironed white shirt. Her eyes filled and she blinked.

'The human flea feeds once only in four, say five days.'

The flea man showed them his thin white arm with the big veins and all the little red spots where he let the fleas suck in the crook of his elbow. 'Now,' he said, smiling, 'who is going to volunteer to feed my little ladies?' and everyone laughed and backed away. Then it was time for the grand finale, when the entire company formed itself into regiments and re-enacted the Battle of Agincourt with little lances and swords, till the victors raised the standard and the vanquished played possum with their legs in the air.

Everyone applauded, the flea man smiled, and they were outside blinking in the sudden light.

'But she's married, Paddy,' Anita said. 'There's my dad. And me. And Robin.'

He said nothing, just stood with his head low, looking away sideways under his brows. At last he raised his eyes and stared at her thoughtfully, gently pushing her blue Alice band back in her hair and caressing her face with his thumbs. 'So there is,' he murmured.

———————

Her mother died in summer, just after her sixty-seventh birthday. They went up for the funeral.

Again the clan gathered, clasped hands in the porch of the church, bowed their heads by the grave. So soon after Bernie's, they said. The Deasys and O'Learys knew how to make a good funeral. Everyone wore mourning. It was like a Mafia graveside or something in a Western. Anita looked around at the craggy Deasy men, the big-faced Deasy women, Anne and Dymphna and Uncle Fred, Connie distraught, sobbing, supported by Uncle Ian. Bloody family, she thought. A pain. She was so tired. All her cousins had turned up, and a whole new generation of label-clad boys with uneasy manners and ugly hair. She was popular, Auntie Geraldine. She was fun. A great laugh, said cousin Barney, and everyone agreed.

Charley wore his good black suit that always hung ready in the wardrobe for occasions such as this. Seeing him when he came downstairs in it, unfamiliar, tall and suddenly striking, she went weak at the knees. He stood by her mother's grave with one arm upon her shoulder. The girls wore their tams. Some of her friends back home had said they shouldn't bring the girls, but Charley and she agreed that this modern death taboo was rubbish.

Tears ran down Anita's face and into her mouth. Her father kept popping into her head, mingling with her mother. She couldn't separate them. All this had been anticipated, but still she didn't believe it was her mother in the box. She kept seeing bright pictures in her head, sudden and startling: her mother when her hair was thick and springy, down at heel by the rag and bone cart, as a mermaid; old, big-stomached, small-shouldered, tubes up her nose. My father should know, she thought. Someone should have made some sort of effort to trace him for this. I could have. But I didn't. Is he dead? Is he an old man somewhere? I wonder if I'd recognise him.

The mourning took on a peculiarly festal quality at the wake. Ties were loosened, arms bared, a lot of whisky consumed. Anita went for a lie down, closed her eyes and heard the voices and music downstairs. She thought she might sleep for a little. 'Mummy,' she whispered experimentally to see how the word felt now, 'Mum. Mummy.'

'Mummy,' said Jasmine, materialising by the bed, 'Daddy wants to know if you'd like a cup of tea.'

Her face was brown, her hair bleached from the sun in France. Anita held out her arms and gave her a cuddle. 'Are you all right, baby?'

'I'm fine.'

'If you get tired just come up to me. Tell Daddy I'd love a cup of tea.'

When he brought her tea, still strange and handsome in his black suit, her heart and thoughts and the feeling in the place between her legs leapt up like flames at the sight of him. He sat down on the bed and smiled tiredly. 'OK, love?' he said.

'I'm OK. I'm just very tired. I'll come down when I've had this.'

'You don't have to. You don't have to do anything at all if you don't want to. Everything's under control.'

'It sounds funny,' she said, 'but you know what I keep thinking of?'

'What?'

'My dad.'

He looked sideways. 'Yes,' he said, 'I can understand that.'

'I keep thinking he might be dead and I'd never know and it's not right, I've never had a chance to go to *his* funeral. I should be able to go to my own father's funeral.' Her eyes filled up again.

'Yes,' he said, 'you should.' He lay down, rumpling his suit, and put one arm across her. 'I was fond of your mother,' he said.

'She liked you.'

'I know. She had good taste.'

She felt him swallow against her neck. She must have fallen asleep because the next thing she knew she was waking up, he was

267

gone and the room was dark. She went downstairs and saw him sitting on the other side of the crowded lounge with Sid asleep on his knee. If I was seeing him for the first time, she thought, would I still fancy him? I can't see him clearly any more. She couldn't take her eyes off him. He looked young, she thought, and she knew how fragile he was under his plain good sense. He glanced across and smiled at her, and she remembered how last Tuesday Michael had said as he lay naked before her that he believed in fate, how he'd felt he knew her as soon as he saw her. How he had suddenly wept and she had put aside her book and they had lain down, she clad, he naked, and she had kissed him and stroked his thighs and buttocks while he ground himself against her hipbone till he came.

★ ★ ★

Robin and Anita sat on the bed in their mother's old bedroom going through the messy contents of two narrow drawers of a table. Old bits of cotton wool and used tissues were mixed in with shopping lists, old postcards, tea-stained envelopes, her birth and marriage certificates, a buff-coloured ration book, a small white foxed card embossed with the words Archie's Chop

House; and a yellowing newspaper clipping about the mass rally of Mosley's fascists at Cheetham Town Hall, mysteriously marked *Livshin* in their father's neat hand. Her heart quickened as she saw this, and at the same moment she realised that she was searching too for some trace of Paddy Riley. There was no sign of any of his letters amongst her mother's things. Now that would have been something. No photographs of course, there never had been any of him. But everyone else was there. The wedding of Geraldine O'Leary and Maurice Silver: Geraldine looked tarty and powdered, her lipstick garish. Maurice looked thin and beaky. The stern young woman with the bouquet was Bernie, and there too were Nora and Mike with baby Bernard, seventeen-year-old Connie looking off to one side, and the bridesmaids, little Anne and Dymphna with their bouquets and acres of ribbon.

'God, look,' she said, passing it on to Robin and picking up another.

Here, fading sepia on a stiff board, were Anita's youthful, unsmiling grandparents. Michael O'Leary stood with one hand on the back of the chair where his bride, Maureen Deasy, sat in thoughtful repose with her hands clasped in her lap. Mullingar, 1918. And here was Mary aged 12 in a doorway in

Dublin. Nice, laughing Mary. And the one Anita herself took, of Mary's grave in Mullingar. And here was baby Geraldine in three-year-old Nora's arms, one chubby fist raised from a froth of white lace.

Here they were, the living and the dead in smiling childhood. She looked at a faded grey snapshot of herself and Robin coming down the helter skelter at Belle Vue and thought that the two children in it were also dead in a way. She did not even remember them so well. She couldn't find the crone who might have been her Russian great-grandmother. Or her father's Bar-Mitzvah picture. He must have taken them with him when he went. For the first time she wondered if he'd taken any of her.

She found something else that day: a scrap of paper on which her mother had written the single word Maurice and a Manchester phone number.

★   ★   ★

She had a feeling of excitement fizzing up, as if something was imminent. She felt like Tony in *West Side Story* singing about something coming, something big, and she didn't know what it was any more than he did. It had her walking round and round the garden, in and out of the wood, up and down the edge of the cornfield like a caged cat.

She decided it was her father. She had not dared ring the number found amongst her mother's things, though there had not been a day in the week that passed since then that she did not pick up the phone and listen to the dialling tone. The number was in her head like a mantra. Maurice. Who else? Who else could it be? Charley thought she should phone, even offered to do it for her. You'll never get it out of your mind otherwise, he said. Robin, surprisingly bitter, said leave it, leave it, Anita, why should we bother? What's the point of raking all that up again? If he'd wanted to see us he'd have done it long ago.

But how did her mother come to have his number? Why hadn't she said anything? Maybe it was just an old number, a dead number.

At last Anita could bear it no longer and called. It was morning. The girls were in the garden, shrieking and running round in slippers and pyjamas. She heard the ringing tone — one two three four. He'd be an old man now. Seventy-one. Surely she'd know his voice? Dad? she'd say. Dad? It's Anita. Further than that she could not imagine. Yes. Hear that, she'd say, that's the sound of your granddaughters. I tell them proudly they are a quarter Jewish and what their ancestors endured. I tell them about *you*, Dad.

A flat-voiced girl answered and she blanked.

'Er — Mr Silver,' she blurted, 'does Mr Silver live there?'

'No. No Mr Silver here.'

'I was given this number,' she said, fiddling with the side of the old basket chair, unaccountably angry with the girl but trying to keep it out of her voice. 'Somebody gave it to me.'

The girl called her mother.

'Yes?' Anita visualised a suspicious matron with steely hair.

'I'm sorry to trouble you. I'm trying to trace a Mr Maurice Silver and I was given this telephone number. Do you know if a Mr Maurice Silver might have lived there at any time?'

But already a lump was rising in her throat and the tip of her nose was burning. He was not there. Of course.

'Well, I don't know,' the woman said, 'I suppose he might have done. I don't know. It used to be bedsits.'

'Did it?'

'I believe so.'

'When was that?'

'Three, four years ago. I don't know. I'm

sorry, I can't help you.'

'Oh, that's all right. Thank you very much.'

She got the phone down before she started crying. Three, four years. Bedsits. Her dad was an old man in a bedsit. She went and sat with Basil in his den. The dog's eyes were horrible to see. His teeth were all gone, his breath a charnel house. She bought him dog breath freshener things to chew but he couldn't be bothered to chew them. A limp little flip of the tail would acknowledge the gift. She went upstairs and crawled under the duvet and cried for ten minutes, then got up and washed her face and told the girls to get dressed. She rang the vet's and made an appointment to take Basil in on Thursday just for a check-over. He hadn't eaten much over the last few days.

She took the girls to the beach and they squabbled and whined as she rubbed on the sun cream, ran to the sea in their flowery swim suits. Jasmine threw herself in, Sid dithered in the tiny waves, scared of jellyfish. Anita tasted salt on her lips. She sat and watched and couldn't read her book because the sun was too bright on the pages. Behind her dark glasses her eyes were sore and red, and her heart felt strange, like a panicking bird going up and down a chimney. Something's coming, *I*

273

don't know *what* it is *but* it is gonna be big. Something like a nerve in her belly told her. It was not something good any more, and it felt huge, like a tidal wave. It was her father but he'd gone now. Finally, she thought, finally gone from me for good. Now something else is coming.

She took the girls to Mr Magic's Merry Maze, Kokoschka's for lunch, bought them sweets and comics and ice cream. She spent a fortune. They fought and bitched all the way till she lost her temper and screamed at them all the things that meant nothing to them and that they couldn't possibly understand. 'You see?' she shrilled, almost in tears. 'I had nothing when I was your age. You've got everything! Don't you understand how lucky you are? You've got everything and all you do is moan. I can't stand it! You don't deserve anything. Just *shut* up, shut up, I'm fed up with you!'

Then Jas turned sulky and Sid cried, and Anita nearly cried too because she hated it when Sid cried. Sid was supposed to be tough. She pulled them both in and cuddled them roughly. The three of them walked along Buttery Lane in a state and met Jane Jarrett with Matthew and Lauren.

'Oh, look at you! You look all done in! Poor Anita!'

'Is it so obvious?' she said with a bitter laugh.

Jane peered at her. 'You OK?'

'It's the holidays. Bloody holidays getting to me.'

'You're nearly in tears,' Jane said, touching her arm.

'Oh, I'm all right.' She sniffed and rubbed her nose. 'I need a couple of days away.'

'Tell you what,' said Jane, 'you give me the girls and we'll take them home and get the pool out. How about that, girlies?'

Sid shrugged.

'Don't mind,' said Jasmine.

Anita laughed. 'Such enthusiasm!'

'You go and put your feet up.'

Weird how you love your kids, she thought, and can't wait to see the back of them. Weird how they'll behave for other people. They perked up, skipping off like little darlings, and she fell into the Dun Cow and drank two glasses of red wine quickly. Her father was a sad old man in a bedsit, doing his competitions. Filling in the forms with an old man's hand. She drank some more and felt better, considered going to see Michael. Luke was away at summer camp somewhere near his grandparents in Dorset. She thought about Jasmine's eczema and Sid's face when she was crying. I wonder if I'm messing them

275

up, she thought. She imagined herself kissing Michael on his full lower lip, taking it in her mouth whole and savouring it like a warm sweet. He was suffering. She was too. She put her face in her hands at odd times of the day or night, overcome. The courtly lover always suffered. It was written. Every time she saw him he asked her to come away with him, just for a week, a few days, a day or two. A night, for Christ's sake. She could. She could go any time.

'Say you've got to go to . . . I don't know . . . sleep with me all night on my boat. Don't even think about it. Please, Anita. Don't think about it, please, just do it.'

She rang Charley on the mobile: 'Charley love, I'm in the Dun Cow.'

'You're pissed.' He didn't sound angry, just factual.

'Yes, a little bit. It's all right though. Don't worry. I love you, Charley, I love you so much you wouldn't believe it.'

'OK, sweetheart.' He sounded tired.

'Charley, the girls are at Jane's and I'm supposed to pick them up at five. Can you get them? I'm going to have to get the bus.'

There was quite a long pause, then he sighed. 'That's awkward,' he said stiffly, and she knew he was with people.

'Well, I'll have to get a taxi,' she said, her

eyes filling up with a stabbing suddenness as she realised she had no cash and that she'd have to go trekking down to the other end of the High Street to the machine, then all the way back up to the roundabout for the bus and after that the bloody long walk at the other end, while he swanned about in the Peugeot. 'See you later,' she said and rang off. She swallowed the unaccountable tears. Let's go wild, she said to herself as she stepped outside nicely pissed. Life is ended before it's begun. A lovely summer rain had sprung up, solemn and silvery, a benediction appalling in its transience. She was scared as she ran down Buttery Lane. She didn't ever want to die. She wanted to have it all and keep everything, even the pulling pain in her chest from the place she thought of as her heart, where all her hurts had pooled over the years and now and again got restless. She bought a bottle of something in the wine shop and went round to Lindsay's.

'Oh, so what?' said Lindsay. 'Wrong time of day? Who cares?'

This could really make me sick, Anita thought, uncorking the bottle.

They watched the rain pouring down over the back garden.

'So what is it?' she asked. 'What's the story?'

'Michael,' Anita said, 'Michael Bastian. What do people think of him round here? Really?'

Lindsay looked thoughtful for a while then said, 'I think he's something of a figure of fun. Yes, he is. A bit of a figure of fun.'

Pantaloon, Stupidus with his long red wig. 'Why?' Her voice came out weak and silly, not hers. Poor Michael.

'Well.' Lindsay screwed up her nose. 'He's just a drunk. There's no mileage in that any more. You know. The day of the stylish boozer is over. Don't you think? Don't you?'

Anita just looked at her. Was there a choice? Really? Did some people have that luxury? And it made her care for him more than she ever had, but in a different way. Poor baby. How on earth could it end for him?

'Anita.'

Tears filled her eyes.

'Anita.'

Never say I didn't care for him, she thought.

'Are you OK?'

Never.

'Are you OK?'

Oh, Paddy Riley.

'Are you OK, Anita?'

Tears spilled down her face.

278

'I'm sorry,' Anita said, 'I was drifting.'

'You certainly were.' Lindsay handed her a tissue. 'What is it with you? You know, I worry about you sometimes, Anita. It doesn't seem to be making you happy.'

'What doesn't?'

'You know. All this. Your thing with Michael. Whatever it is. I know what you say, I know, you don't have to go into it again, but . . . ' She shrugged, shaking her head, sitting frog-like on the carpet. 'Oh, I don't know, you're old enough to make your own decisions, you fool.'

Anita giggled.

'What is it?' Lindsay got up, leaned back in a chair, rolling a fag. 'You fallen out with Charley? You want to stay here tonight? Is that it?'

The woman was mad. 'Me and Charley?' said Anita. 'There's nothing wrong with me and Charley, what are you talking about, woman? I'm going home when I've had this wine.'

Lindsay gave her the cigarette she'd been rolling, lit it and rolled one for herself. 'Eight,' she said, 'and two to go.'

'What?'

'These.' She stuck the fag in her mouth. 'I'm sticking to ten a day.'

★ ★ ★

The taxi dropped her off at quarter to nine. Charley was sprawled on the floor watching a film starring Harrison Ford as a worried businessman in a grey suit.

'I'm sorry!' she cried, falling upon him where he lay, smothering his blanked-out face with kisses.

'Go and see the girls,' he said without expression, 'they're awake.'

She kissed him again and again, then ran up and breathed alcohol all over the girls, calling them her babies and squeezing them fiercely, promising her love foreveranever as they hugged her back with all the strength of their puny arms. When she left them and stood on the landing she was crying. So frail, only her and Charley between them and the void. She didn't want to lose them. She didn't want to die. Charley came up, his face grim, took her arm and pulled her into the bedroom.

'Where've you been?' he asked angrily. 'What're you crying for?'

'Lindsay's.'

'What d'you ring off for?'

'I'm sorry.'

'I was worried about you.'

'I'm so *sorry*.'

'Anita!' He gripped her arms, looked hard at her, a kind of concentration of worry in his eyes. 'Go fucking mad if you want,' he said. 'You'll do what you want anyway. Only don't take it out on us.'

'What are you talking about?'

He let go her arm with a tossing-away movement, stalked to the window and stood there glowering out. She lay down. The light hurt her closed eyes.

'What is it?' he said quietly. 'Am I supposed to have done something wrong or something?'

'You haven't done anything, Charley. I'm sorry. I feel awful.'

He came and sat down on the side of the bed, head deeply bowed, arms braced against the mattress, saying nothing.

'Turn the light off, my love,' she whispered.

'I couldn't get to Jane's till quarter to six,' he said darkly. 'They were in the middle of their dinner. She'd fed the girls.'

'Oh, that's nice of her! Good old Jane! Turn it off, my love.' She put her hand over her eyes.

'What do you think I said when she asked me where you were? 'She's pissed out of her head somewhere,' I said. 'She hasn't got the fucking faintest idea what she's doing.' '

'You didn't!'

'I did.'

'You didn't!'

'I did,' he repeated, very serious, turning his head and looking down at her. 'What am I *supposed* to do, Anita? Tell lies? Does it matter?'

She groaned.

He got up, sighing, turned on the lamp and switched off the main light. 'I don't know what to do about you,' he said in a dull voice, standing over her.

'Give me a fuck,' she said and he walked out.

Round and round went the room.

'Charley!' she called.

He didn't come.

She fell into the pit. When she woke up she was stiff and hot in her clothes and her eyes felt clogged. Still he hadn't come. She sat up. The room had a swollen look, a swollen silence, the whirling slower than before. Slowly she put her feet on the floor, her shoes so tight she took them off, then tiptoed unsteadily out on to the landing. All the lights were off. He wasn't in the bathroom, he wasn't in the study. He wasn't in either of the girls' rooms. She went downstairs and he wasn't anywhere. He's gone, she thought, he's left me. The back door was open, the sooty night icy and solid standing in the frame.

'Charley!' she called, terrified.

Coleman Grey! Coleman Grey!

Her hands shook a little on the back of the chair.

He appeared from the darkness, unsmiling, his hair rough, the collar of his dark jacket up around his neck. Basil was with him. A boy and his dog. For the first time she noticed he was getting grey. How could she have missed it for so long? He was fair, of course, so it hadn't really showed. It made her feel protective of him, as if somehow she could save him from Time.

'What are you doing out there?'

'Looking at the stars,' he said.

'It's freezing.'

He glanced back, as if surprised at the night. 'Go to bed then.' He closed and locked the door.

'I called my dad.'

'Called your dad?'

'That number, I rang it. He isn't there, of course. Dead end.'

Charley crossed the room heavily and put his arms round her. 'Now,' he said gruffly, 'you've done it and you can put it out of your mind.'

'This woman said it used to be bedsitters. I keep thinking he must have ended up a lonely old man in a bedsit and I hate it.'

'You don't know that,' he said. 'Don't make

a picture of something that might never have happened and then treat it as the truth. Come on now.'

They went upstairs and got undressed and into bed and lay talking for ages about their dads, what they could remember of them; how they'd felt when they'd gone, how they used to look out for them on buses, in streets, look for cards that never came. He used to tell people his was dead because it was easier, and in the end he believed it was true. 'He is anyway,' he told her, 'I just know,' and she kissed him tenderly.

The letters had started again. She was still regularly viewing her naked, peeled young man in his burning bath, a jam sandwich in his hand and the radio on the bamboo table playing Roy Orbison. He made her hard and hot all over so that she'd go home and lie down on her bed with a small hand mirror, looking at her private parts, which were like chunks of raw braising steak hiding a miniature pink head of new lipstick. She could touch the raw meat but not the shiny little lipstick. When she did touch that she just couldn't bear it, she could have curled up and died.

Paddy never touched her anywhere but her

face, and never when he was naked.

When he was sad, and he often was, he wrote poems for her mother, misspelt on small, lined scraps of paper. 'You are the Sunday in every week,' he wrote once, the single line, and she had kept the scrap of paper for herself. He was sad the day he took her on the Caterpillar, the day she came down with chicken pox. He tucked an envelope into her pocket and rested his arm upon her shoulders as they walked about the zoo. The pressure of his arm made her tingle and wish she could meet someone from school who'd think he was her real boyfriend. Maybe he was her real boyfriend in a way. All the little hairs on the nape of her neck stood up. They saw the brown bears and the big cats, and she was weak at the knees; the smell of the wild animals was exciting; the giraffes, the rhino, the hippo, the ruminant paddock passed by. She wanted him to kiss her in the burning heat of the reptile house, but he didn't and she didn't know how to ask. But it was the bird house that did for her. They stood with the little crowd that waited to hear the Mynah Bird say 'Hi, Joe,' and suddenly she was faint.

'You're a lovely girl, Anita,' he whispered, 'oh, you are.' Her heart was beating like a hammer and her cheeks and even her forehead burned up.

'Heavens,' said Paddy in a voice that cracked, 'the child's blushing.'

They went outside and the fresh air revived her. He asked her what ride she'd like to go on.

'The Caterpillar,' she replied.

Into a wide dusty carriage they climbed, pulled down the bar and off they went, picking up speed, round and round, faster and faster, hanging on to the bar as they rattled up and down the billows of the track. The ground was far away below, whirling darkly in a pit. One of Anita's legs was bent against the other, her blue skirt flat, her feet in her black patent-leather shoes with the little heel she thought gave her legs a fashion model look. Next to hers, Paddy's fierce brown fists gripped the grey bar. The gravity of the ride pressed her against him. They laughed and his lips smeared her forehead. Then the siren made its coarse, grimacing sound and the old pale green canopy came over the hoops with jerking, determined movements, hiding them in a green tunnel from the swirled faces of the crowds; and the great wind, simoom from the gritty pit, billowed her skirt up off her legs and over their heads, and they laughed as he kissed her inside the billows of her skirt. His warm open mouth slid on hers, then his tongue forced through her lips and was in. His eyes were slits. The siren wailed, the canopy lifted, they parted as the wind blew and she batted down her skirt and laughed.

The world lurched and she felt the sudden futility of the certainty that sooner or later she would be sick. The whole world narrowed to the necessity of getting away from him before she was.

The ride ended. She trembled as she climbed out on to the sloping boards. He took her elbow and guided her out. 'You are a lovely, lovely girl, Anita,' he said, 'but you don't know how to kiss. I could tell you've never done it before.'

'Of course I haven't.'

He leaned down with his face close to hers. 'How delightful,' he said. 'I could show you how.'

She began to shiver. 'I have to go.' She was freezing in the sun.

'Would you come on the Bobs with me next time?' he asked. 'Ah, go on, Anita, say you'll go on the Bobs with me next time.'

'I have to go,' she said tightly, her teeth trying to chatter.

'OK, sweet princess.'

She smiled shakily. Little pains shot through her cheeks. 'Thanks for the ride, Paddy,' she said.

He laughed, showing his toothy smile. 'I'll always be good for a ride,' he said, smiling, putting out his narrow palm and kissing it, blowing the kiss across to her. Then he turned and went off toward the Hyde Road entrance. Anita got halfway down Redgate Lane before she had to sit down on a step. When she felt her forehead it was wet. She wanted to think about how everything had changed now for ever because he had kissed her, but all she could think about was how terrible she felt and how she wouldn't mind dying if only this would stop. She got a little further and was sick on the cobbles in an alley, and when she got home found the first spots on her side. It was chicken pox, not love.

★   ★   ★

Her mother was pegging clothes out in the yard and Robin was at his friend's. Anita used the last of her strength to go to the pot of water on the hob. Drawing the envelope from her pocket like a gun, she held it in the steam till the seal began to peel. The secret was patience, not to go ripping the thing open before it was ready, because then you could never make it good again. She was an expert. No one ever suspected. She'd read them all, she'd read everything. The steam intensified a wave of nausea that was building remorselessly inside her. When it was done she dragged herself upstairs, locked her door and read the poem.

When she set it down, she realised she meant nothing to him, nothing at all. He only liked her because of her connection with her mother.

Oh Geraldine, I'd give the world . . .

It was all thees and thys and starry beams, and he'd never sit down and write a thing like that to her as long as he lived.

At last, as she swooned into a bout of chicken pox that kept her writhing and sleepless for days, she realised the seriousness of Paddy Riley. He had come to put an end to the life they had always had, she and her mother and father and Robin; he had come to take her mother from her father like the brick from the bottom of the pile, then the whole tower would come tumbling down.

———————

'Why don't you go to London for a few days?' Charley said. 'You're always saying you're going to do it, why don't you just do it? See your friend Leah. Have a rest. Do the bookshops. Go for a meal or something.'

'Do you think?'

She'd take Michael. It sprang into her mind.

'I do think,' he said firmly. 'You're driving me crackers like you are. I don't want you bingeing all the time, I can't stand it. You're always like this at the end of the summer holidays. Why don't you make it over the weekend or something and take an extra day?'

Suddenly it was definite. But why now? Why now?

'Alison'd manage, she could get Lauren in,' he said. 'She'd probably be glad of the money. The kids could go to Joanne's. I'll just tell her you're going off your head again and it's a medical emergency.'

He wanted to be rid of her for a bit. To be rid of them all and have the house to himself. He'd bring his work home and do it in the study with Basil draped across his feet.

'I could fix the wall at the back,' he said, 'have a go at the stile.'

'Not London.'

Why now? Why now?

'I couldn't face London at the moment.'

Charley had Leah's number, he could check.

'I wouldn't mind going up to the cottage for a couple of days, get right away from it all.'

'Long way,' he murmured sleepily.

Luke was at summer camp near his grandparents. So many people were away at this time of year. No one would notice a thing.

'I could do some drawing,' she said.

She wouldn't take Michael to Scotland though. She could never have done it with him there, in the cottage where they'd conceived Jasmine. And she could never have done it at home, or anywhere at all connected with Charley. She lay awake long after Charley had gone off. Why now? It wasn't just circumstance, she could have made that any time. It was a kind of madness, she supposed, something to do with fear of death and the way people could vanish at the drop of a hat. She was forty-five. One day we'll all be dead and vanished, she thought, and it suddenly seemed so ridiculous to keep off loving people as if it was a vice.

★ ★ ★

So Michael and Anita went to London, to a hotel in Fulham.

It was wonderfully impersonal: a small lobby smelling like essence of guest house, a bell to ring, a plump little Scots woman who gave them their keys. They could have breakfast in their room if they filled out a form in time and left it on the reception desk. Their room was solid and clean and functional, dominated by a massive frilly bed, with a window that looked down over a small courtyard where a Rombout's coffee sign sat among potted begonias.

It was horribly depressing.

The first night, while Michael was in the bar across the road, she called Charley on the mobile from their room.

'Guess what?' he said. 'There's chicken pox doing the rounds again. What's the betting Sid's got it? What's the betting she's spreading it all around Cheltenham at this very moment?'

'Damn. Did you remember to take Basil to the vet's?'

'Well basically,' Charley replied, 'she thinks we ought to have him put down. But I don't know, he doesn't seem to be in any pain, why should we get him put down if he isn't in any pain? He's just very old and tired and he's got to have some sort of special invalid food. It's all written down. Said to call her if he seems to be in any pain.'

'Won't it be weird without Basil?'

'Weird. How's the cottage?'

'It's fine. Not even too damp. There's masses of wood, so I'm going to light a fire and take that musty smell away. I'm going to have a lovely lie-in in the morning.'

'Lucky devil. What are you doing tomorrow?'

Bookshops, I think, she nearly said.

'Walk down to the village. Stock up a bit. Read my book. Go for a walk.'

'Going to do any drawing?'

'Oh yes.' She had brought her drawing materials and planned to maybe knock off one or two little made-up landscapes to show for her efforts when she returned.

'I've been thinking about the wall,' he said. 'I'm going out to mess about with it for a bit now. I'll get some wood tomorrow. Well . . . have a good time, love.'

Next she called Joanne's and spoke to the girls. Sid said her elbow was sore. Jasmine had gone swimming with her big cousins and had a great time. Their voices piping into this arid place made her eyes moist. When they'd gone she sat still for a long time on the bed, listening to the faint sounds of other people in indeterminate rooms. Her elbow's sore, what does she mean, her elbow's sore? An overblown design of fat yellow roses covered the duvet

293

set, and she was struck by the expressions of hopeless suffering in the eyes of the fishes in the old prints on the walls. She lay back slowly against the bolster.

> *Oh Geraldine, I'd give the world*
> *To live again the lovely past,*
> *The rose of youth is dew-empearled*
> *But now it withers in the blast.*

Years later she'd found he'd stolen it all from an old song called 'Sweet Genevieve'. Once she'd heard it played very slowly on a weeping violin and now, whenever she was in a certain mood, it wandered through her mind, and she'd supply the words:

> *I see your face in every star*
> *My waking thoughts are all of thee,*
> *Thy glance is in the starry beam*
> *That falls upon the summer sea —*

It was such a sweet sound, the tune softly rising and swooning downwards again, full of the glorious romance of mortality. How could her mother resist? He ranged far and wide to steal his words, but then her mother would never have known. As far as she was concerned, they were all him.

Oh Geraldine, sweet Geraldine,
The years may come, the years may go
But still the hands of memory weave
Those dear dead days of long ago.

She'd got the words wrong there somewhere, she was sure. Many of his cribs Anita only realised years later when she became more familiar with English literature. She lit a cigarette. It wasn't sex with Paddy Riley, she thought, though she'd had sticky heats in her body; it was romance, pure and simple adolescent romance, teeny-bop idol agony. She did her make-up and put on her silk knickers and the pink and grey dress. Now that she really thought about it, she wasn't sure she really wanted sex with Michael either. Suddenly she was tired.

★ ★ ★

She went over to the pub across the road where he waited at a corner table drinking a beer. It was dark. Behind the bar was a chalkboard list of about twenty or thirty different cocktails so she chose one at random. It had a little red umbrella and felt as if it was skinning her throat.

He put his hand on hers. 'Here we are,' he said.

Of course she'd told him this made no

difference to the way they were but everything would change now anyway, she knew that.

She smiled at him. 'Here we are indeed.'

'You're not getting cold feet?'

'How could I now?'

'That's not what you should say.' He gave her hand a little shake and started examining it with both of his, spreading the fingers, probing between them, pushing at the palm with his thumb. 'You're supposed to say: no Michael, I'm not getting cold feet. I've never been more sure of anything in my life.'

'But it wouldn't be true.'

He sighed. 'Lie to me sometimes,' he said, sitting close, his head inclining over her. 'That's all I ask. Just lie a little bit now and then.'

'You get the truth,' she said, 'and the truth shall make you free.'

He pushed her away and folded his arms. 'It's not fair. You lie to him all the time but you never lie to me. Why can't you lie to me? Why am I always the one who has to take the truth on the chin?'

She had another cocktail. The second was better.

'There's no one like you,' she said, growing bold with drink. 'That's why you have to take the truth on the chin, because there's no one else like you. You are so strong and unique, you can take this.'

'You've got me all wrong. I can't,' he said, 'I can't take it at all. I'll probably end up hating you.'

'I'll never hate you. Whatever happens I'll never hate you. I'll always still be your friend.'

'You won't.'

She kissed him. That always sorted him out because then he could never stop, just went on and on, his eyelids flickering.

'It's like we're on our honeymoon,' he said.

'Our first night. It's funny to be here, not here the pub, I mean here the hotel. I don't like hotels, I've just realised. It's so peculiar and institutionalised. It emphasises our not belonging. It's like Limbo. That's where we are, we're in Limbo. We're like the lost babies.'

'The lost babies of Limbo,' he said, got up and went to the juke box and hung over it. His face illuminated by its glare was one she'd never seen before, a ghoul with creases in its neck. He put on Talking Heads, 'Once In A Lifetime'.

'I was looking for 'Halfway to Paradise',' he said when he returned, 'but they didn't seem to have it,' and immediately after: 'You'll never leave him, will you?'

'No.'

'I wish he'd die!' He spoke with gritted teeth and a sudden shifty sideways look.

'Don't say that! That's horrible!'

'I do, I wish he'd die! Just not exist. I wish he'd never existed.'

'Don't say it.'

'It's true, it's the truth. You've got to face the truth too, Anita. This is how you're making me feel.'

Nevermore our courtly love, she thought. She hated the twentieth century sometimes. Why could it not have worked? She felt infinitely sad, as if it were the end of something rather than the beginning.

Then he laughed and grabbed her hand. 'Drink that,' he said. 'You can't escape now.'

⋆   ⋆   ⋆

How did it go, the first fuck in three years? OK, she supposed. Perhaps the lycanthropic look of him had influenced his technique, for he growled a low rattle in his throat like a threatened dog as, all hard bone and stretched sinew, he ground himself through her. He seemed in fear and pain. My darling, calm down, calm down, she wanted to say, it's only sex. She couldn't really see him. For her it was as if she'd sent in a proxy, someone who'd read the book of his attraction and

298

knew it all in theory but couldn't quite make the connection with him in the flesh. He was lovely naked, of course, no one could possibly have known it better than she did, but to hold him naked against her, strange and hard and jumpy, with a tough thinness like a racing animal, that was new. Long ago she had learned a trick or two. She had found that perfection was not required as long as you flaunted what you'd got with enough conviction. He was a sucker, a licker, a hanger-on, a hard worker. But nothing moved her.

She was no longer infectious but she couldn't go to Dymphna's wedding because of the spots and scabs that still made her look like an illustration for the plague of boils. Because of this she also couldn't take a message to Paddy, and her mother grew sulky and snappy with everyone, even her. Her mother couldn't get away herself, and Robin was at home too because of the summer holidays. There was a terrible atmosphere in the house. Anita's father and mother had had a huge row because he didn't want to go to Dymphna's wedding, and the air between them was tight and sick. Her mother said her father showed no respect for her family, he looked down on them if the truth were known. 'Ridiculous,' he said, but he was adamant, and when the day came Robin went off with her mother and Connie and Ian and the cousins in a big car, and Anita stayed at home with her father.

She didn't want to go out because of her face, but at one o'clock, after she'd served him up his cheese on toast and lemon tea, he put down his paper and stood up.

'Fancy a walk, Anita?'

'I don't like,' she said. 'Look at my face.'

He peered at her and laughed. 'No one's going to be looking at your face, little madam.'

'I'll stay home,' she said. But her father had made up his mind to this walk, he wanted company and he didn't want to leave her in the house on her own. They took a bus to town then another to Cheetham Hill, and walked around what had been old Hightown in the Jewish quarter. He still held her hand crossing roads, though she was nearly as big as he was. It was a dusty summer afternoon and the whole place was under the bulldozer.

'I used to go down here,' he said, 'with your Uncle Lou and your Uncle David.'

Uncle Lou and Uncle David. She had a picture of them in her mind though she'd never even seen a photograph. He never spoke of them, or of her cousins Sylvia and Adrian and Jessie, or of his father. Occasionally he mentioned his mother, how she'd waded in in her skirts to get him when he fell in the water at Heaton Park, how she spat three times to ward off bad luck.

From time to time he stopped and stood, looking at what was left of the houses and boarded-up shops. His deep brown eyes were glazed with tears.

'That was old Levy's Cap Works,' he said.

'Did you ever work there?'

'No.' He smiled. 'I was only nine when we moved from here to Broughton Park.'

They went to Bellott St Park, where he used to play. 'Look at it,' he said, shaking his head. 'Look at it, it's tiny!'

These scenes of demolition were his past, lost once and now twice. They were clearing the slums, clearing the traces of all that he had given up for her mother and Robin, and for her. Her father was in another world that day. Already he'd left her far behind. What about us? she thought. What about us? What they were, the four of them huddled together in that little house. Everything would change if her mother and Paddy Riley were really in love. They'd all have to go and live with Paddy Riley in his little flat over the top of the hardware store. Never again would she hear her father play his mandolin in the night.

She could not allow that. She thought: if Paddy Riley went away, her mother would forget him in the end and everything would go back to how it was.

But he would not go away.

She thought: if Paddy Riley should die.

———————

There was something proprietorial about the way he gripped her shoulder next day as they strolled about Covent Garden. That was what Candy had been like. Sometimes he'd felt like an arresting policeman. Passing the eternal family of jugglers and human statues, the essential thing about Quack Fair, she thought suddenly, was that it was all fake. They *weren't* parti-coloured fools tripping off the edge of a cliff. They *weren't* medieval. They were just ordinary fucked-up late-twentieth century folk playing Robin Hood. They hadn't got a clue what they were.

Michael put his arms around her. 'I don't know how I ever got into this,' he said, 'I don't know how I ever allowed myself to be so stupid.'

Here, clothed and out in the world, she could see him again. She combed his hair with her fingers. 'You've changed,' she said, 'it was never meant to be anything more than it was. It was never meant to be this.'

'But it is,' he replied, 'you can't do anything about that, it just is,' and when she looked at his eyes she thought his long hard look had a touch of fanaticism.

★ ★ ★

They did the secondhand bookshops in the afternoon, and ate at the Soho Friend that night. 'I should do some drawing,' she said over coffee.

'Your alibi.' He poured the last of the wine.

She laughed. 'It's so funny, so funny us being here like this. I just can't come to terms with it. We don't feel the same.'

'What do you mean?'

'I mean it's just weird. Like we're not real people at all.'

'*I* feel real. I am real.'

No no, she thought, you are a figment of my imagination, and just for a second she understood how a psychopath could really believe it was true. She took his hand. 'Don't be so serious, Michael. Nothing's changed. I'm still your best friend. I promised you, didn't I? Nothing's changed.'

'What are you, stupid or something?' He gave her a sharp look, tossed a cigarette into his mouth. 'That's just the problem.

Nothing's changed.'

'We agreed,' she said.

'We agreed!' He flung himself forward on his elbow, sticking his scowling face into hers. 'You naive twat! Things *do* change! We agreed!'

'Don't you talk to me like that!'

'Did we sign anything? No! See. Here.' His shoulders went back, his hands arched, holding an imaginary piece of paper in the air. 'Our agreement,' he spat, tearing it up and tossing it away. 'Void.'

The bill came. Michael looked at it, lit his cigarette and said, 'What would you think if I said I was going to tell Charley?'

She stared at him.

'After all,' he continued with fury in his eyes, 'bring it all out into the open. You know. Spread a little truth around. That's what you're always going on about, isn't it? You explain it all to him like you explain it all to me. Give *him* a little bit of the truth. What do you think?'

Anita froze.

'You dare say a word to Charley! You dare do a thing like that!'

'And what?'

'I'll kill you.'

The words made her sick. Tears ran out of the corners of her eyes, strangely symmetrical.

'I will never speak to you again,' she said, 'I promise you I will never speak to you again.'

He looked down, frowning, swallowing audibly. 'What cards have you got on you?' he asked in a strangled voice. 'How are we paying for this?'

'Oh God!' She rummaged in her bag and threw the card down on the table. 'What have you got left?'

When she looked up he was staring at her with a peculiar fixed smile on his face. 'I've got nothing to speak of,' he said, reaching out and rubbing away her tears with his thumbs. His eyes looked very soft, as if they loved her, and she started to cry discreetly.

'Don't tell him!' she said.

Michael smiled and shook his head. 'I won't,' he said. 'Not yet anyway.'

The waiter came and took away her card.

'Well, I can't get much more out of our account,' she said, sniffing and reaching for one of his cigarettes, 'not without arousing suspicion.'

'Oh dear dear.' He drooped over his wine glass, muttering dryly, cocky again. 'Mustn't do that, must we? I'll ring my mum. She'll send me something. She'll wire it.'

'What?' Anita said. 'Just like that?'

'Well, I'll have to talk to her, of course.'

Nice if you can, she thought. It's funny

how long you can know someone and still not know them. She'd thought he was just getting by, now she found he was kept by Mum and Dad. Funny how all these weird wild wonderful souls seemed to come from posh beginnings. John's brother rode to hounds. Funny how many of them she'd ended up with. Funny how Charley was the only one from a poor background.

★ ★ ★

Back in the hotel room Michael rang his parents, late as it was. They were still up. His father came on but you could tell it was really his mother he wanted to speak to, she was obviously the softer touch. Anita sat propped up with pillows on the yellow-rose duvet cover, drawing a lake and some mountains from memory. First he had to talk to his father for a while, then she heard him explaining that it was because he was in London and London eats money, and he'd settle it all up at the end of the month. She heard the gentle unintelligible drone of the doting mother, making it all better, then he covered the mouthpiece negligently and said in a half-whisper: 'What's my account number?'
'How the hell do I know?'

'Get my card out of my wallet.'

'How do I know where your wallet is?'

'Fuck's sake, Anita . . . hang on a sec, Mum.'

She watched him stalk about the room looking for his wallet, wondering at his strangeness, the strangeness of a stranger. As he passed he made a sudden dive, grasped her crudely between the legs and tipped her over so that her sketch book fell on to the floor. She sprawled back, open-legged. Might as well just have sex, she thought, beautiful and thoughtless, and that's what they did when the money was all sorted. About three, he fell asleep with one hand clutching her hair so tightly she had to prise his fingers apart one by one to get free, making him twitch in sleep in annoyance.

She couldn't doze off. She looked at the outline of his face in the dark and tried to imagine living with him all the time as she did with Charley. He'd never really love the girls, she thought, not like she and Charley did. She imagined him being there all the time, every morning, every evening, when she was sick, when she was ugly. He turned over against her, dead asleep, burning like a radiator. When she moved, his hand came up, opening like a flower about her face. He murmured in his sleep and she kissed him, whispering soothing nothings. At last she found herself dreaming. She knew it was a dream because she was being rowed by Paddy Riley in a boat on a lake. It was hot summer, the glare from the sun blinding. The lake was somewhere like Italy but at the same time it was the big boating lake at Belle Vue with the sign saying This Way Round. Then the scene changed. She was in a house that was not her own, and Michael was dead. She'd killed him and put him under the floor-boards but she knew she couldn't leave him there. Someone would find him. She had to take him somewhere else, somewhere in the country, somewhere where he'd never be found so that no one would ever know that it was she who'd killed him. A boreen, a fence, wet hedges, a dark sky. No one to help her in her lonely task. She took him out there in a car, the weather was miserable. She was going to leave him in the great wet outdoors, though she loved him, and the knowledge that he was gone was unbearable. When he is under, she thought, when he is under he will never have existed. He will never rise up. Dead was dead and grief was a rock.

★   ★   ★

'I dreamed I was disposing of your body,' she said on the tube to King's Cross.

'It figures.'

When she'd woken up, the relief to find him lying there alive and peacefully sleeping was so great she had almost prayed.

'What did you do with me?' he asked, fiddling with the ticket between his fingers. 'Chop me up into little pieces? Distribute me all over the country?'

'I don't know. I don't think it got that far. It wasn't gruesome, it was just sad.'

She'd been thinking she'd quite like to do a drawing of the tube train, but it would be a bit of a giveaway. Really she ought to go to Richmond Park or somewhere and bodge up something that would do as Scotland.

They went to see where he used to live in King's Cross. It was behind an Indian restaurant and the smell out the back was delicious. They had tea with an old friend of his, a hawk-faced man with an eerie smile, who never looked at her once. The conversation was all of people she didn't know. A round-faced boy of about eighteen with prematurely grey hair appeared and turned out to be the son of another old friend, and they had a long talk about the film *Reservoir Dogs*. They ate in the Indian restaurant for old times' sake. The boy, whose name was

Jacob, tagged along and talked about his plans to go to drama school. She had Kashmiri Lamb with naan bread and Aloo Sag on the side. There was a sense of dread in her bones and it took her some time to ascribe it to her dreams of the night before.

The money had come from Michael's mother and he was throwing it about, treating the lad, making much of him, ordering more wine. She looked at him but couldn't see him again. This is the man who suckled me till I was sore last night, she thought, drinking down the rich red wine. He is forty-one now. His eyes are wrinkled. He has a son.

She took him to Summer Court, but there was nobody left there that she knew. She stood in the courtyard with Michael and he held her hand as she pointed out her old flat. She remembered the time she put the sleeping bag over the lost soul, somebody's son out in the cold. It was eerie standing there like a ghost from another time, and she remembered Candy and Mad John and Rory Gotch and all the others. Probably wouldn't even recognise Candy now. Last time she heard from Leah, she said he'd shaved his head. He looked stylish bald, she said, pretty and slightly brutal.

When Anita stood in the stairwell she felt faint. The same graffiti was there on the same wall and the hairs pricked up all over her body. By the pricking of my thumbs something wicked this way comes. She liked that book. She liked the mad carnival and the carousel that went backwards, making people young. She looked at Michael, so young and old in the dim throat of the building, felt the shadow of her dream fall across him and wanted to save him; so she gave him a vampire kiss, there in the stairwell, with such tender passion that she might have been an ancient queen pleasuring her sacrificial king the night before his death. He weakened against her, moving slowly like a cat.

She took him in the local pub where they'd gone on Candy's thirty-fifth birthday. She remembered they'd sat together, she and Candy, in a corner booth with their backs against the shiny red leather, facing the action in the big, flash, brash bar, and that they had had absolutely nothing left to say to one another, nothing at all. She and Michael had a drink at a table she remembered sitting at. He took out of his bag his battered old copy of *The Little Bookroom*. 'I met you in a little bookroom,' he said.

They went back to the hotel. On the tube, matching his thigh with hers, she grew hard with desire. Getting off, they did not speak but wound their fingers neurotically together and walked scarcely touching out of the tube station, down the street, up the hushed stairs, into their room. They looked wordlessly at each other for a moment, then took off their clothes.

★ ★ ★

Michael was in the shower when the mobile bleeped. She flushed with shame. Charley. She was lying in bed but could reach out easily for the phone.

'What are you doing?' Charley asked.

Her heart jumped. It was his tone of voice.

'I'm, I'm . . . ' Her brain was blank. 'I've just had dinner.'

'Where are you?' he said. 'I know you're not in Scotland. I know you're with Michael.'

She felt physically sick and doubled over as if she'd received a blow. 'Oh, Charley,' she said weakly.

'Anita?'

She didn't know why but her first thought was that Alison had told. But *she* didn't know. How could she?

'Anita, will you tell me what's going on?'

'Oh, Charley,' she said, and giggled, completely out of control. 'What a mess this is.'

Someone told.

There was a dreadful pause. Shower water rattled against the glass panel in the bathroom.

'A mess?' She knew his face from his voice. It was pained. When he really got upset he could never hide it. 'A mess?' His voice got higher. 'Is that all this is, just a mess? What have you done, Anita?'

'Oh, Charley, don't please, don't please get upset, I'll come home now. It'll be all right, I promise you. I'll come home straight away.'

'What are you doing?' he cried again, and his voice broke down.

'Oh, Charley . . . '

He shouted down the phone, 'You *are* with him! I can't believe this! I can't . . . I can't believe it!'

She couldn't speak.

'You bitch, Anita,' he mumbled tearfully and put down the phone.

She sat there with her heavy white breasts hanging helpless, listening to the shower water, then the sounds of Michael's wet feet slapping on the floor. She thought if she moved she might be sick.

The sword had fallen. The wicked thing had come.

★   ★   ★

313

A wild plan to lie: say Michael knew someone in a gallery to see about the drawings, wanted it to be a surprise.

'Wait!' He stood bemused, face pale and stary-eyed, hair sticking out all round. A white towel was wrapped round his waist. 'Wait, Anita,' he said vaguely, 'don't just dash off like this, think. Think. There might be something we can do.'

Too late.

'Do? Michael, he *knows*!' she almost screamed, pushing things into her bag. 'He *knows*!' She'd dressed quickly in the first thing she found on the floor, the pink and grey dress. Tears streamed down her face.

'But he can't know,' said Michael in a weird, calm voice. 'He's guessing.'

She felt physically sick. She heard herself babble uselessly: 'Don't ask me how but he knows! Oh God, Michael, what can we do? What can we do? This is awful! Oh, my God!'

He put his arms round her, all steamy from the shower. 'Ssh,' he said, 'it'll be all right.'

'How *can* it be?'

'Ssh.' He started kissing her, leisurely, seriously kissing as if nothing had happened and they had all the time in the world. She thought he must have gone mad.

'I can't do this now!'

'You're free now,' he said. 'He knows. The

truth has made you free.'

'No!'

He drew back his head and frowned at her, brows jutting. There was thundery weather in his eyes, though when he spoke his voice was still calm and quiet. 'Wait,' he said simply, 'wait, Anita.'

Then they stood apart and she felt suddenly calm too. This part at least was over.

'I will be in touch,' she told him gently. 'I promise. I just have to sort this out, Michael. I can't think at all clearly at the moment. I just have to go home and sort this out.'

He lay down naked and watched her, scowling as she got her things together, then when she was ready and stood by the door took a great bound from the bed as if he were going to attack her, landing on the balls of his feet beside her and hunching there like a demon. He was an ache in her body, an ache in her chest.

'That's right,' he hissed, 'you go. You go running.'

'I'll be in touch,' she repeated softly.

He grinned bitterly but did not speak. She put her hand upon his neck and kissed him goodbye. 'I'll see you,' she said.

'You fucking won't,' he muttered, 'not if you can help it, you won't. I'm finished with now, aren't I? This bit on the side has had its day.'

She couldn't cope with the hate in his face, so turned and left him, closing the door softly and almost running to the top of the stairs. Later she never remembered how she got to the station or anything at all about the journey, apart from the fact that she had one of those funny gaps of time to fill in before her train, the kind where you don't quite know if it's worth going for a coffee or not; she felt sick anyway and wasn't sure that the actual smell of one under her nose wouldn't push her over the top. She just walked up and down on the concourse, looking at the books and magazines and trying not to think. She didn't even ask the obvious questions, such as how could he possibly know? Who betrayed her? High on adrenaline, she was in some dreadful endurance mode, danger antennae raised like all the terrible times, all the packed-away times, on the street, going through all that Paddy Riley stuff.

Not again, she pleaded. Not again.

———————

She was angry with her mother for making her take a message to Paddy Riley when her face was still covered in fading chicken pox scabs. She was better really, but now Robin

316

had come down with the mumps, and her mother was rushed off her feet, fussing and petting and baby-talking him till she'd have driven a saint mad.

'I can't go like this!' Anita moaned.

She was terrified he'd think it was a sudden dose of acne; it could happen to people, Denise had got it quite suddenly.

'Oh don't be silly.' Her mother was in the middle of making a hot poultice for Robin's face. 'They're fading off now, you can hardly see them. He probably won't even notice.'

Her face was nothing. Her mother reduced her to that, just a kid with a face not worth noticing.

'OK,' she said, seething.

Robin screamed when she wrapped the poultice round his face. 'Oh, my Robbie-boo!' her mother cried, 'my baby-baby!'

It wasn't fair. Her and Paddy messing me about, she thought, messing my dad about. She wanted to hit them both. She wanted to cry. Suddenly when she thought of them together it was gross and sick-making.

'OK.' Her mother lit one of the fat cigarettes with big filter tips she'd lately started smoking. 'Now write this.'

Anita got a bit of paper from the drawer and sat poised with her pen.

'Right now,' her mother said, taking a deep

breath: 'Paddy dear, sorry it's been so long Anita's been bad with chicken pox. Is Thursday one all right for you. Just send back yes or no or if not when. Best love Geraldine.'

She didn't write such a good love letter as he did. No thees and thys for her.

Anita walked up to Crowcroft Park and sat down on a bench. She read her own big, flat, loopy writing from Geraldine to Paddy. She could stop them. She could write anything: Paddy, I will run away with you tonight. Paddy, go boil your head. Anything at all. They used her. Her mother didn't care about her having the chicken pox, she only cared because she couldn't run errands. That was the truth. She only cared about herself and Paddy Riley. But Anita could stop them, the silly fools, they wouldn't stop themselves. She just wouldn't go. Why should she? She just wouldn't deliver but she'd not tell them, and each one would think the other had just stopped bothering and give up, and everything would get back to normal in the end.

That's what she'd do.

———

Maybe she fell asleep on the train. She didn't know, it grew dark while she was travelling, and the feel of the station and the street outside was late and deserted when

318

she got off. She was surprised when she looked at her watch to discover that it was only just turned ten, but then as the taxi passed Jak's corner she saw that the soldier clock said quarter to twelve. She felt as if she were in the opening shots of a Bergman film. For a moment her head spun and she had no idea where she was going, just that she wanted to go home but home was home no more and she could never go back there, she had no home. Home never lasted. Fortunately the taxi driver wasn't talkative. She laid her head back and felt sorry for herself, feeling in the dark every familiar bend and pothole of these lanes.

The light was on in the hall. She paid the man off outside the gate and tried to open and close it without making a sound, tip-toed through the gravel and stood for a moment listening to the silence in the tree-tops, trying to get her key into the lock without a sound. Dread mingled with relief at the comforts of familiarity. An owl called, very close. How normal to be letting herself into her own house like this, the hall just as it always was with mess all over the table and discarded shoes lying around to trip a person up. She listened. No sound anywhere. The girls should be home by now. They must all be in bed. She went into the kitchen and turned on the light and checked the time against her watch. Five past midnight. Her watch had stopped. The kitchen looked no worse than usual. Charley had made coffee in the machine earlier and left a big mess of spilled grounds on one of the surfaces. Basil lay in his den so deep in sleep she thought at first he was dead. His tongue stuck out between his snaggle teeth, absolutely dry and foul, and there seemed to be no movement of breath going in or out. But then he made a soft, staggered grunting sound and exhaled with all the energy of a slow puncture. Two grey stones and a fragment of old yellowed bone lay between his paws.

She heard Charley's bare feet coming downstairs.

They met in the hall. He looked very pale and blank and was wearing his ripped blue shirt and oldest jeans, all covered with dust from the wall as if he'd just left off working on it. 'Let's go in here,' he said in a hushed tone as if someone had died, ushering her into the living room and turning the lamp on. The girls' clothes and toys were tossed about here and there. A newspaper stack that should have been emptied a week ago had fallen over.

She felt like an awkward visitor.

'Charley,' she said, 'everything's all right,'

and put her hands over her mouth and laughed. It was terrible, it just came out, she couldn't stop, she couldn't stop it, though really she wanted to cry. She couldn't speak. She sank down on the settee with her hand over her brow and laughed till her chest felt it would burst.

He didn't laugh at all. She couldn't look at him.

'Anita,' he said, 'why did you go to London with Michael?'

She sighed, looking up at him. 'Why do you think?'

There was a terrible moment of silence. His arms were folded, his face eerily still, unreadable. With the set of his head, the heaviness of his cheeks, his loose, childlike lips slightly apart, he reminded her of a boy in trouble, unsure of what was coming next.

'Oh God, Charley, this is a mess!' she said. 'I'm sorry, I'm so sorry, my love.'

'I keep waiting for you to deny it,' he said. 'I keep thinking it's all a dream.'

'How did you know?'

'Luke told me.'

'Luke?'

Of course. Some of the looks he had given her towards the end.

'Yeah.'

'Luke told you?'

'Yeah, Luke told me.'

'Well, what did he say?'

'He rang up. I can't remember exactly what he said, just that you were in London with his dad and he was annoyed because his dad had promised to take him to London soon and he was still waiting.'

All this was delivered deadpan.

'Luke?'

He sat down and leaned forward, loosely linking his hands in front of him. 'And that was it,' he said. 'I thought yes she is, of course she is, yes, and suddenly it seemed so obvious I couldn't believe it.' He was so calm she began to think everything might be all right after all. 'Go on then.' He gave the slightest shrug. 'What's been happening?'

When she went home and said there was no reply, that he seemed OK, he'd given her a shilling for her troubles but said there was no reply, her mother sat down, frowning and biting her lip. Robin, on his settee bed, looked miserable with the white bandage round his face. Her mother had the fire lit and low though it was August, and huddled and scowled over it till it was time to get up and make the tea. She didn't speak to Anita's father all night, though as he wasn't talking much to *her* either, it didn't really make a lot of difference.

Next morning she put stockings on and told Anita not to go out, she wanted her to keep an eye on Robin while she went somewhere. Anita ate her toast, watching her mother with a growing sense of dread. She'd go to see him and say *What's all this about no reply?* and he'd say: *No reply to what?* and they'd know Anita had lied. Her mother was putting lipstick on, staring blandly at herself in the mirror. 'I wish I still had that blonde wig,' she said, catching Anita's eye in the glass.

'The mermaid wig?'

She nodded. 'I wish I had a photo of me when I was a mermaid. Just for a laugh. But that blonde wig — ' she pulled at her hair — 'I could do with it now.'

The doorbell rang. It was Dymphna with an envelope of photographs, yet more of the wedding, so her mother couldn't go out just yet and Anita was saved. She had to act fast. She ran upstairs. She still had the line he'd written down:

You are the Sunday in every week.

It was enough. She studied it carefully, practised feverishly while the muffled voices

323

of her mother and Dymphna came up
through the floorboards, then wrote in
his flowery style and very small neat
handwriting:

Dearest Geraldine,

I hope this letter finds you well. I have
thought very much about things whilst not
seeing you for a while. I will always love
you, dearest Geraldine, whose beauty to
me is as a lovely tea rose growing on the
wall at Alton Towers. But we must not meet
again. Don't be sad, my love for ever,
Paddy.

P.S. I mean this. It has been a very hard
decision, please don't make it even harder
by getting in touch with me. Goodbye.

Anita looked at it critically. She didn't think
he'd have spelled decision right, but her
mother would never know about that. The tea
rose she got from the time they'd gone on the
train to Alton Towers. The tea roses were
massive, like babies' heads, but graceful and
tremulous and dreadfully perfect, and they
gave off a heavy scent that filled the air and
made you want to swoon. She decided to
cut that bit out, however; after all, he might
have said something to her about never
having gone to Alton Towers: let's have a

day out at Alton Towers, he might have said, I've never been there. So she cut out 'growing on the wall at Alton Towers'. Then she added, 'my dearest Geraldine' again, after 'I mean this', because she thought the original looked a bit brusque. She thought it needed some elaboration after 'we must not meet again.' 'You have a husband,' she added quickly, then wrote it all out a second time and read it through. It sounded like a hammy actor getting up and falling down in his death throes again and again, but there was no time for anything else. She sneaked out and lurked uneasily around the signposts at the top of the road, keeping watch on the house. On the main road the traffic was quite heavy. She sat on the wall and crossed one leg over the other. Whenever the cars came up to the sign that said: HALT at Major Road Ahead, they slowed right down and sometimes came to a stop. Sometimes two or three built up. A man in a blue truck whistled at her while he waited. She ignored him. 'Pretty knees,' he said in a low voice. His face was a dark blur.

She didn't tell him everything, of course. 'We didn't actually do anything,' she said, 'we didn't actually do anything until a day or two ago.'

'Depends what you mean by anything,' he murmured.

She talked, her eyes blurring over and her muscles quivering, knew nothing of what she was saying apart from the fact that she must be honest, must tell as much of the truth as she could, hammer it flat between them till he understood how it had really been.

His eyes, firm and steady, never once changed, though his hands stiffened as she talked. Occasionally she even thought he was going to smile.

'We were just very good friends,' she finished.

He actually laughed at that. It is, she thought, it is going to be all right.

'Couldn't you come up with a better cliché?' he asked.

The traffic moved off and she stretched out her legs. She was wearing ankle socks and a pair of blue shoes with a little heel that used to belong to Dymphna. Her legs were better than Dymphna's though, they sloped down to the ankle instead of bulging out. It wasn't fair that Dymphna always had nice clothes when *she* had to go about in rags. Can't afford it, can't afford it, her mother always said. She was going to buy some stockings. And another bra, she'd ask her mother again. Her breasts were the biggest in her class at school. She could get a lad OK. They didn't scare her. She could get a lad.

But Paddy Riley was stuck in her somewhere like a splinter she couldn't get out, and whenever she thought of him, a dark cloud of fear came and hovered just above her eyes.

———

She jumped as his hand hit the table like an explosion.

'What else were you doing?' he said, just as quietly as before.

Anita looked to see if there was blood. It must have hurt, she thought, it must have hurt his hand.

She couldn't speak, though thoughts fell through her mind, that she must explain herself; that she'd been on top with Michael, that Charley was the rock, the solid one, that he should have known back then when she took his arm on the promenade, there'd never been any doubt, *you have to understand the way I am, mein Herr*; that she'd never pulled the wool over his eyes, not his, she'd always been honest and straight, and she loved him anyway, anyway; and that if he was honest too, he'd know it was the danger that had drawn him in.

But she couldn't speak.

He stood by the dark window looking out. Tears began to trickle down his face.

I have been mad, she thought, hating herself.

She saw Dymphna leave. She gave it ten minutes or so then sauntered in. Her mother was in the back kitchen putting plates in the rack over the top of the stove. Robin was in bed on the settee watching TV. Her mother sang:

'*Let him go, let him tarry,*
Let him sink or let him swim . . .

. . . and where have you been, pray may I ask?'

Anita said she'd been to see Denise but she wasn't in.

'Well you've no right to go sloping off like that! I thought I told you I wanted you to stay here.'

'Well, Dymphna came.'

'So what?'

And then Anita gave her the letter and she looked at it with a nowty face and walked into the back kitchen. Anita followed.

'I'm sorry, Mum,' she said awkwardly. 'I

328

knew you were upset so I went over to Paddy's when Denise wasn't in and I told him you were annoyed that he hadn't sent you any reply, so he said to bring you this. I'm really sorry, Mum.'

'What are you on about?' her mother snapped, and slapped her across the face. Anita was so shocked she burst into tears.

'Honest?' he cried so loudly she thought he might wake the girls, his face breaking up. 'Oh, you wanted to be honest! You weren't very honest with *me*, were you?'

He cried then with childlike abandon, face all droopy, mouth a slack grimace.

'You're sorry!' His voice cracked.

She went to him but he flinched and warded her off with one raised arm and a fist, face all wet. 'For Christ's sake! Don't you dare to touch me just now.'

She knelt upon the carpet and watched him cry. Her own tears had eased off, but her eyes felt stiff. A low buzzing started in her ears. Charley's crying became bitter and muffled, full of long sniffs and pathetic gurglings in his throat. His eyes, when finally he opened them and looked at her again, were desolate.

'I should have known,' he said. His nose

sounded blocked. 'He was always more your friend than mine.'

'It's all right, Charley,' she said, 'it's over now, I promise you it's over.'

He didn't have a tissue and sniffed and wiped his nose with the back of his fingers. 'I mean, I don't know, I can't believe that you did this anyway. Do you love him?'

There was no answer.

'I want the truth, Anita,' he said, and his voice shook. 'Don't you think it's time I had it?'

The buzzing in her head was like a faraway swarm. 'I do love him,' she said through it, 'but not in the same way.'

His eyes closed.

———————

'You've no bloody right going up there asking people for messages when I've not sent you! Let him bloody rot! I'm not chasing after people begging for messages!'

Anita wiped her eyes, standing up straight and staring her mother out. I am in a lot of trouble, she thought. Her stomach felt queasy and hollow.

'Well, go on,' her mother said, 'read the bloody thing out now it's here.'

Anita missed out all the P.S. in the end. 'Dearest Geraldine,' she read, 'I hope this letter finds you well. I have thought very much about things whilst not seeing you for a while. I will always love you, dearest Geraldine, whose beauty to me is like a lovely tea rose. But we must not meet again. Don't be sad, my love for ever, Paddy.'

Her mother didn't say anything, just scratched her head vaguely as she looked out of the back kitchen window.

'Do you want this, Mum?' Anita said, holding out the letter.

'No,' she replied quietly, and started going about getting the tea in her usual way.

Robin saw Anita's red eyes.

'What's wrong?'

'She hit me,' Anita said.

That night whenever she closed her eyes she saw images of Paddy Riley in his bath or walking across the room naked with a cigarette loosely held between his gentle dove fingers. She clung on to her pillow and tried to force the images away so that she could go to sleep. But when the images retreated the fear rolled in, the terrified realisation that, come what may, her mother would go and see him or he'd contrive to see her and they'd find out what she had done. She couldn't let it happen. But what could she do?

Her brain went round in circles.

———————

A paralysis fell upon them. They might have been frozen by a wizard's pointing finger, her all watery with tears upon the carpet, stiff-kneed and nauseous; he sitting hunched, pale and washed out, wide-eyed at misery. And nothing to be said.

They sat like that for an age, till he lifted the big hand she'd seen soothe her babies asleep, and, very slowly and comfortingly, rubbed the place where his heart was as if it felt sore there.

———————

Her mother's face was awful. She walked about swearing, kicking the cat if it got under her feet, pushing Robin away when he snoozled up to her. Then she cried terribly, arms rigid, hands grasped together, sitting by the fireplace not caring that Robin was staring at her. Her face, turned away at an odd and awkward angle, was strained and clenched and trembling. Racked, thought Anita. Racked.

She felt as if she had shot an arrow into her mother and was watching it slowly fester.

Later, her mother washed her face and started angrily doing her make-up. 'You know, it's his birthday soon,' she told Anita, 'he's going to be 22. What d'you say I give him a nice little present? Something like a sock in the eye?' Then she laughed wildly and started crying again.

Anita went upstairs to where Robin, who was up and about again now, was hovering pale-faced on the landing, his freckles glowing. 'What's up with her?' he whispered. 'We ought to get Auntie Connie or Grandma.'

'Maybe she'll be all right tomorrow,' Anita said.

By the time her father came home her mother had tied up her hair and fixed her make-up again and was walking about hard-faced, plonking things down on the table with constant little angry clearings of the throat. Robin and Anita wouldn't have dreamed of telling their father about the crying. He was grumpy anyway and it would only have made him worse. They just kept out of the way.

Charley looked at his watch. 'I'm very tired,' he said. 'I don't want to talk about this any more tonight. I want to think.'

He sniffed, and wiped the remains of tears from his eyes and the sides of his nose. 'I'm sleeping in the study,' he said.

She too was tired, overwhelmingly, and she was scared. She kept thinking Michael was going to come knocking at the door. The shadow, the demon lover.

'You don't have to sleep in the study,' she croaked.

The steadiness was back in his eyes. 'I know I don't but I want to,' he said, and smiled wanly at her, as if smiling at her was a habit hard to break, before remembering and shaking his head vaguely, getting up abruptly and walking out.

Her knees cracked when she stood up. She followed him towards the kitchen, where he had stopped at Basil's den and was inspecting the old dog.

'Is he dying?' she asked timidly.

Charley rose to his feet. 'I don't know,' he said, moving away from her. 'He doesn't seem to be in any pain. He's not eaten much. I've wet his lips a lot. I don't know if I should. Don't know if we should just let him go.'

They stood there in silence for several moments till he turned and went upstairs and into the bathroom. When she followed she saw through the open study door that he had anticipated, and already made a bed up.

★   ★   ★

She checked on the girls. She didn't want to sleep alone. She could take one of them in with her, but Jasmine was awful to sleep with, she twitched and scratched and sighed and flounced all night. Sid was a good solid little sleeper, but Anita didn't like the look of her, her cheeks were all flushed and she was mumbling a little in her sleep and champing her teeth from time to time.

She stood in their darkened room in their darkened mess and listened to them breathe, and the thought of losing them was worse than anything, worse than the streets, worse than what happened with Paddy Riley. She heard Charley blowing his nose in the bathroom, but when she came out he'd gone into the study and closed the door, so she went back in and sank down on the floor at the foot of Jasmine's bed and stayed there for so long that the things in the room became clear, their things, all their stupid broken dirty little things that they loved.

She went into the bathroom and tried to make herself sick but it didn't work. When she looked in the mirror her make-up had all gone, and her eyes were mad and red and tiny, so she ran from the room and climbed into bed and thought about Michael. Little ape. Where was he? What was he doing now? Had he just gone back to his boat as if nothing had happened? She couldn't imagine the next step along that road. Whenever she saw his face in her mind it was that deep-eyed, suffering look he had, his lips a sulky plateau. What if she ended up with him after all?

They could make something together. It might last a few years. She did love him after all, and there was always something to be made out of that. They couldn't stay here. Impossible. The girls. Impossible. None of this should be passed on to them.

Her blood sounded in her ear against the pillow, like footsteps trudging endlessly through sand. When she turned over it was in the other ear too, regular and mindlessly robotic. The night was full of lurid imaginings. The sea came flooding up from the shore to carry them away. She was on the streets. The streets swallowed her, grey and sinister as an alleyway in the chamber of horrors. She died alone in the doorway of a derelict building. They did not know her name. Anita felt her pink house fading around her like a fairy palace in the first light of morning. She felt her children, the golden naiad and the little fat dark one, slide away down a sucking plug-hole.

Her brain felt like a giant slug oozing in her head. Was he asleep? Why couldn't she just go in now and talk to him, explain. Explain what? She'd done it. She was guilty. But if she could just talk to him, she thought. He had always been so kind.

———

So a couple of days passed with their mother weeping around the place or falling into bouts of catatonia, and always, for Anita, the fear that the bell would ring or a shadow appear in the yard, and it would be Paddy Riley. Anita took to sitting out on the front steps with her legs spread out to catch the sun, in her hand a book whose pages she never turned. Her eyes checked continually all possible approaches to their house. On the third day when he appeared at the mouth of the alley across the road, a crumpled suit loose upon him, a crumpled bunch of big pink daisies hanging down by his side, she ran to him. She had rehearsed this in her mind.

'Paddy,' she said dramatically, 'my dad's home.'

His smile faded. He stared at the house. Her mother would appear at the door any minute and it would all be up with her. She was terrified: her palms sweated, her mouth was dry.

'So what?' he said softly.

She grabbed his arm and hung on. 'Please,

Paddy!' and burst into tears. 'Please don't make trouble!'

'What's the matter with you?' he said, shocked. 'What's this,' touching her face, 'chicken pox?' She hadn't meant to cry, but at once she knew she could use these tears. She ran a little way from him into the alley, and he followed. Good, he was out of sight now if her mother should happen to glance out of a bedroom window while making the beds, or come to the door to see what Anita was doing.

'What is it?' he asked again. 'What's happened? Why hasn't she come?'

'I've been ill,' Anita said.

'No, why didn't *she* come?'

'She did,' Anita said. 'You were out. She wanted to tell you, oh she really did want to tell you herself, Paddy.'

'What?'

'Come away from here,' she said nervously. 'Let's go somewhere else.'

They walked up to Jackson's and sat in the long grass watching the little carriages going along their tracks, carrying rubble.

'It's my dad,' Anita said, twisting the sharp grass round and round her fingers till it hurt, 'he's dying.'

He crossed himself. 'God forgive me,' he murmured. She didn't understand it then, but later she did; 'God forgive me' meant that he was glad.

'He's got cancer,' she said. 'The doctor says he's probably got two or three years left.'

She could see that he believed her. He'd taken her nerves for grief.

'She doesn't think it's fair on him,' she said. 'She doesn't want him upset.'

Paddy made strange delicate movements with his left hand before putting his forehead into it.

'She wants you to promise not to come round, she said. She thinks it's better this way. I would have come and told you before, but I've been stuck in for ages with this stupid chicken pox.'

Lies, lies, they thrived and multiplied.

Paddy stared at her, his knuckles in his mouth. Oh, he was a handsome, charming young thing, Paddy Riley. No doubt about it.

She felt as if she were sinking in quicksand. All this time she'd been thinking, if I just do this, say that, all this will stop. But it never did. Every move just sucked her down more into the muck.

★ ★ ★

The trouble was, people weren't predictable. How could she have known he would become this melancholy phantom beside her, with his glowing skin and huge staring eyes? He was the knight-at-arms in the poem 'La Belle Dame Sans Merci' that they had done at school. Oh what can ail thee? He jerked into life, searched his pockets frantically. 'Take this,' he said, and scribbled on an envelope. 'Give her this and come and see me tomorrow no matter what she says or anything. Just come. Come before six.'

She left him. She looked back once and saw him dark against the sky, alone and palely loitering, still holding his big pink daisies but with no one to give them to.

On Pink Bank Lane she stopped and read his note. It said: *Dearest Jewel, Prescous Jewel, I am very very sorry for your trouble but don't turn me away or I will go mad. Send me by the girl some word return please. Send me anything. Paddy. I'm scared of what I might do.*

Send me by the girl.

The girl?

The girl?

The cat's mother?

* * *

When she got back Robin was riding idly up and down the alley on his bike and her mother was slamming around in the kitchen in a terrible mood. 'Where've you been?' she cried. 'I'm sick of you doing this, going off as if you own the place, leaving the door open and your book on the step, what am I supposed to think? You might have been kidnapped for all I know.'

'Well, I wasn't,' Anita said.

'I suppose you went up to Denise's.'

'No, I didn't as a matter of fact. I went to Belle Vue.'

'Oh.'

Anita sat down at the table and started picking up grains of salt from the cloth with her fingertip, putting them on the tip of her tongue and feeling it recoil.

'Don't suppose you saw a sign of His Majesty while you were there?' her mother asked sourly, turning to the grate and straightening the fire irons.

'I did actually. He was on the Bobs.'

'He's on that?'

'Not working,' Anita said, 'he was *on* it. Riding on it. With that blonde girl we saw him with once.'

Her mother was cleaning round the grate viciously, her strong arm making wide circular motions. 'The one with the arse on her like a barrage balloon,' she said.

Anita laughed nervously, unsure why she'd

341

said that about the blonde girl. She'd just wanted to close another door.

'Did he talk to you?' her mother asked.

'Of course he didn't. He was on the Bobs.'

'Was he with her like? You know. Did he have his arm round her or anything?'

Anita had to think about that. 'I think he did,' she said.

Robin came in wanting a jam butty and her mother told him in a clipped voice no, it would ruin his tea. When he argued, she screamed at him, making them both jump: 'I said no! No! It'll ruin your tea, you stupid boy!' threw down her cloth and walked from the room. Robin and Anita looked at each other.

'Screwy,' Anita whispered, pointing to her head. She followed her mother upstairs.

Her mother had composed herself and was fixing her makeup in front of her dressing-table. 'I hate this dress,' she said.

'Get a new one then.'

She snorted.

★   ★   ★

The next day was a Saturday and very hot. As soon as Anita woke up she remembered she had to go to see Paddy Riley this afternoon. There's no reply, she'd tell him. No reply. Don't make things any harder for her than

342

they already are, please, dear Paddy.

A kind of fixed tension had taken her over. She couldn't eat anything. She couldn't remember why she was doing what she was doing but it didn't matter, only the next move mattered now that she was in so deep. She had to think very hard to remember that it was for her father she was doing all this, for her father playing his mandolin alone downstairs late at night. At first the remembrance of this, and his real stony-faced presence in the house, made her feel weepy; but strangely, as she sleepwalked through the morning, watching her mother very closely for any signs of aberrant behaviour, she began to feel a sense of weird elation. Of power. She was fencing with time and reality, changing the world. Surely she'd be safe. Every day that passed saw her safer. Anyway, her mother and Paddy Riley could not meet now because their meeting would be her downfall. It must not happen. It was like contemplating the nuclear bomb or a meteorite landing on their house.

———————

Just after nine she woke feeling hag-ridden. At least her watch, still on her wrist, said just after nine. Then she remembered it had stopped, or at least she thought it had; it

343

could be any time.

It felt like Sunday on the landing. Yes, there was the big fat Sunday paper lying on the mat downstairs. Normally he'd have picked it up by now and brought it back to bed with him. There were voices downstairs. The children, as if everything were the same. Music playing softly. She smelled porridge. When she went down Charley was standing in the open back doorway, dressed in his oldest clothes. It was chilly. She looked straight at him. Please don't over-react, she tried to say with her look.

But it was running away, the walls, the world running away around her.

'I'm finishing the stile,' he said.

The girls were eating porridge and Sid was making an awful mess with the honey.

Jasmine jumped up and gave her a kiss. 'Mummy,' she said, 'did you have a nice time?'

'We thought you weren't coming back until tonight,' said Sid.

'Well,' Anita said brightly, 'I missed you all, didn't I?'

'Basil's not very well, Mum,' said Jasmine, getting down from the table.

'You shouldn't sit in there,' Charley said, but something in his tone told the girls his heart wasn't in it and they both left their breakfasts and got down in Basil's den, one on either side of him. His ginger feather beat slowly up and down.

'How is he?' Anita asked.

'Better this morning, isn't he, Dad?' Sid said, kissing the old dog between the eyes.

'Surprisingly,' said Charley stiffly, 'he does seem to be.'

'He's had some scrambled egg,' said Jas.

Anita sat carefully down at the table and Charley and she looked a peculiar raw look at each other.

'Come on, girls,' he said gruffly, 'time to go and get dressed.'

'Or something,' Anita added.

'Yes, go on and sort yourselves out.'

This morning everything seemed to take them five times longer than usual. They ran in and out endlessly in their silky pyjamas, fooled around in the hall, stood arguing by the sink with pained expressions, till Anita screamed at them and they retired in umbrage to the living room and put on the TV much too loud.

'Turn it DOWN!' she yelled.

They did, a fraction.

'Turn it DOWN!'

Charley started to laugh, in a grim, unfriendly kind of way.

'Are we going to talk, Charley?' she said.

He glanced at her but said nothing.

'Charley, I don't want this to finish us, please. If ever I'd thought that — '

He went on stoically spooning coffee into mugs, getting the milk out of the fridge, ignoring her completely. His face was blank and resolute.

'Charley,' she said sharply, 'do you hear me?'

He turned and looked at her, his gaze intent yet shielded. 'I hear you,' he said with a mildly sarcastic inflection in his voice, scarcely moving his mouth.

'I don't want this to finish us,' she said again. 'Do you believe me?'

'Why should I believe you?' He put down his hands, splayed out as if in pain, flat on the table among the breakfast bowls, leaning over her in a very slow, soft, predatory manner, as if he was going to kiss her. 'Why should I believe anything at all that you say?'

———

She got to Paddy's about three. The door at the bottom of the stairs was on the latch. 'It's open!' he called when she knocked on his door. He was getting drunk in his bath, a brown bottle in his fist, more lined up along the duck-egg blue tiled shelf. His body lolled beneath the suds. His curls were dark and damp and shiny, dripping over his heavy, questioning eyes.

'Oh Anita, Anita, my little Anita,' he said, 'what terrible news have you brought to me?'

'No reply,' she told him.

He put the bottle to his lips like a hunting horn and took a long drink. That's when she remembered that he was teetotal. She sat down on her usual chair. 'You'll be all right, Paddy,' she assured him. She looked around. 'Would you like me to make you a cup of coffee?'

'I have decided,' he announced, ignoring her offer, 'to drink myself into oblivion. O-bli-vi-on. Your mother is mad. You can tell her that from me.' He slurred his words, brandishing the bottle with an arm that wavered about all over the place like a drunk weaving home. She watched him, fascinated. The radio on the little bamboo table, now over-populated with empty brown bottles, played 'Ginny-Come-Lately' by Brian Hyland.

'Ah, I love this!' he sighed, and fiddled the dial to get it clearer. His hand was wet.

'You shouldn't touch that with a wet hand,' Anita said. 'That is incredibly stupid. I'm not sitting anywhere near you while you're doing that.' She moved away to stand in the doorway. She could see them both, the whole room, crackling and buzzing with lightning.

He laughed.

'Your mother will be a widow,' he said, and sang liltingly, conducting the air with his bottle:

'*I'm a buxom fine widow, I live in a spot*
In Dublin, they call it the Coombe . . .'

She could push the radio in, she thought. He'd be gone. She could do it. No one knew she was here. No one had seen her come up.

'Have to go,' she said.

'Anita!' he drawled drunkenly. 'Anita, my little Anita, you are not saying I'm abandoned!' He tilted his head to look at her, his wet curls in his eyes. When he held out his dripping arm to her she took his hand, even though she half believed they would combust on contact. Tears sparkled like ice in his eyes.

On the way out, a tiny little flick on the flex as she passed.

'I'll come and see you,' she said. 'Shall I?'

'You will come and comfort a dying man,' he said pompously, letting go of her hand.

$$\star \quad \star \quad \star$$

Anita found her mother in a peculiar state, just sitting on the bed as if waiting, staring straight ahead with her lips moving slightly as if she was silently praying. She'd done her hair and was all got up in her nicest clothes and make-up. When Anita spoke she jumped and leapt up in a fury. 'You gave me the fright of my life, you stupid girl!' she cried and hit her on the side of the face with the full force of her open palm. 'Get away from me!' she cried. 'Get away, you stupid girl!'

The fury and something more in her eyes frightened Anita. She had never seen her mother like this before. She ran out. On the landing she stopped and listened. Her mother was crying in there, terrible hard crying that scraped her throat raw.

———————

'Who else knows?'

'Alison,' she said after the briefest pause.

'Alison? Who else?'

She hesitated.

'Only Lindsay.'

'Lindsay! Fucking *Lindsay*!' His face expressed horror. 'Oh God, Anita, why didn't you just stand on top of the town hall with a megaphone? If fucking Lindsay knows about

349

it, the whole bloody world knows about it.'

'Well, I'm sorry! She hasn't told anyone else, she wouldn't, not a big thing like this.'

'Oh no,' he said sourly. His forehead was all churned up.

They sat for a while not speaking, not drinking their coffee.

'You could at least have been discreet,' he said bitterly, reaching for the phone. He tapped in a number fiercely.

'Saying sorry's pointless, isn't it?' she said.

He didn't reply.

'Because you're just not accepting apologies, are you? There's nothing I can do, is there?'

———————

'What's the matter with Mummy?' Robin asked Anita, coming into her room that night.

'I don't know.'

'It's both of them,' he said. 'Something's going on.'

'I know.'

'I'm on her side,' he said.

'Do you realise,' Anita pondered, older and wiser, 'if they get divorced, we'll be children of a broken home. Do you realise?'

In bed she remembered how she had almost pushed the radio into Paddy Riley's bath. A second it would have taken, then all her troubles would have been at an end and he would never have existed. He would be a figment of her imagination.

A second it would have taken. She could have done it. When a thing was done it stayed done; dead was dead. Her blood ran cold.

She was upstairs lying down, worrying that the sound in her head might be the start of a brain tumour. She heard the car return, the engine die, and then much later the sound of the car door. She heard him come in, sensed his pause at the foot of the stairs; then a couple of strides like pounces and the door flew back on its hinges. He'd worked himself into a fury somehow between taking the children to Doon's place and returning home. His fists were clenched and he trembled. Anita flung her hands over her head and cried out but it wasn't her he hit, it was the little angel church made of matchsticks. With an incoherent shout he swept it from its place on the bookshelf and kicked it to pieces against the wall.

She screamed.

'I hate that fucking thing!' he sobbed. 'I've always hated it!' Then he sat down on the bed with his back to her and bowed his head.

'Charley!' she cried.

She touched him but he ran into the bathroom and locked the door.

When he came out he was composed. He stood in the doorway with his thumbs in his belt and said: 'I think you ought to leave this house.'

She was sitting rigid on the bed. Nothing was real. 'I don't want to go,' she said.

'Well, I'm sorry,' he replied gently, 'but I think that would probably be for the best.'

'Charley, you can't . . . '

'*Please*,' he said, 'don't make this harder than it already is.'

She started to cry. 'Where could I go?'

'You can go to him,' he said nastily.

'I can't!'

'Why? Won't he have you?'

'I don't want to!'

He laughed. 'Should have thought of that, shouldn't you?'

'You want it like this?' she said. 'You want it all out in the open? Everybody knowing? Think about the girls, please, Charley . . . '

He laughed again. 'Did you? Think about the girls? When you were stealing away for your dirty little sessions?'

'It wasn't like that!'

'Oh yes it was. That's exactly what it was like.'

'No!'

'Oh of course not, it was love, wasn't it? Sorry, I'd forgotten.'

He was so cold, so hateful. She put her face in her hands.

'Anyway,' he said, 'with Lindsay spreading it all over town I suppose they'll hear about it in the playground when they go back to school, so I don't think you can very well talk about sparing their feelings.'

'They need never have known,' she said, and her voice gave out.

'They have to know,' he replied brusquely. 'It's happening, they have to know.' He turned as if to go downstairs.

'Charley!' she cried. 'I don't want to go!'

'Well, *I'm* not going,' he said testily. 'Why should I have to go anywhere? Why should the girls?'

'I *can't* leave the children!'

'Well, you're not taking them. I'm not having my children living on a boat with you and your boyfriend, you must be joking.'

'It's not like that!'

'Oh yes, it is,' he hissed. 'Oh yes, it is.'

————

She put all the letters she had kept from Paddy Riley to her mother in the fire when no

353

one was looking, one or two at a time. The only thing she kept was the line *You are the Sunday in every week*, and that she kept folded in two between the pages of her page-a-day secret diary with the little gold lock.

Then she lay down on her bed quite still with her arms crossed over her chest like a figure on a tomb, and her mouth moved silently. It was too big to think about, the pain that was in her mother, the pain that was in Paddy Riley. Too big for her.

'I shouldn't think it'll be big enough for the three of you as it is. It's poor Luke I feel sorry for. He doesn't even like you.'

Anita gave up and lay down and cried.

She didn't know how long it went on for, whether he was there all the time or whether he went away and came back; all she knew was that when at length she became aware of him shaking her shoulder, it was like being slowly brought round out of a long deep sleep. 'That's enough,' he said roughly. 'That's enough now, Anita.'

'I can't stop!'

'Yes, you can. Now, calm down.'

'Where can I go? I have nowhere to go! I'll be back on the streets!'

'Stop it!' He shook her. 'Stop it now!'

'I can't! I've got this noise in my ears!'

'Lie down.'

She lay down and he peered into her face, stroking her arm awkwardly and speaking in a soft, gruff voice: 'Don't be so dramatic. We can sort out money and stuff, don't worry, you won't go short.' He was unshaven, his eyes bleak, dark-shadowed. 'You don't have to do anything just yet,' he said, 'I mean about moving out or anything. It wouldn't be fair to spring it on the poor girls. We have to work out the best way to break it to them.'

She sat up again, rested her arms on her knees and looked at him. 'Are you saying that's it?' she asked him, trembling. 'Is that it, Charley? That's it?'

He looked bewildered.

Surely now, she thought, surely now everything will be all right.

'I've got this noise in my head,' she said.

'What like?'

'Like a buzzing. I'm scared.'

'Oh, it won't be anything.'

'I've got a headache,' she said. 'It's hurting my eyes.'

'You probably didn't sleep.' He got up and went out and came back a moment later with two Paracetamol and a glass of fizzy water. 'Why I am doing anything at all for you I don't know,' he said.

She thought: if I had met Michael first, I would have had an affair with Charley.

'Get some sleep,' he said.

He went out and closed the door.

She lay down. The buzzing in her head grew worse. Now it was not a bee, it was more of a low-flying aircraft constantly over the house. It would never let her sleep, she thought, but somehow when she closed her eyes she was swallowed, and the next thing she knew she was waking up with a feeling of someone having just blown a trumpet inside her brain. She heard the kids rushing through the house, and Doon's voice. A little later she heard footsteps on the landing, Sid shouting, Charley saying, 'Ssh, Mummy's tired, she's lying down.' She wanted a drink, anything, but when she'd gulped the fizzy water he'd brought her so kindly she was angry and hated him. What does he mean, she stormed, being all nice and friendly when he's leaving me? Oh, that's how you really twist the knife! Much more lethal than a smack in the chops. And he *was* leaving her. Dress it up how he liked, that's what it was. *She* wasn't leaving *him*. She'd never in her life be such a fool as to leave him. First opportunity and he was out. Couldn't wait. No talk of second chances, it was the chop for the first offence.

Was she so bad? Was she so evil? Why had he got all the money anyway? Why was it like he was doling money out to her?

She thought of her mother getting it doled out by her dad and always being short. Charley with his good job. She might have known. We were never suited, she thought. He's realised. He'll get rid of me now. I'm losing my looks too.

*　*　*

She got as far as the kitchen before she heard Doon's voice. They were outside. She could see them through the back door. He was holding a rock, standing with one leg bent at the knee and grinning at Doon, laughing at something she'd just said. Doon stood holding a mug of something hot between her hands, the pearlised lilac of her fingernails shining in the sun. They hadn't seen her.

How could he just carry on messing with the stupid wall as if nothing had happened? How could he have that merry look in his eyes, turned on *her*, when Anita was dying? She backed away, fled unseen back to bed and lay there thinking of Charley and Doon. It was weird to think they'd slept together once. She'd been with Michael, of course, too. What is it about her, she thought, that she keeps getting to my men first? She remembered being with Charley at a party once, and Doon passing them in the hall: 'How are the banks and braes of bonny Doon?' he had said, and Doon had thrown back her head and flung her hair about like someone in an advertisement, laughing with her mouth wide open and all her teeth showing. How are the banks and braes of bonny Doon, indeed.

Anita listened. From time to time she crept out on to the landing. Doon stayed around. She heard her fussing over Basil, talking baby to him. She heard her calling Jasmine from the back step.

The sky was beginning to fade when Doon's car pulled away.

★ ★ ★

Soon after, the door opened and the girls came in and sat on the bed. Anita smelled cooking and her stomach lurched with hunger.

'How are you feeling?' Jasmine asked. 'Are you awake now?'

'Yes.'

'Did you have a headache?'

'Yes.'

358

'Shall I tell Daddy to make you a cup of tea?' asked Sid.

'Yes please.'

'Look, I'll draw the curtains for you.'

'I'll put the lamp on.'

'Oh, Mummy!' cried Jasmine. 'Your lovely little church!'

'Oh yes. It fell off.'

'But it's all smashed up! It's all in bits!'

'Daddy stepped on it by mistake.'

'Clumsy twerp,' said Sid.

'Oh look! This bit here. That's one of the angels.' Jasmine held up a fragment about the size of a domino. 'Can I have it?'

'If you want to.'

They flitted about tidying away the mess, putting it neatly in a pile on the bedside table, making the room cosy before they dashed off. Anita leaned across and stirred the matchstick debris with her fingers. Her watch still said just after nine. Pretty soon, she reckoned, it would have caught up with itself. Well, she couldn't hide here all night. She stood up. It was like a lull in battle, a brief rest in her tent before she sallied forth to lead her armies once more into the fray. She was fighting for her life.

The door opened and Charley came in and plonked a cup of tea down on the bedside table next to the bits of broken church. He was all pink about the eyes and nose. 'I don't know,' he said in a strange voice, half sour, half resigned, 'it just seems really peculiar to me that I'm bringing you cups of tea after what you've done.'

She sat down again.

'A thank you would be nice,' he said.

'Thank you.'

Her head was frightening her, the hum as if something had been left on that should have been switched off; she was going to have to see the doctor. There might be some awful thing in there she didn't know about, it might be going to explode for all she knew. How could she tell? She felt vague and light with physical fear.

'How's the head?' he asked grudgingly.

She swallowed. 'Not very good.'

'I did some pasta. Do you want some?'

'Yes please. I can't remember the last time I ate.'

He looked at her intently. At last a very small smile appeared. 'Are you coming down,' he asked, 'or do you want it up here?'

She tried to smile but her mouth felt all shivery. 'I'll come down,' she said.

★　★　★

He stood at the back door looking out.

'What do you think of the wall now?' he said. 'It's quite a big job, that is, you know.'

She sat at the kitchen table eating cold pasta with warm mushroom sauce. They'd sent the girls up in their pyjamas to watch *The Lion King* for the hundredth time.

'It's great,' she replied.

'Michael's back.'

'Is he? How do you know?'

They might have been discussing the weather.

'Doon saw him.'

He walked out a little way and stood looking up at the sky through the trees. 'It's going to rain tomorrow,' he said. It didn't feel anything like rain to Anita.

'What did Doon say?'

'She saw him in the Co-op. She just went up to him and asked him what the hell was going on and told him to stay away till me and you had had a chance to sort things out at this end.'

He came and stood looking in at her, leaning on the door-frame with folded arms.

'Oh God!' she said.

'What?'

'Everyone discussing our affairs. *Doon* getting involved.'

'You're just jealous of Doon.'

361

'Of course I am! What do you expect? What did she say about us?'

'Who?'

'Doon!'

'What did she say about who?'

She flung her plate across the room and out of the door and it smashed against Charley's wall. 'Charley!' she screamed. 'Don't you dare mess me around at a time like this!'

'I'm not messing you around!' he shouted back. 'I don't know what you're talking about. Do you mean what did she say about us meaning you and me, or what did she say about us meaning you and him?'

'Meaning you and me, of course. I mean, you've obviously been telling her all about it. What did she say?'

'I don't know.' He looked exasperated. 'She just said what a shame and all that sort of stuff. What do you expect her to say?'

'So everybody knows now. It's the talk of the town.'

'*You* told first, precious.' He pushed himself off the doorframe with the weight of his shoulder and came back into the room. 'I suppose it's worse for you, people knowing. You've got something to be ashamed of. I haven't.'

'Oh don't be so bloody smug!' she

screamed at him. 'Saint bloody Charley!'

The girls must have heard that.

He turned away from her and dropped to a squat in front of Basil's mattress. 'Anyway,' he said, 'she needn't have bothered. Telling him to keep away, I mean. I mean, no doubt you and he will have a lot of things to discuss. Come on, Basil.' He put cheerfulness in his voice. 'Come on, you stupid mutt, time for walkies,' practically lifting the old dog on to his feet. 'Think about where you're going to live,' he said as he passed Anita. 'Don't just let it go.'

Yawning squeakily, shaking his paws out feebly one by one, Basil stumbled through the kitchen with a mild, blind, smiling look in Anita's direction, following Charley out the back for his slow drift round the right-hand side of the garden. He always seemed to go that way these days, as if pulled by some perverse force, a kind of sideways gravity.

———————

Paddy was working on the Bobs that day. The fat man with a goitre had just taken over. She'd walked up from the Longsight entrance, past the exotic birds, lingered by the floral clock and watched the gibbons. Paddy was leaning on the rail and smiled when he saw her.

'My little Anita,' he said, 'dare I ask? You have brought me no words. No words from the whore of Babylon.'

She didn't like him calling her mother the whore of Babylon. She was not that bad. He'd been drinking again, she could tell by the sleepy look in his eyes and the grand way he delivered his words.

'This time I have,' she said. 'She said please don't send any more messages.'

He nodded, looking away, getting out a cigarette. The man with the goitre was clearing his throat wetly in the booth.

'Doesn't take me all that seriously, your mother, does she?' Paddy asked.

'I don't really know what you mean.'

There was a great scream and splash and shouting from the Water Chute. He smiled. 'How's your dad?'

She didn't know. How were people with cancer? 'He's not too bad at the moment,' she said, 'but it's knowing there's not much time.'

He nodded again, narrowing his eyes. 'Ever smoked a cigarette, Anita?'

'No.'

'Never tried one of your mum's?'

'No.'

'Now's the time to try. Here.' He placed his cigarette between her lips with the slightest caress to her cheek from his thumb in passing. 'We will share this,' he said, 'it's not a good idea to have a whole one straight off. Make you sick.'

'I don't want to be sick,' she said.

'No no, not if you just have a little puff. Just to start you off like.'

She was a natural smoker. She didn't cough too much. Paddy told her she'd done very well. When she handed him back the cigarette his hand and his whole arm were trembling finely.

'She *should* take me seriously, you know,' he said.

A siren made a sound like someone being sick.

'I have to be going now,' Anita said, her head spinning excitingly.

'I'm going for a turn on this thing.' He waved his arm extravagantly behind him at the hulk of the Bobs. 'You coming?'

'Oh no, Paddy. I'd never dare.'

'Sure you would. There's nothing like it. Come on now, Anita,' he offered her his arm, 'I need you to look after me on that thing, don't you think?'

'Paddy, I'm terrified of it. I'll never go on the Bobs.'

'In this life,' he said, 'the only sin is to miss an opportunity.'

Michael called on Monday.

'What are you doing?'

She froze at the sound of his voice.

'Oh, Michael.'

'What are you doing, Anita? What decision have you come to?'

'Decision!' She almost laughed. 'Decision! Michael, I can just about decide to stumble from one second to the next!'

* * *

'This child's ill,' Charley said, with his hand on Sid's forehead. He still had his suit on.

She wouldn't eat her tea. Anita had cooked a sausage casserole. She'd used red onions.

'Well, I don't know,' she said, 'she was all right till about an hour ago. Weren't you, baby?'

'I just feel funny,' Sid said irritably.

'Come and sit on Daddy's knee.' He picked her up and carried her away.

'Is it chicken pox?' asked Jasmine, from Basil's den.

'More like some horrible disease she's caught from the dog,' Anita replied, turning to the sink and thinking: God, I wish the summer holidays were over.

His plate still sat on the table, untouched. Jas never ate anything anyway, she was probably working her way up to being anorexic for her early teens. A whole pot full of food sitting there completely untouched. I don't know why I bother, she thought. She had to tell Charley about Michael's call, which played over and over in her head as if she'd taped it.

Now or never.

'Shall I call the doctor?' she said, going into the sitting room where Charley had flopped down on the sofa with Sid.

'I'd give it an hour or so,' he said, yawning. 'See how the Calpol does.'

'Do you want to go to bed, Sid?'

'No.'

'Yes, I think you'd better. Charley, take her up.' She stared hard at him. Get rid of her, she said with her eyes, I have to speak to you.

He looked away. 'Come on, Cleopatra,' he said softly, standing and scooping Sid up in the same movement. Anita wandered through the house in a mild trance while she waited for him to put her to bed. The front and back doors were open and a breeze blew through. Jasmine was up a tree above the wall, Basil's eyes twitched in dreaming. Anita felt as if the breeze was blowing the house down from the inside, playfully pushing at the walls till they started to bulge, raising the roof, gently exhaling till the bubble burst.

Poof! All gone.

When he came down he closed the doors, then stood and looked at her with his hands in his pockets, waiting for her to speak. He looked gormless with worry and lack of sleep.

'How is she?'

'She's OK. No spots or anything. Probably just a bit of a temperature.'

'Michael rang this afternoon,' Anita said. 'He wants to talk to me. I said I'd meet him at the Simnel Arms at seven.'

His jaw tensed up. 'Whatever,' he said.

'I'm telling him that it's all over.'

'If it's all over why are you going to see him?'

'Because he deserves it,' she said. 'He at least deserves a face-to-face meeting.'

'He deserves nothing.'

She sighed. 'Don't you want me to go?'

Charley laughed. 'You're mad,' he said contemptuously. 'God, all these years I've never realised how stupid you are. I don't give a fuck what you do, I've told you. Go and move in with him, lock stock and barrel. Just do it, for Christ's sake!'

'Don't shout!' she cried. 'I'm not moving in with him! I'm just going to talk to him. He deserves that much.'

'He deserves nothing. He's just nothing. He's less than nothing.'

She listened for Jasmine.

He looked over his shoulder. 'This is hopeless!' he exploded.

'It's not fair, Charley. You're looking for villains. None of us are villains.'

'You are,' he said quickly.

———

Paddy gave her back the cigarette and jumped over the rail. Halfway up the ramp he turned and beckoned with his arm. 'Sure you won't?' he called but she shook her head. She would smoke his cigarette to the bitter end and then she'd go home. She'd not be sick. She watched him climb into the carriage at the front. A few couples got on behind. Paddy waved to her as the carriage began to move.

———

There was a round table set beneath a chestnut tree on the big lawn, where they could drink their drinks and watch the families eat their sesame-seeded burger buns and swat away the lazy early evening wasps that drifted up from the nasturtium beds. Children swung on tyres attached to other trees. Michael held both her hands very tightly and glowered upon the innocent scene. 'You can't,' was all he kept saying.

She had often been two people when the

situation required it. It was a survival technique. Sometimes she wondered if she came close to being like those people with multiple personalities she'd read about. That evening under the tree with Michael she split in two. One of her wailed and bled and wept over him, the other stood aloof, waiting for him to be through, knowing it had to be done, that she was tossing him aside like she tossed Paddy Riley all those years ago because that's what you end up having to do with the ones you want but don't want enough.

She watched him going round and round on the Bobs, smiling. He was shouting something the third time he passed but the noise of the carriage obliterated everything. She threw down the dog-end, stamped on it with her toe and went home. She walked round by the sideshows, the Rifle Range and Coconut Shy, the Hook-a-Duck and the Darts. She had no money. Outside the King's Hall they were dismantling the old Midgets' House. Paint cracked and faded, the signs lay on their sides. Dancing Midgets. Real Live Tiny People. She watched for a while, then walked home down the Tree Walk.

He held her hands so tightly that they hurt, repeating in a calm, hollow tone: 'You can't.'

Everything was said. Nothing more could help, so she stayed silent.

'I can fight,' he said, glowering. 'How do you think I got through school? I can fight for you.'

She was trying to forget him. Oh but he was so beautiful, so beautiful, she thought, she could kiss him all over again, start it all again, but she sat still as a stone, lips closed.

At eight she said she had to go.

'Anita!' His tone was wondering, shocked. 'Look at me.'

She did, full in the face. He was a gargoyle, an ugly child.

'You said we were friends.'

She kissed him quickly on the cheek. When she stood his goatish blue eyes followed her.

'We are still friends,' she said.

Halfway across the lobby of the hotel he caught up with her. 'You don't leave your friends!' he said loudly.

She turned at the top of the steps.

He came close and put his face into hers. 'You got me into this. You came to me. You've taken three years of my life. Now you tell me I'm redundant.'

'I'm sorry!' she cried and dithered for a

second, shrugging forwards as if she was going to put her arms round him, then thinking better of it and running down the steps towards the car park. He did not follow. As she drove away she could still see him standing at the top of the steps, the yellow arc lights that had just come on turning the scene to sickly chrome. At the next bend of the road she had to blink hard to keep her vision; as soon as she could she pulled into a layby. If she'd had a god she would have prayed. Please, she would have said, let him be OK. Don't put him on my conscience with the others. Let him go and find a nice free single or otherwise unattached woman, not too insane, one who'll stick by him to the bitter end. Give him a constant friend.

She sat in the layby for ten minutes, crying in a dull, tedious kind of way. Be happy to assuage my conscience, she meant. Be my friend to assuage my conscience. He had to be OK. Luke would take care of him. Luke was a clever little sod. It was the phone call that had given them away apparently.

'What's my account number?'
'How the hell do I know?'
'Get my card out of my wallet.'
'How do I know where your wallet is?'

'Fuck's sake, Anita . . . hang on a sec, Mum.'

Luke's granny had asked him who Anita was and on such things futures hang.

* * *

She locked the house up very carefully. The girls were fast asleep.

Charley wouldn't come out or answer, even though Anita knocked three times. His silence and the very faint music inside the study drove her mad.

'If you saw the fire, Charley,' she said to the door, 'most likely you survived the plague. You were a survivor, Charley.'

He didn't answer.

She sat down and cried outside the door.

'Charley!' she sobbed. 'Charley, please come out!'

She felt so lonely.

The door opened.

'Oh Charley, you can't,' she said just as Michael had said to her. 'You can't. Please Charley, can't we sort this out? It's all over now with Michael, I promise. Oh Charley, I promise! I've told him.'

She stood there literally wringing her hands. Charley looked perplexed. 'What a state you're in,' he said. That was all. And he watched her. She couldn't stand his indifference and ran away into their old bedroom. His things were disappearing from it furtively when she was not looking: his books, his shoes, his shirts from the back of the chair. He'd be needing new shirts soon. He wouldn't have them. Serve him right. Now let him see how hard it is to live without me, she thought. He hadn't wanted to touch her, she'd felt it, though she'd wanted to touch him. I have to make him cry, she thought. God help me to make him cry again.

She heard his door close quietly. Then the lock.

———

At tea-time her father always got the *Chron* first. He'd read it while he was having his tea, then cast it aside broken-backed on to the floor beside his chair while he watched TV. After a while her mother, yawning, rubbed her hair back from her forehead as if life were very hard, picked it up and smoothed out all the pages and put them in order with a martyred air. Then she began to glance through it with scant interest, passing the time between eating and doing the pots.

They weren't talking any more. They hadn't

talked for ages. A frosty silence ruled in the house when they were both in it. Robin and Anita got out of it as often as possible. Robin had gone up and was messing about in his room and Anita was halfway out of the door when a terrible sound stopped her in her tracks. It was the sound of her mother laughing, a sudden deep, prolonged, embittered laugh from the depths of her chest. Anita looked back. Her father was staring at her mother with a look almost of terror on his face.

'Geraldine!' he said sharply.

She held the *Evening Chronicle* between her hands.

'Oh wept!' she said.

Anita's father sprang from his chair and hovered over her mother, who dropped the paper, turned her head on one side and let her face distort, as if some dreadful force were pulling it backwards, stretching it, mouth and eyes and everything. She looked hideous. No sound came from her but she shook with something suppressed.

'Away!' Anita's father said urgently to her. 'She's all right. Let me handle this. Off you go. Go on!'

———————

They did not speak at breakfast. It hurt to be in the same room. The girls knew something was wrong and shovelled their porridge in dutifully. She caught him just as he was sneaking out of the front door.

'Will you go with Doon again when I'm gone?' she asked. She was genuinely interested.

'Oh, don't be stupid,' he said icily, and slammed the door.

Well, she thought, a slammed door. That's something, I suppose, and went to put some newspaper down for Basil. Jasmine came and watched her. 'Are you getting divorced?' she asked.

'No we are not,' Anita said smartly. 'We're just having a row, that's all.'

'Pretty long row.'

'Well, some of them are.'

He'll never do it, she thought. He'll never do it to them.

'Now look,' she said, taking hold of Jasmine, 'you are not to go worrying yourself about stupid things like that. Daddy and I are *not* getting a divorce. We're just in the middle of a big argument and it'll take some time to sort out. All right?'

Jasmine didn't look convinced.

'Get your shoes on,' Anita said, 'and tell Sid to get hers on. We're going.'

'Has Daddy got a girlfriend?' she asked, sitting on the floor and tying her butterfly laces.

Anita laughed out loud. But as they sat on the bus going over to Jane's she thought, well, he could. There was nothing to stop him now, was there? She couldn't very well complain, could she? She imagined seeing him with someone else. Charley and Doon were in her mind as she rang Jane's bell. Jane would know, of course. Every bloody person she encountered from now on would know all about their commonplace little tragedy. Lauren answered the door. All smiles and normality, no time to chat, Anita left the kids and ran.

★   ★   ★

Charley didn't come home that night. The girls thought it was funny she hadn't said where he'd gone and picked up on her fear, which was constant and sour now, hovering about her like a smell. Sid burst into tears

'It doesn't help, you know,' Jas told Sid, 'you bursting into tears. All you do is make people feel worse.'

'Leave her alone,' Anita said.

She opened a bottle of wine, gulped one glass quickly and recorked it. She couldn't afford to get drunk. She might need to drive. Who knows? He might be dead somewhere. She might never see him alive again. Charley didn't go out on his own an awful lot these days. He always went with her. Anita sat down and held on to her head as if it was about to fly off. Why, she thought, here's the buzzing coming back and I hadn't even realised it had been gone. She tried to slow her breathing and relax, but instead of peace she kept getting to the impossible abyss of her birth dream, still dredging itself up from the deeps. There they stood on that mythical cliff top, calling her on, her father and mother and all the rest, vague shades in legions at their backs, the charnel pits of her own lost ancestors, the ones they dug themselves, the ones they were shovelled into, dead being dead, her father lying back in his chair with his long white fingers gracefully twined, taking sights down the mountainy crag of his nose.

What a swine nature is, she thought, making men and women like this.

It grew late and the girls wouldn't go to bed. They kept running up and down the stairs wanting things, creeping about, whispering. She took Basil out in the lane and he stumbled along a pace or two. 'You and me, Bas,' she said gamely. 'You go find him.' When she came back in Sid was sobbing in the hall.

'I thought you'd gone,' Sid wailed.

'I just took Basil out for a wee,' Anita said, 'silly girl! As if I'd go off. Now come on, I'll take you up. Daddy'll be back soon.'

'Will he?'

'Course he will.'

'Jas says he's not coming back.'

'Course he's coming back,' she said with forced jollity, 'he's just gone out for a drink, that's all. Poor man, he's allowed to pop out for a drink now and then. Come on. And you, Jas, stop saying such ridiculous things and upsetting your sister. Now get into bed, he'll be very cross if he comes back and finds you're both still awake. Lights off!'

They were asleep by eleven.

Anita sat on the sofa zapping the TV on and off. When it was off she listened to the buzzing in her head. When that got too much she zapped on some noise to drown it out. She thought about ringing the police but of course it was ridiculous, it wasn't even closing time.

But then it *was* closing time, and then the really late-night programmes began, the ones she normally didn't see. She turned the TV off and listened to the falling of the rain and thought about the nights under canvas, listening to the rain on the canopy and drifting in and out of sleep. She dreamed she had a little box and in it was the Feejee

Mermaid all scrunched up, poor thing, and when she awoke she remembered clearly Tom Shafto, all wrinkled and brown himself, telling her about the creature exhibited in London by P.T. Barnum, who had acquired her from a museum, which had acquired her, poor thing, from the son of a Boston sea captain. The Feejee Mermaid was a withered, hairy little corpse, Tom Shafto said, with an expression of terror on its face.

If mermaids exist, thought Anita, that's what they're like. Certainly not like my mother, applying her lipstick under the sea.

———

The talking ground on and on downstairs, on through the night, her mother and father's voices, deep, serious, endless like rain that's set in, that's there when you fall asleep and there when you wake, there in your dreams.

Her mother had lost control. Gone mad.

She didn't know what to do. All she could see when she opened her eyes was darkness and no answers. She sighed a long deep sigh and shivered, saying please God, let it all be over, please let us all be happy. She closed her eyes and watched Paddy Riley going round and round on the Bobs, smiling, endless, round and round, endless as the voices grinding on and on downstairs.

He was shouting something the third time he passed but the noise of the carriage obliterated everything.

Charley got out of a taxi at ten past one. 'What are you doing up?' he asked her, mildly surprised when he saw her sitting there on the sofa. He was soaking wet. He must have been waiting for a taxi in the rain somewhere. She hadn't even noticed that it *was* raining.

'There's something wrong with my brain,' she said.

'What?'

'I've got this terrible noise in my head.'

He came and peered down at her, leaning close. He was getting a little chubby in the face, she noticed, and his eyes were heavy and stormy. He was drunk too. Funny how people always drink in these situations. If I didn't have this helicopter sitting in my brain, she thought, I would too, I'd drink the rest of the wine and know what to do.

'I'm scared,' she said. 'There's something wrong with me.'

He went on peering closely into her face like a doctor looking for clues, or as if he might kiss her, except that there was no softness in him at all. 'Are you really ill?' he asked.

'It might be a brain tumour!' she cried.

Miraculously, he smiled, a very small, awkward smile, typical of him. His eyes softened. One of these days she would draw Charley. Really catch him.

'You haven't got a brain tumour,' he said. 'You need to go to bed, that's all. What you waiting up for?'

'You,' she said.

The smile was gone. He was all winter again when he stood, took one of her hands lightly and pulled her to her feet. 'You shouldn't wait up for me,' he said. He held her hand going upstairs but did not look at her. On the landing when she tried to draw a little closer to him, he shifted away from her touch as if repulsed but trying to hide it; then let go of her hand, went into the study and closed the door. Anita wanted to fly after and kick the smug door into splinters and scream hatred and abuse at him. But she could hear Sid, sleeping lightly, mumbling a little through her teeth, so instead she went into the bedroom and undressed and put on her willows nightie and lay down carefully in the half-dark. She closed her eyes. He doesn't want to touch me any more, she thought. That's it then. When that goes, it all goes. I've lost him. What does he want me to do, crawl and beg? I'll never crawl and beg. She'd gone two days without food on the streets before she'd begged before. She could hear the rain now, pouring softly, the kind of pleasant sound that should have lulled her to sleep. It went on and on, singing and gurgling, happy-sounding, as if everything was OK. She was so tired she actually slept, and was dreaming something about being in a little rowing boat off the coast of France, when the ringing on the bell woke her up.

★ ★ ★

Michael looked small and withered, his white face coming out of the dark. The trees dripped but the rain was over, and his hair was only a little damp. His gaze went right past Charley as if he didn't exist. 'What are you doing?' he said sternly to her. 'What are you doing?'

'What do you mean?'

Jasmine and Sid were on the landing.

Michael looked at Charley, whose face was tight and hard. 'This has to be sorted out,' he said, swaying a little.

'What is it?' called Jasmine in a voice of controlled anxiety. 'What is it, Mum? What's happening?'

'So this is how you go about it?' Charley said. 'Waking up the kids at three in the

383

morning?' He stepped away. 'Anita, this is your thing. You sort it out.'

'What is it, Daddy?'

'Nothing.' He dashed upstairs. 'Nothing to worry about. Go back to bed. It's only Michael,' and set about shooing them into their rooms.

Michael's face was set and hard. 'You owe me,' he said, with an intake of breath.

'I know.'

'You owe me for the hotel.'

'Of course. I'll write you a cheque.'

'I don't care about that,' he hissed, thrusting his face into hers. 'You owe me. After all these years you owe me.'

'I know,' she said gently. 'I know I do. Come in.'

'I've walked,' he said fiercely in the kitchen as she walked about making coffee, rinsing mugs, wiping things down, anything to keep moving, 'all the way from the sandings. Gave Luke the slip. I just kept walking and walking and walking, thinking: what is at the other end of this? What am I doing? But you owe me something, Anita, you owe me.' He was beginning to breathe unevenly. 'Do you think I don't have any feelings?'

'No.'

'Do you?'

'What exactly do you want, Michael? What

do you want me to do?'

'You made a mistake with Charley,' he said. 'See the way he wants rid of you? I'd never want rid of you.'

'Michael, there's no point . . . '

'You can't do this.'

'You went on and on,' she said, turning and speaking directly into his face, 'till I went away with you. You never let up about it. I kept saying I didn't want to, I kept saying it was better as it was. You insisted. It's my fault, I know, I never should have gone. We were fine as we were, Michael.'

'You were,' he said, 'I never was. You think you're the only one in the equation.'

'I always tried to be honest. I never lied to you.'

'You did! I'm your friend, you said. Well, what are you now? You're not my friend. You're not my friend.'

His eyes filled with tears.

Charley came in.

'You're going to have to keep your voices down,' he said grimly.

Michael was the first to speak. 'He doesn't want you any more,' he said to her, ignoring Charley. 'Even if he thinks he does for a bit, it'll work against him.'

'Listen,' said Charley, walking about, 'you don't know anything. She can do what she wants.' He stood still and looked at her. 'You can take the car,' he said. 'If you're going, go.'

'No.'

She began to feel sick. Michael took a step and gripped her arm, high up. 'Don't be stupid!' he said. His thumb dug in.

'Let her go.' Through the sickness she was vaguely aware of Charley standing off to one side, his face a blur.

Michael let go and put his head in his hands, staring at her with an expression of horror. He is ridiculous, she thought, this is ridiculous. She did not understand how she could feel this and feel too that she could have taken him into her arms as if he were one of the children.

'What are you doing? What are you *doing*?' he said. 'You're making the wrong decision. I *know*.'

'What are you doing, Anita?' Charley echoed. 'Are you going with him or what? If you're going, for Christ's sake, go.'

She shook her head.

Charley threw his hands up in despair. She wanted to burst into tears and run upstairs crying 'I don't know! You two sort it out! I'm going to bed!' She was in too deep. She wanted to fall on the floor and cover her head. She wanted to laugh. For one awful thrilling moment she thought she was going to have hysterics.

She shook her head.

'Anita!' Michael cried.

'Sit down,' ordered Charley, 'sit down before you fall.'

She sat down.

She thought that she was speaking but she was not, there was no sound in the air. The words were from inside, in her head, in the core of her body: I didn't mean any harm, oh God forgive me, I didn't mean any harm.

'You should go now,' Charley said.

She covered her eyes but he was not talking to her.

'Oh, should I?' It was Michael.

'Yes, you should.' Charley spoke very quietly.

She heard no movement but suddenly Michael spoke very close to her face. 'It's all up, isn't it?' he said.

When she opened her eyes his face was in hers. He looked old and weathered, weary.

'Yes,' she whispered. Tears spilled down her face.

He straightened, jerky, sniffed loudly and started to cry in a hard, stifled way, then rushed from the room. She followed.

'You can't walk all that way back.' Her

voice was sticking in her throat. 'I'll call you a taxi.'

He made a harsh sound, striking the air in her direction. With the other hand he shielded his face from her, crying with serious intent, quietly and with great dignity. She thought of her first sight of him in Tesco's, he and the beautiful child going up and down the bread and cereal aisles with their basket. She wanted to go and put her arms round him. She loved him. He'd been her fantasy for so long and was now this drunken ruin. With a great sniff he shook his shoulders erect and looked at her. The skin under his eyes was wet, his mouth tightly closed.

He breathed audibly through his nose for a while.

'I'm leaving.' His voice was strong. 'This is all just too painful for me to stay. I don't know what I thought I was doing, coming here.'

'I'll get you a taxi,' she said again.

'I mean leaving. Leaving here. Leaving England even. Go somewhere.'

They hovered for a moment by the front door, a peculiar take on an everyday scene: seeing out the guest.

'There was a time there when I actually thought you would come with me,' Michael said. 'I thought we could swing it somehow.

Back in the hotel there, just for about ten minutes.'

'I had no idea you ever thought that, Michael,' she said.

'You did,' he said firmly with a quick nod of the head.

And of course she did.

He opened the front door and walked out into the darkness.

'Please let me get you a taxi,' she said. 'Luke'll be very worried about you. He does, you know.'

'I know.' He sniffed and wiped his nose with the back of his hand. 'Luke's asleep. He's OK. I want to walk.'

He stood on the path looking back towards her. He looked sideways and his lips moved slightly, as if he were thinking deeply to find the right words. A few cold little raindrops blew down from the apple trees. At last, with an effort, he spoke.

'You have treated me very badly,' he said.

Then he walked away down the path to the gate. His back was very straight, and there was a pride in his bearing that never left him. It was one of the things she'd loved about him. In spite of bullying and failure, lost love and addiction, he'd never lost his pride.

He was gone. For a little while she heard his footsteps, then nothing.

She closed the door and went towards the kitchen. Charley sat on the mattress in the den, head thrown back against the wall, Basil's head and front paws across his legs. He was pale and washed-out and his eyes were tired.

'You got away with it this time,' he said. 'You won't again. I promise you that.'

'There'll never be a next time.'

'Basil's dead,' he said, 'I saw him go. About a minute ago. While you were saying goodbye to *him*.'

Anita got to her knees and hung over the dog's whiskery face. He looked as if he were asleep, though his grey lips were drawn up over his back teeth, all yellow-brown with age. She looked at the hard, dirty pads of his feet, at his stones and his bones.

'Oh dear,' she said, 'dead is dead is dead is dead is dead,' and started to cry.

'Don't cry,' said Charley.

She couldn't look at him because something had gone out of his eyes, something she couldn't define as yet. He was changed.

'Look at me,' he said.

She did. Now his eyes were raw, as if he'd just crawled over a battlefield. 'You won't get away with it again, Anita,' he said.

'I know!' She bit her knuckles.

'Ever.'

He closed his eyes.

'But I have!' she cried, 'I have, I have . . .' and she rocked and keened and gave herself over to drama and despair, which he hated.

'It doesn't help,' he said, crushing her face against his chest till she was suffocating, 'it doesn't help, all this drama, it just makes things worse. For God's sake, Anita, come out of it!'

I'll tell him, she thought, now, while everything's wide open, then if he still wants me after that I'll know that there's a God.

The morning after her mother had gone hysterical while reading the *Evening Chronicle*, Anita came down very early when no one else was up. The *Chron* lay discarded by the back door and she picked it up and read, standing by the window in the ashy grey room, how an amusement park employee named Patrick Thomas Riley of West Gorton had been killed in a fall from the top of the Bobs coaster at Belle Vue. He'd stood up just as the train approached the highest point of the ride, some eighty feet, and the force of the carriage going over the top had thrown him up and out, right over the wall of Belle Vue to land in the heavy traffic on Hyde Road, causing a double-decker bus to mount the pavement and one car to go into the back of another. No one else was hurt. A spokesman for the amusement park defended the ride's safety, saying that if people behaved responsibly accidents could be avoided. Riley had been drinking. The spokesman urged anyone who used any ride always to read the safety notices and abide by the rules. 'Unfortunately,' he said, 'this would appear to be a case of a foolish act of bravado that resulted in tragedy.'

It was not bravado. It was goodbye to her mother. It was because of all the letters Anita had not brought, all the words she had not repeated. She was the cause. She alone was the cause.

He must have flown out in a wide arc of the sky, she thought, so that for an endless moment he would have been able to look down like a bird on Hyde Road and the swimming baths on the corner of Belle Vue Street, and the bus stop where he'd waited with them for the bus to Ardwick Green to get Robin's shoes the day her mother caused a scene. And she remembered him sitting on the settee that first day when Connie was there, saying: Wouldn't mind that, shooting off into space, looking down on the earth, by

God, I'd go like a shot.

'Wouldn't you be scared?' Connie asked.

The kettle steamed on the hob.

'No! Well, yes, but even if it all blew up, wouldn't it be worth it just for one second looking down?'

Past and gone, past and gone. Forgotten.

He kept saying it, over and over, like a mantra: past and gone, past and gone, forgotten: till the words began to melt into each other and she felt as if her brain was collapsing in on itself.

She couldn't understand his words, only past and gone, past and gone, forgotten.

'I'm falling asleep,' she said.

'Me too.' His eyes were teary. He grasped her hand so that it hurt. 'Now keep a grip,' he said.

His hand trembled.

He put the old dog blanket over Basil, just up to his chin. Anita put the dog's bones under the blanket with him, and his stones, the current favourite by his head. Then they closed the door, and locked it, and looked at each other.

★   ★   ★

She'd thought she could have slept but it was impossible. How could *he* sleep?

Sometimes she really believed deep down that one day she would meet Paddy Riley again, then she longed and ached to see his face and tell him how many times she had died within because of his mother in Tipperary, whose son went to work in England and never came home. Came home dead. All scrunched and withered like the Feejee Mermaid. Dead is dead, Anita, said her father. And Paddy Riley, who never went back to Ballyjamesduff, leaned down out of the sky and whispered, 'The only sin in life, Anita, is to miss an opportunity.'

She woke with a start.

Charley put his thigh under hers.

'It was a dream,' he mumbled, 'a dream.'

THE END

We do hope that you have enjoyed reading
this large print book.

Did you know that all of our titles
are available for purchase?

We publish a wide range of high quality
large print books including:
Romances, Mysteries, Classics
General Fiction
Non Fiction and Westerns

Special interest titles available in
large print are:
The Little Oxford Dictionary
Music Book
Song Book
Hymn Book
Service Book

Also available from us courtesy of Oxford
University Press:
Young Readers' Dictionary
(large print edition)
Young Readers' Thesaurus
(large print edition)

For further information or a free
brochure, please contact us at:
Ulverscroft Large Print Books Ltd.,
The Green, Bradgate Road, Anstey,
Leicester, LE7 7FU, England.
Tel: (00 44) 0116 236 4325
Fax: (00 44) 0116 234 0205

Other titles in the
Ulverscroft Large Print Series:

STRANGER IN THE PLACE

Anne Doughty

Elizabeth Stewart, a Belfast student and only daughter of hardline Protestant parents, sets out on a study visit to the remote west coast of Ireland. Delighted as she is by the beauty of her new surroundings and the small community which welcomes her, she soon discovers she has more to learn than the details of the old country way of life. She comes to reappraise so much that is slighted and dismissed by her family — not least in regard to herself. But it is her relationship with a much older, Catholic man, Patrick Delargy, which compels her to decide what kind of life she really wants.

BLACKBERRY SUMMER

Phyllis Hastings

Debbie converted a wing of the old farmhouse into an Academy for Young Ladies. She hoped this would enable her to make provision for her children's future careers. But she could not foresee the disastrous fire or the regret and guilt she would feel for giving her youngest son to be reared by her twin sister Dolly. Next to the farm, Dolly's wealthy husband Christopher built an imposing mansion in the Gothic style, and planned to run a racing stable, but his schemes were doomed to end in tragedy.

THE SANCTUARY SEEKER

Bernard Knight

1194 AD: Appointed by Richard the Lionheart as the first coroner for the county of Devon, Sir John de Wolfe, an ex-crusader, rides out to the moorland village of Widecombe to hold an inquest on an unidentified body. But on his return to Exeter, the Coroner is incensed to find that his own brother-in-law, Sheriff Richard de Revelle, is intent on thwarting the murder investigation. But Crowner John is ready to fight for the truth. Even faced with the combined mights of the all-powerful Church and nobility . . .

SLAUGHTER HORSE

Michael Maguire

The Turf Security Division is surprised and suspicious when playboy Wesley Falloway's second-rate horses develop overnight into winners. Simon Drake investigates, but suddenly there is a new twist — someone is out to steal General O'Hara, the star of British bloodstock, owned by Wesley Falloway's mother. With a few million pounds at stake, lives are cheap; Drake finds himself both hunter and quarry in a murderous chase where even his closest associates may be playing a double game.

THE SURGEON'S APPRENTICE

Arthur Young

1947: Young Neil Aitken has worked hard to secure a place at Glasgow University to study medicine. Bearing in mind the Dean's warning that it takes more than book-learning to become a doctor, he sets out to discover what that other elusive quality might be. He learns the hard way, from a host of memorable characters ranging from a tyrannical surgeon to the bully on the farm where Neil works in his spare time, and assorted patients who teach him about courage and vulnerability. Neil also meets Sister Annie, the woman who is to influence his life in every way.